I0636775

THE BLOOD CROWN

THE BLOOD CROWN

M.S.Y

In a world of heroes, everyone is a villain.

GULF BOOK SERVICES

The contents of this work, including, but not limited to, the accuracy of events, people, and places depicted; opinions expressed; permission to use previously published materials included. and any advice given, or actions advocated are solely the responsibility of the author, who assumes all liability for said work and indemnifies the publisher against any claims stemming from publication of the work.

All Rights Reserved
@ M.S.Y
Cover Illustration & Design by Shaziah Shamim

GULF BOOK SERVICES

Published by Gulf Book Services Ltd
20-22 Wenlock Road, London,
NI 7GU, UK
Email: info@gulfbooks.co.uk
Office No: G23, Sharjah Publishing City Free Zone
Sharjah – UAE

First Published by Gulf Book Services Ltd

No part of this book may be reproduced or transmitted, downloaded, distributed, reverse engineered, or stored in or introduced into any information storage and retrieval system, in any form or by any means, including photocopying and recording, whether electronic or mechanical, now known or hereinafter invented without permission in writing from the publisher.

ISBN: 978-1-917529-11-2
Year: April 2025

Typeset in Cormorant Garamond, Cinzel Decorative and Bonheur Royale by Forging Minds, India

FOR ALL THOSE WHO REMAIN IN DUTIFUL SILENCE,
REMEMBER WHO YOU ARE AND WHO YOU WERE
MEANT TO BE

PROLOGUE

Victoria Ironhart,
Day 1o,

~

I was drenched in blood, head-to-toe.

No worries—I would kill a bit more, and then I would be finished.

The bomb in my hand felt strangely light that day. Ferrumisle was in ashes, and I could make out the slight metal glint of our fortress gleaming in the twilight stars. People clamoured about, grieving the deaths of those who plunged forth into my ambush yesterday.

Why would you cram four thousand people in one spot?

I lifted my arm behind the jagged rock. I was too close. It was okay, though. I couldn't die.

I aimed, watching as a man turned his head, capturing the sight of the metal orb I held. Oh, the dread in his eyes that ratted onto the features of his face—I wanted to gorge it whole.

I hauled the bomb higher, a flicker of a smile grazing my lips as he lurched back, hollering words I could not apprehend as the people began to create a racket.

Three.

A lady tripped, staggering against the gravel.

Two.

People crashed into each other, and I trembled out from behind the rock.

One.

I hurled the bomb into the mass, and a thunderclap resounded as I was thrust back, the harsh, sweltering wind whipping my face. I struck against the rock I had hidden behind, sagging to the earth.

Fire lapped furiously as flesh trickled off the faces of those inferior varmints like a melting candle, and the fallen desperately consumed their blood like it would return them to life.

I let out a small chuckle.

The skin peeling to flesh, flesh dripping to blood, blood soaking into the ground to white, fresh bones. Oh, how I would adore licking them clean. Make certain they all suffered what I did.

How dare they disobey their rightful majesty? How dare they taunt me for who I am?

I would show them all. I staggered up, tensing against the rock. The sharp point pierced through my hand, trolling through flesh and bone as it peeked out from the top, but I fell again and dropped back to the rugged earth, my hand remaining glued to its position. I shut my eyes.

I needed rest. It had been a long week, or at least that's how long I reckoned it had been, and as I nodded off, his face burst forth in my mind. The memory came to me urging sympathy, but it left me in the wake of more open wounds willing to bleed.

CHAPTER 1

'Just smile and wave.'

Elysande stands beside me, and I mimic her actions. I paste a smile on my face, moving my hand to and fro as the citizens of Ferrumisle pass by, bowing and saying, 'My Queen,' my heart sinking with every sentiment repeated. Missilians, they call themselves. I'm not sure why. Maybe it's to show that they will rebel against the bastard of a family that rules them when the time comes.

Xavier and Father are seated upon the thrones on the dais, shaking hands with all those who have arrived to congratulate Xavier for his ascension to the throne. Elysande is ecstatic, of course. Her son—my step-brother—is to become King. I swallow the lump clogging my throat. So much for being the eldest child.

The red velvet curtains are draped across windows, coveting the sunlight that emanates through the fortress's iron walls. The skin at my fingertips bursts open, and I hear the clink of every tiny crystal that drops down, humiliation heavily tinging my cheeks red.

I follow the gaze of those dressed in an ebony tweed suit—their partners in an uncomfortable crimson chiffon dress—the badge of honour strung through the rough material, with two swords clashing over their hearts to King Avalorian. Metallures, all of them. My hands burn at the thought.

Ferrumisle is a land of sorcerers and sorceresses, and every land has a Lord and Lady. Our Kingdom's lords and ladies represent the three powers: Metallures, Crystallites, and Stollars. Both Father and Xavier possess the power of metallurgy-the ability to manipulate metal.

However, a rare heart is birthed every few millennia. An alloy of metal and crystal; a concoction of flame and fury. These individuals are known as the Calamoris: the calamity of death itself.

When a Missilian is discovered to have powers that defy nature herself, they are transported to Caelumterra to be trained in their powers, to be controlled like a puppet until their each move is decided by the High Council to do their bidding.

Unfortunately, Caelumterra failed to compensate for the help of the Calamoris. Only one such heart has lived to tell the tale of the corruption of good, and it is the Queen of Inferis, Nyx Darkryn herself.

She could create land with crystal and coal, twisting the tragedies she inflicted upon us into blessings—much like death itself.

'My Queen.' I look back to see a man in a snug black doublet, smirking at me as he bows before Elysande. I try to smooth the frown that creases my face before she notices. I should not be letting her control my every step and action. She is my step-mother, and I have every reason to hate her.

The man wears an amethyst crystal ring, a sign of his prowess in the ability of crystal manipulation.

I am a Crystallite, unlike the rest of my family. We have the power to form and manipulate crystals as well, which respond to our feelings. The other downside? Metal can burn us. I bite my lip, watching as Xavier crushes a metal goblet in the air, eliciting gasps of astonishment from those that surround him.

Elysande smiles briefly, a glint of disgust plaguing her shockingly white eyes, before they make their way to the dais, and finally, the last of the Missilians approach us.

'My Queen.'

The Stollars. It is as if Aetheria blessed them herself. They are deeply rooted to the earth, having the ability to manipulate stone itself—and at their best, crack even the widest and strongest lands in two. The ancient cracks on the rim of each land are a sentiment to the War of Aetheria and Queen Nyx, who created a rift to form the six lands we witness today.

Caelumterra had split a hole before departing as the forefather of all, surrendering a patch of brazen land for the likes of trade and alliances, now known as the Center.

Dear step-mother is an arguably feeble Stollar. Rumours whisper Elysande could split a hill in half, but whatever strength she had then has been drunk from her soul for she is now only blood and bones.

'Victoria, such a pity you couldn't be up there. We forever look forward to it,'

I stop in my tracks, my jaw set. I turn to see Lady Celestia Stone shove through the crowd in her majestic sky-blue gown that flows around her body, and barely manage to hold my smile. I loathe her with a passion. She clasps onto Lord Auric's arms, who nervously shifts in his black tunic. A sheathed sword is at the strap of his belt, and a bit of his stomach juts out. An emblem of a rock hovers above his heart.

I suddenly feel underdressed in my simple pink ball gown.

Elysande laughs, a light, high-pitched noise that sends shivers down my spine. Her voice sounds exactly like Xavier's. Like Mother, like son. I wonder if my laugh sounds like my mother's. I join in, my voice hollow, grinning shakily.

'Oh, but of course, not everyone is fit for royalty.' Celestia lets out a haughty chuckle as Elysande daintily pats her eyes before ushering the couple to the dais. I clench my hands into fists but don't say anything. It's alright.

Elysande's white gown flows behind her, and I do my best not to trip over each layer of the snowy train I follow behind. As we walk, a small gasp elicits from behind. I turn to see what the matter is when a dwarf woman with a scrunched face collides into my dress. I stagger back. There is a smash of glass before wine seeps through the thick layers, and I feel the heavy bulge of liquid sink into my leg. Silence plays out, morphing into low murmurs and a few giggles. I wince slightly as the woman falls to the floor, apologising hesitantly.

'P-P-Princess! A-Accept my sincerest apologies! Please, do not—'

She halts, eyes wide.

'Take it,' I say. She sits still, jaw wide open. I notice the cavities in her teeth and her skin folding into each other as she awkwardly grabs my outstretched hand, her fingers hard and rough from scrubbing dishes. I pull her up gently, aware of her age.

'Your apology has been accepted.' I smile, this time genuine.

'N-no p-penalties?' she stutters, and I shake my head.

'Of course not, accidents happen all the time.'

I can feel the scathing glares that burn into my back. Was I not allowed to show even a slight bit of kindness now? The dwarf gets to her feet, hurriedly cleaning the glass off the floor, pulling the shards onto her dress before she scurries away. Elysande places a hand on my shoulder, her lips formed into a cruel smile.

'Come, Victoria.'

We pass the six carefully carved stone chairs surrounding a table and make our way to Father and Xavier, where Father guffaws at something his son said. They look our way, and I have an instinctive feeling the joke was regarding me.

'Ah, Victoria!' Father lets his pudgy fingers encircle my wrist, pulling me closer to him. 'How do you plan to celebrate your brother's ascension?'

I don't want to.

I keep quiet, but when Elysande glares at me, all traces of the lingering thought dissipate into thin air.

'She won't. She's too royal to do so.' Xavier chuckles wryly, chocolate curled hair bouncing with every hearty chortle that escapes his throat, and Father laughs.

'Well, what a joke if I ever heard one!'

I feel my heart splinter, but I don't say anything. There is no use and there never will be.

'Well, Victoria, Elysande,' Father looks to each of us. 'We shall have a brief celebration—us Missilians and the King. Elysande, take the Ladies to the Palace Gardens.'

He turns to me, eyes squinting. 'You may head to your chamber, Victoria.'

Victoria Ironhart,
Day 9,

Oh woe,
thy trickery hath no mercy,
every card is dealt ever so stealthily,
every hurtful meaning shadowed so carefully,
but I never understand,
why you allow me to never learn,
for thou's foul hands never fail to torment me
more than I can ever hold.

'Victoria!' Xavier yelled from behind. I turned away from the stone I was sharpening my sword across, tossing the burnt rock aside.

'What?' I asked sullenly.

'There's an army outside!' He burst hurriedly, words spilling out together in a blur.

'An army?' I enunciated, dragging my sword. It scratched against the stone, sending the perched doves screeching into the air. The Palace Gardens were most beautiful in the day, and I had looked forward to spending my time here after lessons.

'You need to go and let them in!' Xavier exclaimed.

'Why should I? Go ask Father!' I snapped, turning away from him.

'Father's busy.'

I sighed. 'Then why didn't you let them in? You know it's bad manners to keep people waiting.'

'They wanted to meet the Queen,' Xavier said. I turned to face him, his arms crossed over his chest.

'So you've already spoken to them?' I raised an eyebrow.

'Of course,' Xavier answered.

I shook my head as he looked to me tentatively. 'Get Elysande.'

Xavier let out a strangled sigh. 'Just go and open the damned gates to the army!'

'It could be a trap,' I snapped.

'If it was, they would've barged in already.'

'You don't know how Briarthorn Atoll plays,' I hissed, wiping my hands against my red dress, staining it with mud. Elysande would get mad. No matter. It looked a lot like blood.

'It's not Briarthorn Atoll,' Xavier said gruffly. 'It's Fames.'

I stared at Xavier in silence, taking in his tanned skin and muscular physique. In the sunlight, he didn't look a bit like the young boy I knew. He looked like the devil himself. The sun batted down ferociously, sparing no mercy with its heat waves plundering down upon me.

A few beats passed, and the wind blew a strand of my ebony hair onto my face.

'Very well,' I said. Xavier looked me in the eye, a small smile tugging at the edge of his lips.

'Perfect.'

I followed him cautiously, remembering the last time I let my guard down around him.

The walk was barely five minutes, but upon arrival, I could hardly breathe.

The sight was horrendous. Hundreds and thousands of armed soldiers from Briarthorn Atoll, with catapults and bombs at the ready. It was all a trick. I rounded to Xavier, but could see him nowhere. My heart began to pick pace. If they were let in, Ferrumisle would be burnt to the ground. I would no longer be Queen. I would no longer be worthy of the crown.

A metallic tinkle sent shivers down my spine. I turned hesitantly to see Xavier holding an oblong key, inserting it into the large lock.

'Xavier,' I said calmly. 'Don't you dare.' The wind rustled my hair, the ground eerily silent. I took a step back, and the clink of metal echoed as the lock made contact with the Palace grounds.

All I heard was the Prince of Briarthorn Atoll's guttural roar before everything went dark. When I awoke, the land was in ruins. A quarter of our population had died. A quarter had left. The rest remained in spite, having nowhere else to escape. Father was devastated. Xavier was not.

There is no greater betrayal than that of your kin.

But if I have none, what betrayal would it be? As soft as a feather or as sharp as a dagger to the heart?

~

'Your Majesty, more have been killed,' one of the soldiers said. Confident, considering he was in charge of the army I had bombed.

'Already?' the voice growled. 'I want her dead!'

I was behind the soldier, throwing an arm into the air.

The figure turned as the soldier started, 'We have been trying-'

A crystal speared his gut through the back. A splatter drenched me in blood, and I spat the crimson liquid out. Collective gasps erupted from behind the man as the demanding figure staggered back, startled. Gosh.

How many men did they have? I watched him back away as I moved closer, in awe of the thousands of men behind him. Strangely, they did not make a move to do anything, their arrows whizzing into the dirt barely a metre away from them.

'How petty. Am I so powerful I need thousands of soldiers hunting me?' I gasped softly, grinning.

'No, you are not,' the figure bit out. I couldn't remember who he was. 'Victoria, you don't ne—'

I'd estimate twenty-thousand soldiers rounded up. I almost felt sorry for what I was about to do.

From where I stood, the earth cracked beneath my feet, splitting open into a cavern, a hole that could swallow them whole.

I stood, watching as all of them scrambled for their life.

Some of them escaped.

Most of them fell into the void below, their worthless lives never to be seen again.

I weave around the spiral of stony stairs adjacent to Xavier's Chamber. The humid gusts of wind rashes my bare arms after days of war against the titanium windows, shoving them open with such force that it created a monster of our crimson curtains.

The Missilians had departed, and the celebration was over. I swallowed. So then why was Father calling for me?

I had been in my room peacefully, drowning in my deepest thoughts, wondering how my whole life had come to an end.

From the corner of my eye, I watch Ferrumisle's sun set. Rya, we call her. After the War of Aetheria, the complete sun—Sol —was split into five, and our days were treacherously long and foetid, sparing no mercy.

Desmond Nathaniel Thorncrest, the Prince of Briarthorn Atoll—I clench my jaw as I hop over the last stair. If it weren't for his power thirsty heart, I would still be Queen.

I growl in exaggerated frustration as a tight squeeze obstructed my path from entering the hallway.

How I wish I could get my sweet revenge, but I would be stupid to do so. Squeezing through the blockage, I pull up my pink dress laced with pearls in an effort to skim the hall swiftly, abruptly bumping into General Steelborne.

'My Princess!' a thick accent erupts from a burly, olive-skinned man. I look up at his towering figure, his silver hair tied in an elegant bun.

'It is alright,' I answer lightly, throwing him a small smile. I hesitantly walk toward the great obsidian doors, both fists clenching the cold, brass door-knobs in unison, embedded with the symbol of Ferrumisle, a phoenix.

Breathe in, breathe out.

With a heave, summoning as much strength as I can, I bang the brass. A low, deafening crash thrums through the hall.

I feel it in the walls, the floor, in my shoes vibrating to my brain, the sound deeply engraved in my veins.

I drop the metal, and my head follows suit. I feel the sting reverberate through my body, sharp needles pricking my hands. It is all I can do not to drop to my knees and stifle the scream threatening to emit from my throat.

The phoenix tattoo on my neck burns in agony, the black turning to a bloody red and a fiery orange outlining the intricate details, each line a knife scarring my throat as it always does. A gasp escapes me, and a thunderous voice rumbles from the Great Hall.

'Enter.'

With bleary eyes, I watch the doors unravel the beauty that lies within the castle's mutinouscales, each deafening click of the bolts unlocking, burying my confidence.

The obsidian doors creak open, sliding effortlessly across the red carpet that adorns the floors of the Great Hall. Golden chandeliers hang high on the ceiling, massive pillars made of crystal looming overhead.

I curse silently while letting my dress flow as if it were the calm of the sea, hoping he was not seated in that throne, wishing it was empty, desiring his blood soaked, obscured and drenched in my velvet gloves. Yet, there upon all luxuries and extravagance sat the King of Ferrumisle, the storm that was destined to bring doom.

'Victoria, dear, what took you so long?' thunders King Avalorian.

I remain silent.

'You take pleasure in avoiding Father,' Xavier scorns, his brown hair a mess, the perfect epitome of a bird's nest. I grimace at the truth in his words, the pain in my palms growing.

With a knowing smirk, Xavier adds, 'Of course, it is not every day where the youngest is chosen over the eldest for the remarkable duty,' he emphasises his last words, *'as King.'*

My mouth remains glued shut. All I can do is stare and fumble with the layers of my ball gown.

'Precisely what I have requested you for,' Father coughs.

I stiffen, my breathing coming out in slow, quiet rasps. *Requested?*

'Of course, all heirs that are unworthy or have failed ascension to the throne are thrown into Mors Regium,' his voice carries through the hall.

Carcerem Regum Mortuorum.

The dungeon of dead kings.

'However, I have come to an agreement with the King of Briarthorn Atoll, King Thaddeus Thorncrest.' I try not to collapse to the ground, rephrasing his words. *I successfully blackmailed King Thaddeus into eradicating your expulsion.* But how? And with what? I wait—patiently—my breath hitched in my throat. What could possibly be worse than the dungeon of the dead?

'An arrangement of marriage has been agreed by both Kings.' Father's hands clamp together, lips pursed tightly. 'Prince Desmond Nathaniel Thorncrest shall be your betrothed, and you will be Queen by his side.'

Suddenly, I can't breathe. Everything stops and I feel like I'm falling and falling and falling until all the air has left my lungs. I bore straight into my Father's eyes, unable to mask the crash of waves that pulls me under.

Then I turn on my heel—and run.

CHAPTER 11

I stumble into my chamber, gasping, staring at my palms. Half-moons are imprinted across my skin. The burning sensation has subsided.

Elysande's taunting lecture echoes in my head: '*You should be grateful for the leverage provided by your Father! Do you know how much he sacrifices to bestow such luxuries and keep you, a petty child, in perfect norms? The least you can do is have some formality and respect, Victoria.*'

Crystals sprout from the windowsills of my room, jagged like vampire fangs. I catch sight of myself in their reflection. My wide, terrified eyes gleam a searing red, and I feel a spark ignite within them. It's as if they could scorch the crystals and melt them until the fortress reeks of burnt serum—another offence for which my father would punish me.

My heart plummets harder. I hate looking into something that shows me a pitiful woman staring back down, disappointed by the lack of her achievements.

Ebony hair cascades down my back, crowned in a braid—a cruel mockery. Father assigns a servant to style me like a hopeful, delicate princess, knowing I'll never wear the true crown. I flinch, the realisation of everything throwing me off guard.

Marrying me off to Desmond Nathaniel Thorncrest—the oldest of three siblings? What is the point of being Queen when I will have barely any land to rule?

And what's worse is that he is a half-blood werewolf. When the five suns and moons of Aetheria come together, aligning in a pattern of darkness and light, drowning the world in a void, then only will he shift into his rightful form. Every half- year, a werewolf is met with this destiny.

I take in a deep breath, attempting to calm myself.

The soft, velvety pillows embrace me as I plop into them. How on Aetheria did Father manage to achieve such a feat? Blackmailing the kingdom in ownership of The Blood Crown? What was he thinking?

Bile rises in my throat.

A thump echoes against the wooden door, distracting my train of thought.

'Who is it?' I call, staggering to my feet.

'Soon to be Ki-'

I cut him off before he can boast further: 'Go away!' My heart stops as a beat of silence passes by. Why had I said that?

Before I could crumple in front of the door, begging for mercy, Xavier's rough voice breaks through the quiet.

'We shall be leaving for Briarthorn Atoll. If you're least interested in learning about our strategies...'

That was enough to make me groan inwardly and slump to open my room door, witnessing Xavier leaning lazily against the mud-brick walls. He raises an eyebrow. 'I thought I was told to go away?'

And I thought servants carried messages through the castle. I brush past him, a scowl etched across my features. A scuffle echoes behind. Then a few footsteps. And Xavier is beside me.

'As you know, my coronation is set to proceed on Junius eighteenth, when I turn twenty- one, and you, still twenty-four.'

Another dig. I purse my lips grimly, following Xavier as he passes me. I realise we are turning for the Keep. The fires around us flicker softly.

'You are well aware Briarthorn Atoll is in possession of the Blood Crown.'

I nearly choke at the revelation of Father's plan, drinking hope like a thirsty child gulping water for the first time in years. Before I can stop myself, the words are out of my mouth, echoing through the hall.

'Father wants me to kill Desmond so I can get the crown?'

Xavier chuckles. 'No.'

A flustered flush grows in my cheeks. Did I really have to act like that?

The walls echo back Xavier's response louder, as if mocking me for my foolishness. I cringe. When would I stop being the reproachful person I am?

We halt near the entrance of the Keep. Xavier places his hands on the brass, clenching his fists around it as his knuckles go white.

'Whatever you do, play along. You shall not dare to scheme against us.' He rounds on me, biting out his last words, 'Do you understand?'

He turns, muttering softly under his breath. Loud enough for me to hear, but not loud enough to echo through the hall.

'We don't need any unnecessary laybacks, although it's ironic because you already are one.'

I stare at Xavier, stunned. His ironic threat simmers heat in my cheeks, splodging them bright red. How dare he think I would betray our family? I resent his ascension, but I would never kill someone of my blood. I am being married off to a scoundrel! Did he really think I would somehow break the marriage and return to Ferrumisle after disobeying Father?

'Very well, King Xavier,' I sigh, pulling my hand up to push the door open.

He smacks it away.

I gasp. A singeing shock of pain stings through me, and I feel my surroundings blur. Rings. Victoria, you idiot. Xavier wore metal rings. He smirks, a tug of pride arching his back.

'Princess Victoria, know your limits. You ought not to disobey a King.'

I cling and pinch my hands, acid burbling inside me. I don't understand how his rings pain me. They're made of crystal too, and I should have enough strength to withstand if there is another element present alongside metal forged into an object. Xavier bangs the brass, shoving the door open, grabbing my arm as he does so. He pushes me to the front, ushering me to walk toward the lean table at the centre of the Keep.

I plop down daintily beside Elysande, offering Father a wry smile. Father grins back. I can see the pride etched in the old lines of his ancient facade. At a hundred and fifty, it takes guts to fight back against the curse of The Blood Crown. Most would have killed themselves. But Father's immortality has been an unyielding trial—a call upon death, rejected tenfold.

The table in front of me has been covered with an old map of Briarthorn Atoll. Four goblets surround it—one on each side. Father sits on my right, eyeing me carefully.

'We will be leaving for Briarthorn Atoll, as you know it,' he says. I nod, plastering a smile. If I get married to Desmond, I will have no control over my life.

Not like I have control over any part of my life already.

'Victoria's marriage is merely a cover for the abduction of The Blood Crown.'

My smile falters.

'What a wonderful plan, Avalorian,' Elysande says. Xavier meets my eye, and I hurriedly look down. Even if we may be thinking the exact same thing, I could not let my emotions write themselves across my face.

Xavier is Father's puppet; one wrong move and I could be six feet under the ground. I should be privileged to even remain a princess.

'But why the Prince of Briarthorn Atoll?' Xavier asks suddenly. 'He attempted to kill you.'

A burning sensation rises in my stomach. This was only half the story. The Tribal War was one of the greatest combats in Aetherian history. Briarthorn Atoll had retaliated because Father had tried to steal the Blood Crown, and now he makes the same plan all over again. Had he not learned his lesson?

Those who dared attempt to steal the crown were doomed to live for eternity. Even at the cusp of death, your immortality would forbid the entity from wrenching your soul from the taverns of your heart. However, poison can kill. The High King of Caeulmterra was wise in one thing when he forged the crown. You were immortal to murder or any natural cause of death if you attempted to steal the crown, but what's better than beating nature with its very own creation?

Wraith Berry could kill—only if one was clever enough to unearth it.

Having a chance at your life again was a tiring yet enticing opportunity, but for Father, it's a chance at redemption.

'Because they are the only land in possession of the crown,' Father replies, cocking an eyebrow.

'We could ask for backup,' Xavier suggests, tilting his head to get a better view of the map of Briarthorn Atoll. It may seem plain, with the palace towering to deafening heights and the forests that covet the land, but the traps in the palace armoury are a smidge bit too thorny.

Father chuckles. 'Equity is a rare luxury, my boy. Think of yourself first, and the next if you must. Personally, pondering over aiding another is a waste of time.'

I resist the urge to roll my eyes.

'Why, yes. We are at too much loss if we question for aid. Betrayal runs in royal blood,' Lord Lysander says from behind.

'You would know about betrayal,' Father murmurs, and I tilt my head upwards, surprised that he was here.

Lord Lysander sighs. 'Well, it seems I have arrived in time,' he says sarcastically, pursing his lips. He brushes back ebony locks, gritting out his next words. 'May the King continue with his plan?'

Father dismisses Lord Lysander's begrudging tone. 'Victoria, you will be moving in with the Thorncrests,' he instructs.

I nod.

Wait, what?

Father goes on. 'Your job is simple. You must acquire the Blood Crown. Do what you must—kill the king, kill the princesses. *However,* do not, and I repeat, do not, kill the prince. Once we have the coronet, we will not have one, but two kingdoms!'

Father bangs on the table in triumph, the sound reverberating through the dungeon, taunting me.

Move in with the Thorncrests *before* marriage?

I swallow.

'This way, Xavier will rule in Ferrumisle, and I will rule Briarthorn Atoll,' Father finishes.

I could practically feel Lord Lysander's depleted groan echoing through the Keep.

Father was too old, but his pride still young.

'Victoria will be doing the dirty work for us,' says Xavier, nodding his head in understanding. I flinch. I wasn't a servant, so why was I so readily agreeing to everything? The audacity to use your own daughter. I was already worthless, and using me would indeed make me seem even more the desperate princess. My fingers turn bright red. I'm the oldest. I should have the respect, the privilege.

'But you will be the King of Briarthorn Atoll?' asks Xavier.

'The Blood Crown can only be claimed by the heir, the killer of the heir, or through a hundred thousand kills. I, my dear boy, will have the satisfaction of slaughtering Desmond's neck.'

I stand up abruptly and the wood clatters against the marble floor. Father's small eyes cut through me like blades.

'Excuse me, but nature calls.' I smile and bow slowly, staggering off the chair and nearly tripping over my dress. 'Another reason why she deserves to be married,' Elysande tuts from behind as I make my way to the door, the clink of my heels echoing across the room. I feel shame gush over my face and instinctively quicken my pace.

'Maybe with a husband she shall learn some etiquette—and wit.'

I feel like a dozen rocks have been placed upon my chest, threatening to crush the tiny organ within me. My heart cannot bear this any longer. Every day for three years, I have been shunned for leading a battalion into Ferrumisle's lands when it was Xavier who forced the gates open and I told him not to.

No one listened to me as I helplessly pleaded.

Everyone mocks and ridicules me for not ascending to the throne. I kick a piece of marble that has chipped from the floor. I need to do something. Something to prove myself. Something I should have done long ago.

Something to get me out of this marriage and save me from the humiliating doom that lingers above me. If I get married to Desmond, I would be seen as a toy to be played around with. I pass Xavier's chamber, and the fresh aroma of spice and musk smacks me in the face. I notice that my room door has been left open. I must have forgotten to close it as we left. I look back and forth, peeping through the hallway to see if anyone had passed.

It was clear.

I hesitantly enter my chamber and quickly close the door behind me, slinking against the door. *Breathe in, breathe out.* I close my eyes and inhale deeply, and deflate onto the floor.

Desmond Nathaniel Thorncrest.

The Blood Crown, given to the most powerful being in Aetheria.

Forged by the High King himself to undo a monster he thought would aid. Instead, it was given to Briarthorn Atoll, and now Desmond would soon have the power.

The Blood Crown could control Aetheria if placed in the wrong hands. Anyone with the crown on their head thirsts for a power so eminent they would go to great lengths, even to the point of murder, to have it upon the tuft of even a strand of their hair.

'Kill them all! And the princess should not survive!'

My heart pounds in rhythm with the obedient soldiers on the day of the Tribal War. Desmond's voice is embedded into my mind, refusing to provide me solace. The command blurs my thoughts, and I grip my clammy hands tightly.

I survived him once, but will I survive him again?

You need to kill the heir, or have the blood of a hundred thousand on your hands to claim the Blood Crown as your own.

Desmond Nathaniel Thorncrest is a war strategist and chief commander in the field.

Such petite nicknames for a murderer.

That day, the number of civilians and soldiers killed exceeded sixty thousand. The following day, fifteen thousand soldiers of Fames were slaughtered near the Queen's Forest. They had been visiting King Thaddeus for an interesting trade.

Even if Desmond was the heir of the Blood Crown, I am most certain he is absolutely solidifying his rule by achieving a hundred thousand kills.

I may as well do the latter, but it is not easy. It would be fairly obvious a person was attempting to claim the Blood Crown if they went on a killing rampage. Yet for Desmond, it was easy. He is the head of his army and undoubtedly earns a fresh, free kill every five seconds.

I groan and thrash, flinging my arms into the air.

Of all the men I could get married to, I had to be wed to the most cunning and bloodthirsty man in Aetheria?

A sudden thought hits me, and I turn abruptly, breath caught in my throat. Maybe that could help.

I scramble up from the floor, nearly slipping over my dress. I feel my hands tingle in excitement, the crystal chandelier above me quivering.

The Blood Crown.

That's what I need to get. Not my kingdom. Not anything else. That bloody crown, the source of Father's stupid plan, Xavier's betrayal and Desmond's hunger for power.

If only I could get my hands on it, no one would be able to stop me.

That's exactly why Father wed me to him.

Under Desmond, I would no longer be able to fight—if I killed him, I would die under the humiliation of the cowardice of my plans. I seethe, my hands balling into fists.

Life isn't fair; I had learnt that on countless occasions. It is only when you make a change that it becomes just.

Bile rises up my throat as the thoughts force into my head. I should not be thinking this. If I were to be caught, I would most certainly be executed for treason.

But here we are again.

Why do I have to be the good person? I rub the phoenix tattoo on my neck, boring into the crystal mirror hung above my desk.

All I need to do is kill.

'Alright,' I breathe, taking in a sigh of air as if it were water.

I need to kill a hundred thousand people—or kill the future

King of Briarthorn Atoll, so the Blood Crown can claim me as its rightful owner.

It's simple. Which has more worth?

Once the crown was mine, everyone would realise that I should have been the Queen of Ferrumisle. From there, I could destroy the Scroll of Eternity—the parchment that prevented the individual in possession of the Blood Crown from taking over the world. It too was forged by the High King to prevent absolute tyranny.

The King of Briarthorn Atoll has signed it, meaning the crown's power is fully dormant until the scroll is destroyed. Desmond was yet to do so. If he did not, he would be hunted down and killed.

All I needed to do was claim the Blood Crown and somehow destroy the Scroll of Eternity.

I exhale loudly, frantically shaking my head.

'Damn it, I can't do this.'

'Mama, can you tell me a story?'

I sat on my mother and father's bed, nestled in the maroon coverings. These were the puny recollections that remained of her. I could scarcely sense the touch of her gentle hands, the warm embrace that wrapped me in a blanket of dawn whenever I had felt under the weather.

'What story, Victoria?' she said. Her silky voice echoed Elysande's. I had loathed it.

'The War of Aetheria,'

'Bellum Aetheriae,' she sighed, but I could sense the small smile touching her lips. She had recounted the tale to me multiple times, but I wanted to hear it from her lips just one more time. And I was glad I did because shortly after, she vanished.

Calypso Berenice Magnus, her name was.

She who hides, she who brings victory, she who hails from the greatest. That's what her name meant. That is what a part of my name meant. Victoria: the goddess of victory. At the time, I hadn't thought much about it. I still don't, to this day. It isn't worth pondering over.

Mother's hands came around and drew me close enough to hear the rumble of her words echo in her chest.

'Well, Victoria, the War of Aetheria struck exactly at midnight.' She splayed her hands in the air, forming visions of a hauntingly alluring nixie storming the darkness, demons creeping behind her. The nixie's hair and skin were as white as snow, her body slender as a salamander, but her prowess in sorcery was as powerful as a dragon-breathing fire.

'Five thousand years ago, Nyx Darkryn, Queen of Inferis, conspired to conquer the four lands in Aetheria: Caelumterra, Ferrumisle, Briarthorn Atoll, and the Land of Fames.'

The scene veered to the three lands soaring at each point of that of a triangle. Aloft, Caelumterra blurred the skies like a halo, the motherland uniting all four.

'Caelumterra had presumed she would be one to bring harmony to the world, but Nyx was famished. Hungry for power. She believed she should be the superior queen, and the rest of the world her servants, for in history, Nyx had provided the lands necessities to furnish for their kingdoms—but they had never returned.'

I hadn't questioned how. Queen Nyx was a Calamoris. She had been bestowed upon with the power of witchery and dark magic; vile enough to corrupt, yet decent enough to grant. And when her Father refused to abdicate his throne to thank her for blessing the lands, she spiralled.

'She resolved to take matters into her own hands. First, Nyx triumphed Ferrumisle, our motherland, the land of metal.'

A vivid notion of our Kingdom with its aged stains appeared, a stony-like fortress pulverised into smithereens, blood splattering across the bland life.

'Next, it was the Land of Fames.'

A wilderness that extended for miles powdered into ashes as the blaze lapped ferociously like a parched mongrel, annihilating the thousands of creatures that hailed from the land, including nixies.

'Finally, Caelumterra.'

A celestial burst of fog blurred the room, dragons soaring high, floundering with the demons that coloured the land dark. The wingmaidens flew into cottages, and the High King and queens quarrelled amongst one another, against their kind, against Nyx.

'But Briarthorn Atoll defeated all hopes for Nyx.'

King Caspian Thorncrest, a burly young man with muscles the size of bludgeons, came thundering into the scene. The glow shifted to inevitable twilight, the reverberating chime of a clock ringing in the galaxy. It was exactly midnight.

A foreboding tone penetrated Mother's soft voice. 'Caspian Thorncrest vanquished Nyx Darkryn by sheer luck. He created Carcerem Regum Mortuorum, the Dungeon of Dead Kings, and condemned Nyx to banishment until the end of time.'

'The story doesn't end there, Mama!' *I squealed as Mother made way to get off the bed, groping for her hands. She threw back her head and laughed. The high-pitched cackle always had me rolling on the floor. But not today. Today felt different.*

'You're right, my little queen.' *Mother tucked me back in bed, brushing a hand over my jet locks.*

'Nyx escaped, but this time, Caelumterra was prepared. They had forged the Blood Crown, a coronet only granted to the most powerful individual, one that allowed them to rule over all of Aetheria, but it came with a steep price: it consumes the very soul of its wearer. They swore if Nyx had the crown on her head, she would end her reign. That's why...'

Mother swung her hands once more, revealing a coronet forged from dark steel and obsidian, rusted in gold and bejewelled with clear selenite on four points that reflected the five sun's colours, and a crimson garnet crystal towering in the centre. It was said the gems had been infused with the blood of fallen kings and queens, but none knew for sure.

'When Nyx returned to the High Court, she bartered a deal. The crown for leaving the Kingdoms alone. Caelumterra agreed.'

Oh, how absolutely stupid the council had been. The High King and queens of the past were ones to be ashamed of.

'What's next?' I asked breathlessly, bounding hysterically on the bed. My knees ached against the cotton on hard stone.

Mother sighed.

'Briarthorn Atoll was the last land to be overthrown and one that first bested Nyx. You know what happened next. The Blood Crown chose Caspian Thorncrest.' Mother had gotten off the bed and placed a kiss on my forehead. I knew the ending of the story like the back of my hand, but I still asked.

'Then what did Nyx do?'

She let out a chuckle. 'Then did Nyx form Inferis, the final land in Aetheria. Ever since her creation, Nyx Darkryn has not shown Aetheria the face of darkness.'

Whether she was alive or dead, no one dared to figure. Nyx concealed herself in the deepest caverns of her charcoal kingdom, and since she had no heir, to this day, history titled her as Nyx Darkryn, the Queen of Inferis.

'Mama,'

'Yes, Victoria?' she hovered over me, faint blue lips forming into a small smile.

'If Nyx comes back, I'm going to defeat her, just like Caspian Thorncrest,' I said, determination scrawled over my face. Oh, how naive I was. I could laugh if I had the heart to. I had held my arms up to flex my muscles, and Mother let out a chuckle.

'Sure you will, my little queen. Now go to sleep. I'll be back soon.'

Mother blew me a flying kiss and left the room, leaving me in darkness.

~

The next morning, Mother never came back.

CHAPTER III

The carriage rumbles against the rocky floor.

It's the next day.

I'm in a carriage with Elysande on our way to Briarthorn Atoll.

I'm about to meet my future husband—the man I need to kill to get my hands on that crown.

Is it worth it?

Yes. Yes, it is.

Destroy his ego. Crush him. He killed more than sixty thousand for his own sake—surely taking the life of one man won't do any harm.

Oh, but it will. Everyone will suspect it was me.

That's why I must eliminate anyone who could be a threat.

'Victoria,' a soft, silky voice pulls me back to Aetheria. I shudder quickly, blinking rapidly as the grass blurs into view. I feel a deep pit form in my stomach and refuse to look Elysande in the eye.

'Elysande,' I force out, my eyes darting around. The sun's rays are the only source of light shimmering through the pale curtains that I peek through.

'Have you come up with a plan yet?' she asks.

You trust me so much to create a plan that I could betray you through?

I swallow.

'Yes,' I reply instead.

A beat of silence passes by.

'Well,' I feel her wave her hand in the air, a tingling sensation erupting at the back of my head. It sends shivers down my spine, and I cannot bear but to turn towards her.

'Tell me your plan. You left early yesterday and never returned. Avalorian must be filled in,' she says, raising a delicate, white-threaded eyebrow. The striking resemblance between her and Xavier makes me bite the inside of my cheek.

I nod my head, smiling a bit as I repeat my mantra from last night, hoping I stick with it. 'I silence anyone that would distrust me. I wi-'

I cut off abruptly, mouth hanging open. I can't continue. I can't. I can't say something I know I won't do.

A princess's promise is just as valuable as a prince's.

Elysande gives me an expectant look, nodding her head up and down. When she realises I have no intention of completing my sentence, she exasperatedly sighs before continuing for me.

'You will make Desmond fall hopelessly in love with you, so much so that he will willingly offer himself as a sacrifice when the time comes.'

I clamp my mouth shut and nod tightly, my throat constricting.

'I will make Desmond fall hopelessly in love with me, so much so that he will willingly offer himself as a sacrifice when the time comes,' I repeat monotonically.

He's a war strategist. Why on Aetheria did they think he would be stupid enough to fall in love with the enemy's daughter?

Elysande smiles. 'Wonderful. Don't make it too suspicious, though.'

I nod again, goosebumps rising on my arms.

Desmond wouldn't really offer himself as a sacrifice. He's

more likely to kill me before our hands even touch. But I had to do this right, for my sake.

A gong chimes outside, and our carriage screeches to an uncomfortable halt. I hold in a gasp as I grab onto the curtains, pulling them down. The sun blinds me. The fanfare band blasting outside the gold embezzled gates pierces through my eardrums, and I squirm. One of our guards dismounts his horse, hurriedly scuffling to pull open the door.

I shake my head.

I can do this. I can do this. I can do this. I can do this.

Break the rules. Kill a King—or kill a thousand others. Whatever the choice, I had to decide now. The moment I stepped into this palace, I would be enamoured by its deception. I push up from the velvety cushions, pulling up my ombre dress before Elysande grabs my arm suddenly, her stale breath gusting down my neck.

My heart races.

'Avalorian put his soul into trusting you,' she whispers. A thump echoes in the deepest caverns of my lungs, like a single boulder dropping into the gaping taverns and reverberating in the empty silence.

'Remember what will happen if you break it.'

I resist shoving her away from me as the carriage door is flung outward, just as the heavy, looming gates sprawled with ivy ease open, the golden sun rays glowering down at us. Four vast towers stood at either side of the palace, drowning in a pool of aureate, adorned with garnet stones and selenite crystals reflecting a prism of colours through the sky.

The large, crimson garnet gem is fused onto the Blood Crown used to achieve what your heart desires. The selenite crystals were used as a means of protection, costing the Kings of Briarthorn Atoll to live for centuries till end.

I ignore the outstretched hand of the guard, daintily stepping out of the carriage, Elysande following behind.

I turn to see Father and Xavier dismount the carriage in front of us. Father merely chuckles, waving a dismissive hand.

General MacQuoid, the King of Briarthorn Atoll's most trusted advisor, bows low, dressed in forest tweed.

'Welcome, Your Majesty.' His staff thumps the floor as he pulls himself up, a daunting smile under his thin, magician-like moustache.

'This way, Sir. High King Thaddeus awaits in his throne room.'

I let my hands fall in the middle of my dress as I catch sight of the three figures hovering behind him. Genevieve, Lorelei, and *Desmond*.

The three siblings nod in unison as if they were all puppets in a masterful theatre before General MacQuoid turns on his heel, ushering us to follow him. We do, with Desmond leading up front, and Genevieve and Lorelei falling back with me.

'You're going to be Queen,' Lorelei mourns, pulling her jet umbrella higher over her to eradicate the sunlight.

Her voice is prim, her dress proper, the dove-like gown blowing along with the wind as if it were an elegant bird. Her hair is a deep contrast in ebony, defining her high cheekbones. She smiles, the two pointed teeth grazing her lips as they drag up to each side.

I was going to be Queen, indeed, just not in the way they expected me to be.

I witness the heavy, jet wolf face that is scratched across her jaw, and I follow the mane's trail until the tattoo is obscured by her gown. Atop, Sunniva dips low into the horizon in a bright shade of pink, casting a blush onto Lorelei's carefully permed cheekbones.

I smile hesitantly, willing for these disastrous thoughts to evaporate from my mind. I had to make a decision soon; otherwise, I would undoubtedly be my own calamity.

'What an honour,' I muse instead, flicking my hair back. 'I had no idea,'

Genevieve snickers as Lorelei grunts. Her teeth resume their position over her lips, disapproving. It is obvious she bartered nothing more than arrogance out of my ascension with Desmond.

'Someone's not in a good mood today,' Genevieve grins wickedly.

She is dressed in all green, like the miles of earth that surround us. Her beauty is ethereal—so bewitching, yet oh, so ugly. A curse placed upon the stollars of Aetheria for dividing the lands with Nyx instead of uniting.

I could say the Thorncrest family and I are related in many ways, seeing that Genevieve's mother had traces of Acidum originating from Ferrumisle. It came as a shock for all when Lorelei was announced a vampire, and her sister a stollar.

Desmond is a creature of the night—a werewolf. I shudder. Just what would that beast do to me? He attempted to kill me once. Will he do it again?

We walk through the cobblestone passageway, plants trimmed in honour of each creature that inhabits Briarthorn Atoll, lining the bumpy stone. I hardly remember when we last met—though I would not call the war an exchange of pleasant greetings. Three years seem to be such a long time ago; I can't seem to fathom it.

We approach the looming palace, standing at least five feet away as the doors thunder open, doves squawking overhead as the obsidian chunks unveil, and I have to shade my eyes to prevent the light from blinding me. Genevieve smiles at my form, draping my head in green cloth to shade me from the gold that has been electrified with sunlight. I let my hand down gratefully, pulling closer into her.

Sometimes, Genevieve was the warmth I needed on a cold day. Most of the time, she was a bastard. A stinging burn erupts on my hand, the feeling lasting longer than most. I bite my lip hard, drawing blood and gasping as Xavier shoves past.

'You—' I start, and Genevieve pulls me back.

'You what? Going to cry about it?' Xavier chuckles, not bothering to turn around as his voice floats in the winter air.

It was enough being the worst royal family in Aetheria; Xavier didn't need to add more to the ideology. 'You're as weak as the crown you'll never wear.'

I want the ground to open up and swallow me whole when Desmond turns, casting a mirthless glance at Xavier. I pull out of Genevieve's grip, swallowing as I catch Lorelei barely conceal the giggle that betrays her demeanour. I clamp my hands together, bowing my head as my locks cascade around my face.

I wasn't weak. I am not weak. Right?

We enter the elegant gold hall furnished with forest ornaments and woven tapestries, a dark emerald carpet flooding the ground beneath us. I notice Xavier has approached Desmond, but although they are a mere distance apart, I regard their soft exchange of words. Our families have been brought up together; to anyone, it would look as if they were catching up. Unfortunately, small talk isn't embraced in royalty.

It had been three years since I last visited Briarthorn Atoll. In fact, it has been three long years since I last stepped foot in another land.

I thought I would feel refreshed, maybe even a bit joyous, but instead, a pit yawned deep in my stomach, threatening to overflow its contents.

Briarthorn Atoll has not changed much, nor have any of the siblings. Desmond was the same as ever: quiet, secluded. I had never exchanged a word with him, save for the glares thrown at each other whenever our fathers met. Our parents made sure that a distance remained between the two of us, in hopes that love would not make us lose sight of the responsibility of our soon-to-be thrones.

I attempt to move farther from the doors, hoping I could somehow disappear. I don't want to be here. I don't want to be in a room where every individual loathes me for my uncanny ability to destroy my own kingdom, but Xavier catches sight of me and I—

'Halt!' Desmond thunders.

A bellowing thump echoes through the hall. Xavier and I hold our gaze before I drop it, looking away.

Guards are placed on either side of the throne room entrance, coveted in gold armour. If I squinted enough, I'm sure I would be able to glimpse the flicker of quicksilver lacing through their rough bodies.

Every fallen soldier who dared to betray their own homeland, Briarthorn Atoll, was punished with immortality, their loyalty pledged to the rightful ruler for eternity.

General MacQuoid is stagnant beside Desmond as Xavier retreats, eyeing the guards aggressively. The rest of us stand behind as if we were ornaments waiting to be adorned. I watch Desmond, noticing his stiff figure. He has no intention of being here, it seems. As if he had sensed me staring, his gaze turns to me.

His face remains cold, a contrast to my own. I attempt a smile, immediately noticing the mark of a wolf sprawled across his neck.

His eyes are droopy and a dull, lifeless gold, thin lips set into a firm line. Gold studs were stoppered into his ears, hardly distinguishable from his skin. His nose is turned up, breathing conceit from every snout possible. As welcoming as he may intend to seem, his outfit is undoubtedly a stark disparity from his glistening features.

His attire is suited for a funeral.

Nothing I wouldn't give to have one right now.

He turns, seeming to have taken me in, taking a step forward.

I drop my gaze, embarrassment flooding my face. Why had I shown a gesture of interest?

'The High King Thaddeus Thorncrest has requested the presence of my betrothed's blood, the Ironhart family,' Desmond's voice is cool and composed. 'Burden us no more, and allow his Majesty to greet his guests.'

The guards strike their swords on the floor and pull the handles of the brooding door, squirming with bronze serpents.

A flurry of whispers suddenly erupts. I feel a shove on my back, and I'm thrust between Desmond and General MacQuoid. Without another word, Desmond loops his arm through mine and pulls me forward into the emerald throne room.

The air shifts as we enter—thick and tense.

I fake a dainty smile as we approach King Thaddeus, gliding easily over the velvet. Instead of pillars, massive barks of tree trunks shoot their way up to Caelumterra, storming the earthy roof, dressed in shades of green arrowheads. Vast golden chandeliers are hung high, with guards and royal generals in every corner and every shadow.

I notice the King, his shiny bald head bearing the Blood Crown. He wears a complete grey suit over which a green mantle shapes his pudgy body. He raises his goblet in gesture, a small smirk playing on his lips.

My heart rackets wildly, threatening to break free from the prison it is held in.

My cheeks flush, heat rushing through them fiercely. It is all I can do to not pull away from Desmond under the stinging stares of our audience. His grip is tight and uncomfortable, barely leaving me any space to walk. Queen Isolde seems bored beside King Thaddeus, her long, flaky void of a dress snaking its way down the stairs.

I hear giggling behind and recognise Genevieve's screeching voice lapsed over Xavier's cackling laughter. I'm about to turn when something cold brushes my arm. I gasp, my heart in my mouth as I slip on my dress before a hand grabs mine.

Cufflinks.

'Sorry,' a gruff voice unapologetically pardons. Desmond bores into my eyes, but both his gloved hands have resumed back inside his pockets.

The silence echoes in my ear, shattering every last nerve in my body.

'Get up!' growls Xavier, pulling me up towards him.

My heart still thunders, pumping furiously. Of all the times, something had to go wrong now? Why did fate love to play me?

'King Thaddeus,' Father booms, brushing his way past us. I notice Desmond watching Father as he pushes me aside. I stagger back, trying not to fight Xavier's grip. I will have a bruise by tomorrow. Desmond raises his eyebrows, staring into my eyes... shocked?

I hesitantly look away, turning my attention back to Father, who is halfway through his hollow statements.

'- and I am most pleased you accepted Victoria's hand in marriage.'

Queen Isolde turns her head sharply.

Father's drawl makes me squirm, but it seems to have a worse effect on King Thaddeus. I squeeze my hands tightly. King Thaddeus Thorncrest is now a pink, plump peach. Of course, he would be embarrassed accepting the marriage of the daughter of the worst King Aetheria has ever witnessed.

Despite his sheepish demeanour, he seems to overcome his humiliation in front of his royal court. He bows his head a bit, the selenite crystals on the Blood Crown reflecting in the sunlight pooling in from the windows.

'Of course, if it weren't for Xavier's involvement, my inclination would have been to decline this proposal. Unfortunately, Victoria's qualifications for the role of Queen in your Kingdom are not on par with those recognised in mine.'

I resist the urge to roll my eyes. Is King Thaddeus really trying to demean Father using me? Father doesn't regret choosing Xavier as King, and he never will.

'Threatening each land with the Dungeon of Dead Kings is the only reason you garner support, Thaddeus.'

Father smiles pleasantly, as if he had not just shamed the entire Thorncrest family of their respect. His hands come forward out of his red mantle, stubbornly clamped together.

'Fortunately, my daughters are too destined for leadership. What could be more favourable than the rule of one immature King when you have the prospect of three astute rulers working together?'

Queen Isolde suddenly erupts into a cacophony of coughs. A servant immediately rushes toward her, holding a glass of crystal water. She takes it gratefully, swigging it down in a second.

'Pardon me. Please, go on.'

I notice the slight wrinkles etched into her skin and the dark bags under her eyes. She looks sick.

Father purses his lips. King Thaddeus places a hand on his chest and lets out a haughty laugh, one that ripples goosebumps throughout my body.

'A King lost for words? Truly, your land is doomed.'

I hear Lorelei's soft remark carry through the room and stiffen.

'A Queen lost her power. A King lost his words. The land was doomed before it was even created.'

'Oh, no,' Father drags his O's grandly, 'I differ in arguing with the peasants; they are utterly worthless when it comes to playing with blood.'

King Thaddeus's eyes widen in stupefaction. I could practically hear Xavier's ridiculing laughter echoing through the throne room and across the five lands. Tension fizzes in the air, and I feel if the Kings do not pause their glares, one of them would surely be set alight.

Desmond's face creases into a frown before turning to Genevieve.

'When will dinner be set? I think our guests feel quite ravenous from the ride.'

I look at the glass pane taking up half of the right wall, draped with snaking ivy. Briarthorn Atoll's sun plunged low, already vanishing behind the tumultuous peaks bristling with silage.

Desmond beckons to me, and I smooth the front of my dress, swallowing. The uneasy quiet choking the room is too great to bear. Xavier lets go of my arm, and I rub where he had held me as I reach Desmond. His crystal rings had scorched into my arm.

'We have a lot to prepare for the upcoming occasion,' Desmond adds. 'I think a feast is in order for our engagement.'

'But the ring?' Genevieve pipes up. Murmurs arise, and I instinctively pull my hand away from Desmond's outstretched arm. The guards curiously shift towards us. The world pulls in.

'Oh, that,' I flinch visibly as Desmond pulls out a crimson box from his suit and removes the shining ruby from its saviour.

He turns slowly, pulling my hand to him, and pushes the ring onto my index finger.

His hands are cold. The ring is colder. But his next words are ice.

'Welcome to the family, Venefica.'

He called me a witch.

He *called* me a *witch*.

How dare he. How dare he offer me a ring of mercury emblazoned in melting diamond? If he was trying to kill me from the outside, it was a terrible plan for a war strategist, but from the inside?

I brush the ring softly, the silver metal coursing through the diamond coating, a gentle thrum echoing in my body as heat flares beneath where it rests. My first instinct is to yank it off and hurl it into the abyss, but my heart refuses it, forcing me to cling to the possessive prison Desmond had bound me in.

We sit at a long table, obnoxious blabbering exploding from each side. Father and Elysande, and King Thaddeus and Queen Isolde sat at opposite ends of the table, while Lorelei, Genevieve and I sit across from Desmond and Xavier.

Desmond had removed his blazer, revealing his white button-up shirt. It was uncharacteristic for a prince, especially one who was about to become King. Royalty should always maintain their decorum, even when no one is watching.

Roasted vegetables adorn every dish, and tiny bowls of caviar are placed across each royalty. The stench of wine floods the room and I suddenly lose my appetite, playing around with the juicy meat. I reach out for a goblet to have a sip of water, my heart still thundering yet stagnant in its position. Unease is holding it down.

'When is your coronation?' Desmond asks Xavier over the chatter.

'Junius eighteenth,' Xavier replies stoically.

'Thaddeus,' says Queen Isolde.

'Victoria must be envious,' Desmond says again. I stop shifting the food on my plate.

'Of course, she cannot handle the truth,' Xavier shuts Desmond down once more.

I bite my lower lip hard.

'Thaddeus,' Queen Isolde repeats. She coughs a little.

'It's not every day the youngest is chosen for such a duty over the oldest. Usually, it is the mature who have better sense.' Desmond innocently takes a swig of wine, inclining his head toward me.

'Unfortunately, although I may appeal to you as childish and senseless, I have more spite than you could put together,' Xavier lashes.

'Thaddeus Thorncrest!' Queen Isolde roars.

The table falls quiet.

Slowly, I turn to King Thaddeus.

His head lolls up and down, purple foam spewing from his mouth, his emerald eyes losing colour. The Blood Crown clatters from his head onto the floor, shading a dull gold. What if I grabbed the crown and ran? I shake my head aggressively, placing a hand to my head.

A chair clatters to the floor.

'Fa-Father?' Lorelei breathes shakily.

Desmond looks unnerved.

Another piercing screech echoes. Only, it's not Queen Isolde—it's Elysande. I jolt up in a rush, spilling the water all over the table. I frantically look around before concentrating my gaze on Elysande.

'Oh my lord!'

'What is it?' I say, my heartbeat rising with every word uttered. But when the deed is shown to me, a daunting feeling in my chest renders me silent.

I couldn't be happier.

'He's dead! M-My hus-husband! King Avalorian! He's dead!'

CHAPTER IV

'I demand to know who killed my husband!' Queen Isolde cries.

I heave. Father is dead. Father is dead—and I am happy?

I turn to Xavier, watching his gaze crumple. He wouldn't kill Father, would he? I shake my head. Why am I even thinking that? Xavier would never do such a thing, would he?

My gaze slips to Desmond, who can barely control his reaction. He bites his lip nervously, swallowing. If I weren't so sure about his grief, I might have confessed to lying as a tiny tear drop rolls down his cheek, spilling to the floor. He quickly wipes his eye before looking away. I plop down daintily into my seat, a rush of apprehension sloshing over me. My plan was to kill King Thaddeus. Instead of one dead body, we had two. And if Father has been killed, then the next target would be Xav—

'Y-Your Highness, m-maybe the w-wine was poisoned?' General MacQuoid splutters, splaying his hands, unsure of what to do.

I flinch as I watch a flustered Queen Isolde wag her arms in the air.

'Nonsense, Elysande and I both drank the wine. Why, so did Desmond!'

'Could it have been slipped in later?' General MacQuoid tries again, attempting to calm Queen Isolde.

It didn't work.

She screams fervently in Latin, cursing loudly at the General before exploding into coughs. I shake my head in frustration. What had I been thinking about?

'Possibly,' Xavier suddenly says, walking over to the corpses. He seems to have recovered from his short stupor.

Instinctively, I feel something gnaw at my back. I turn, noticing Desmond watching me. I look away quickly. What was going to happen to our plan now?

Was it strange that I did not feel any remorse about Father's death, but instead felt more concern for the future of the Kingdom?

'Wraith Berry.'

'Pardon?' Queen Isolde exclaims, her voice drenched with a mixture of anger and astonishment. I turn to see Xavier eyeing the violet foam dubiously.

'Wraith Berry,' Xavier calmly repeats.

'Impossible,' Desmond kicks off his chair, striding over to where Xavier stands. 'We do not harbour such poisons in our Kingdom.'

'How dare you accuse us of such vile doings!' Lorelei seethes, her hands balled into fists. 'Only the Tribe of the Famished possess such deadly venom!'

Genevieve places a hand on her sister's shoulder.

'But it has come to my knowledge that a hidden stash has been stored in the castle's dungeons,' Xavier replies lightly, beckoning towards Desmond. 'Is Desmond not in charge of the trade of provisions between all five lands?'

Genevieve's face drops, and Lorelei is at a loss for words. I look between Desmond and Xavier. Had he just accused Desmond of killing his own father?

'I have had enough!' Queen Isolde bursts, hand over her

chest. 'We accept the Ironhart family graciously into our abode, only to witness the deaths of our dutiful kings. And by the heavens, you accuse us of hoarding the most powerful bane in the world?'

Her words echo through the throne room.

Elysande sheepishly plays with her snowy braids, and I tug at the golden locket laced around my neck. It is... bewildering. Only our family knew of killing King Thaddeus. Could it be that Xavier foolishly filled in Desmond in our plan, allowing him to take revenge?

But why has he not informed his family of our ploy?

I splay my fingers, legs shaking rapidly. What was happening?

'My Queen, why don't we provide the Ironhart family a place to sleep? Until then, we can inform the kingdoms of the unfortunate... murders.' General MacQuoid sighs, ushering us to the hallway.

'King Xavier, I— '

'King?'

The word escapes my mouth before I can stop myself. I meet Xavier's steely gaze and pull an arm around myself protectively.

It was that look, the one he had given me when I promised to breathe not a single word of his participation in the Tribal War.

All heads turn to me.

'E-Elysande is still queen,' I splutter. 'You cannot dethrone her without—'

'Victoria dear. I cannot handle the burden of your father's death and the stress of ruling a kingdom,' Elysande places a hand on her chest, breathing raggedly. 'I abdicate my ruling.'

My heart thunders, like a steed stampeding across iron, each thump pounding in my ear.

'Then it is agreed,' Xavier announces, triumphantly grinning at me.

You can't just abdicate your ruling. There are formalities. I open my mouth, then shut it again.

What's the use?

I would be brushed aside anyway.

Xavier clamps his hands together and Lorelei eyes him in stupefaction.

'General Steelborne and I will travel to Ferrumisle to inform our Land of the demise upon us, while the ladies stay here, if that is all right with you, Queen Isolde?'

'Very well,' Desmond replies without missing a beat. 'Mother, will you—'

'I will remain as Queen until a solution has been garnered!' A near choking echo catches me off guard.

Desmond shakes his head, Lorelei moving towards their mother and caressing her back, eyes wide open.

'General?' he sighs, removing his gloves and massaging his temples.

'Yes, my Prince?' General MacQuoid steps forward.

'King Xavier and I have certain issues to discuss. Would you be so kind as to take the ladies into their chambers?'

Issues?

General MacQuoid hesitates, then claps his hands. 'Alright then, Miss Victoria and Prince Desmond can—'

'I would prefer my own chamber,' I say quietly, ignoring the look in Desmond's eyes.

General MacQuoid nods, a bit surprised by my interruption.

'Hemsworth, escort the princesses and the Queen to the guest room,' he signals to a servant, who comes forward with a bobbing head, imitating that of a duck. 'Our Prince, and, er, King, prefer solitude.'

I look to Xavier, tilting my head. *What are you doing?* I want to ask him. *Tell me, so I can plan my—*

'We will see you in a while, Victoria,' Desmond says. I squint and stare at him. There is something in his eyes that I cannot seem to put my finger on. Did he think I was nervous? I mean, I was nervous, but why did he care?

Lorelei grunts, shoving her dishevelled hair back as she storms into the hallway, Genevieve trailing behind her like a lost shadow, her eyes glassy and vacant like those of a zombie. Queen Isolde lets out a weary sigh, her fingers gently brushing over King Thaddeus's head as she mutters something inaudible.

With a wave of her hand, the Blood Crown floats loftily behind her, shimmering in the dim light. In moments, I am the only one left among the little cult, the air thick with tension.

I attempt to follow, pulling off the chair, my legs slick with sweat. I walk, aware of the eyes boring into my back. Just a few more steps.

Five more steps.

Click clack.

Four more steps.

Click.

Three more steps.

Clack.

Two more steps.

Click.

I'm almost out—then I can finally breathe again.

One more step.

I feel his shadow behind me before he places a rough hand on the door.

'I hope you aren't too close to your little brother,' Desmond breathes. He reeks of mint.

My breath catches. What was Desmond going to do to him? Why do I even care?

Desmond notices my movement and edges closer until the faint smell of charcoal fills my nostrils.

'He may no longer be King.'

Victoria Ironhart
Day 8,

~

You bring me peace,
but you tear me apart,
like I am nothing but a misery to be dealt,
an obstacle to destruct.
I try not to focus,
but your complexion is too focal,
and I cannot help but beg
and wonder why Woe fills me in such distress.

~

'Victoria Drakewell Ironhart.'
I looked down, but I felt the searing burn of Father's eyes digging into my forehead.
'On countless occasions—ah—' Father scoffed before continuing, 'Tell me—what are you doing loitering around the castle?'
I didn't say anything.
'Do you not have a duty as Princess?'
My head stayed down, my position stagnant—one foot forward, one hand on the floor—as if waiting for a crown to be placed upon my locks.
'Answer me, Victoria!' his voice thundered through the throne room.
I still didn't say anything. After the incident with Xavier, he had made it his daily duty to remind me of my naivety in falling—literally—into Xavier's trap. I was forcing myself to keep quiet. I knew if I said something—anything—it would be the end of my reign.
It was true, what Xavier had said.
Father did hate me.
I could see it simmering in his eyes, burning in his flesh with

every flexed muscle. I wasn't enough for him. Underneath my feet lay a freshly coveted burgundy carpet stretching to the throne. I felt the little thud of my teardrop shake the iron earth underneath and clamped my hands into fists to stop from trembling.

Don't cry, I had told myself. He wasn't worth your tears.

A small sigh, barely audible, escaped Father's lips.

'This cannot occur ever again.'

I jolted my head up.

'Accept my sincere apologies, but the fate of our Kingdom is at stake.'

His voice held no remorse.

He rose from his throne, thrusting his cloak behind him and glared down at me. You let me down, said his eyes.

'From this day onwards, Prince Xavier has been elected as Heir to the throne of Ferrumisle!' he boomed. His voice was carried by the iron bricks into the homes of the peasants as if they were speakers on full volume.

'We let no unworthy heir sit upon our throne! You shall bow to your future King!'

I could practically hear the whooping and cheering. Every vile, filthy emotion slithered into me, hissed and bled until—

Something bloomed in me. But this time, it was no resentment, no feeling of how I had let down Father. My whole life I had been trying to impress him. This time, it was strong, wild, fearless.

I wanted to do something. Something that would bless me to witness the deaths of my Father and my brother and Briarthorn Atoll's entire lineage.

All I needed was patience.

This was not a wish.

This was not hope.

It was pure, raw desire.

~

I woke up on a ship, strained and tied to a column with ropes. They dug into my ashen skin. I won't bore you with the finer details, though. I escaped, and that's all you need to know. They didn't kill me on the spot.

Fools.

I would've laughed, but I was busy strangling a guard who had attempted to run a spear through me. The thud of his dead body against wood was all the affirmation I needed to know that no more soldiers hid under the deck. I sighed, pressing at the bruise on the back of my head.

The rock had hit too hard—enough to knock me out for a while.

I could make out the figures on the land and the short, stubby buildings that outlined the horizon. It suddenly clicked where I was.

Ferrumisle.

Oh, home sweet home.

Now wasn't the time to ruminate on my past, though. I barely remembered it.

I saw the cannons first. I don't recall what exactly happened, except that I stood behind the large metal barrel, scooping the bomb in one hand and shoving it down the nozzle. Then I heaved, pushing the cannon to where the men stood—and fired.

I did the same thing over and over. You would have thought the bomb must have stung, but I was beyond it.

Even pain realised that an adversary such as me was beyond defying. Even pain realised I could inflict more agony than it ever could.

Another bang. Another crash. Another piercing roar that struck the land, but I did not stop until I witnessed the last lifeless body on the cracking earth.

Then did I thunk down the plank, boots thumping against the wood, and greet my land with the ruler it deserved.

CHAPTER V

'Father's dead,' I mutter. He's really dead.

'No one cares about your bloody father,' Lorelei spits, her arms folded across her chest. 'Our father is, and that means the Kingdom will be in upheaval!'

I swallow the bulge in my throat. They were right. Everyone would be ecstatic about father's death and would hope the entire family is wiped out.

But who could have killed him?

Supposedly Desmond—but why?

'I'm surprised you're sad, considering what your Father has done to you,' Genevieve sneers, plopping down on the neatly folded bed.

I flinch. She was spoiling the carefully made covers. I feel bad for the servants here. It must be tiring to clean up after this family.

We were in the guest room. The beds were high off the floor and on either side of the walls, requiring ladders to climb. I would be scared to sleep in here; it was large enough to conceal monsters that could be lurking in every shadow.

'We should talk about why Father treated me the way he did,' I murmur pointedly.

'What?' Lorelei scoffs, laughing. I look up, not realising they must have heard. Heat floods my cheeks. 'What did we ever do to you?'

'You mean whatever did Desmond do to you,' Genevieve corrects her sister, clicking her tongue.

'It is because of him Xavier has that crown and I don't,' I bite out.

Desmond's words come flooding into my mind. *He may no longer be king.*

I should be happy about that, right? I curl my fingers. It still didn't change the fact that I wanted to prove myself.

No, resuming my position as queen in Ferrumisle would do nothing.

I needed the Blood Crown. Lorelei glares at me, and I pull into myself even more.

'It's your fault for opening the gates,' she shrugs, chuckling wryly.

No, it was not. It was not. It was Xavier's, right?

Right?

'Why did your land attack that day, though?' I ask, shaking the thought out of my head.

Genevieve shrugs before sarcastically adding, 'Desmond felt like dethroning a princess and killing half your land.'

I gawk at her. What if Desmond really did want to kill us all?

She sighs. 'Why would I know? He barely ever tells us anything. That one's in his own shell and hardly ever utters a word unless absolutely necessary.'

Lorelei bursts into cackles. 'Don't tell me you believed that. Desmond doesn't kill without reason,' she pouts mockingly. 'So don't worry too much about your head being chopped off.'

I bite my lip, sheepish.

I couldn't tell if that was an insult or a compliment, but if it's from these two sisters, it should most certainly be taken into offence.

'W-will there be any food left?' I stutter, trying to ignore their barbs. My stomach grumbles, but a heavy pit had already long formed. If I ate, I would throw up. Why had I asked that? I should have kept my mouth shut, like I always do.

'If you want dinner served in your quarters, then sure,' Genevieve answers. I nod, curling deeper into the bed.

A beat of silence passes.

'I'm off,' Genevieve announces to no one in particular, bounding off the bed. 'I'm going to be back with a few kills.'

Lorelei scowls. 'Don't tell me you're leaving me with this pathetic form of life. She doesn't even talk.'

I swallow. Crystals begin to jab the inside of my palm. She could have worded that better; I wasn't that bad.

'I didn't say you had to stay with her,' Genevieve points out, grinning.

My heart drops to my gut.

Lorelei smirks. 'Oh, right. I forgot I was given the freedom to go and do whatever I want.'

'Have a good night's sleep, Victoria dear,' Genevieve croons as Lorelei follows. I quickly pull off the bed, watching as the green-haired stollar saunters over to the pulley.

'Wai—'

I nearly scream as darkness engulfs the room. I dart around wildly, but I see nothing—only pitch-black shadows pressing in. I stumble, my hands shaking as they flail against the walls, searching frantically for the door.

A gust of wind breathes down my neck. I stiffen, my breath coming out in shallow puffs. My heart beats erratically, and my soul is in my throat.

I whip around, feet tangling in my dress. A crash reverberates as I stagger to the floor. Did I trip—or did something pull me down? I choke back a scream, scrambling to get up as panic threatens to drown me. The laughter grows, mocking and relentless. I'm trapped. No way out. The darkness is alive, and it wants me.

It wants to kill me and swamp me in its void, just like everyone else around me.

I pull up against something cool, hard—and hot. I yank my hand away. That was metal, and that meant this was a door.

Breathe in, breathe out.

An eerie sigh escapes from somewhere in the room, and I act on my instincts, trembling hands wrenching the bar and heaving it open. The dim chandelier casts an iron warmth over my skin, and I gasp for air before staggering outside onto the rough carpet.

I try to stand, legs wobbly as I slam shut the darkness that threatens to envelop me whole, and break into a run.

I pass by chamber after chamber, panicking. Desmond's chamber. I need to find Desmond's chamber. Where could I find his chamber?

I try to remember the map of Briarthorn Atoll's palace, stumbling over my dress—and it clicks. Next to the Chief Commander's Office. I dart down the stairs, glimpsing a look behind for a shadow or anything of the sort.

I see a hazy figure emerge from behind the wall.

I stumble, catching onto the railing and muffling a gasp as it stings my bare hands. I place a cool palm over the burn and rush down the flight of stairs, panting heavily before turning right and—oh, sweet oblivion.

I crash into the door, flinging it open and diving straight onto the bed, leaving the door wide open behind me. My body trembles as I clutch the blankets around myself, gasping for air; my breath comes in wild, erratic bursts.

Breathe in, breathe out.

It was alright; everything was fine.

I thrash around, ducking under the blanket. Father is dead. My eyes flicker wildly around the dark room.

Breathe in, breathe out.

Distract yourself.

Today. What happened today? Father's death.

A tinkle of a bell echoes, and I shiver. Everything would be fine. I'm fine. It's alright. I am in the most fortified palace in all of Aetheria. Nothing could hurt me.

I let out a shaky breath.

Curse Genevieve and Lorelei. I couldn't even do anything to them.

I clench my hands into fists, my nails digging into my palms. We have no course of action, and if I know any better, I would be thrown to the dead.

I swallow, clutching the blankets around me tighter. I am of no use to either Xavier or Desmond. I am no use to anyone any longer. Father could not kill me for the plans I was conceiving—so I could go ahead with them.

My heart stops.

All I had to do was kill Desmond. A simple plan, yet equally complicated.

'Kill Desmond,' the words taste bitter on my tongue. Like I shouldn't be saying them. But I can.

A shuffle echoes. I stiffen.

I throw the blanket off my head and slump when I realise what was making the noise. I was still in my dress, and each movement of the flaky material against the rough blanket caused my pulse to beat erratically.

Breathe in, breathe out. Desmond. Think about Desmond. Killing a hundred thousand people would take too long. Now that both Kings were out of the question, Queen Isolde would have to forcefully abandon the Blood Crown to Desmond.

She couldn't wear it anyway if she tried to.

I rub my hands together, watching the open door that had begun to close because of the wind.

I hope it is the wind.

The Blood Crown can only be worn by a direct descendant of the ruling bloodline—meaning the sons or daughters of the current ruler. However, if the rightful heir is killed, the crown passes to the regicides.

I could hear Mother echoing those words as she warned me of the crown's power. I didn't care then. My job was to be a dutiful princess. Yet here I am today, plotting to steal that very coronet.

If I could get the crown, the world would be at my feet. No one would see me as the pitiful princess I am, and I could finally vow revenge over every single person who had wronged me.

I shiver.

The threat of my own death lingers uneasily in the air, like a dagger about to cut straight through my heart. A crack echoes.

I grope under the pillow. A knife.

The door begins to creak open, slowly.

'W-who's there?' I sputter, jolting up and brandishing the knife.

The door slides open wider, a bright light flashing for a mere second before a shadow engulfs it whole. My heart pounds furiously until a voice sighs.

'Desmond.' The door clicks shut as he emerges. 'I thought you insisted on having another chamber.'

He trudges in, flipping on the light. The room is filled with maps and books of all sorts: writings during the War of Aetheria, the Tribal War between Briarthorn Atoll and Ferrumisle, their course of action and strategies. Lush green plants sprout from under his table, swarming his aged wall with squirming ivy, and stone covers each end of the room. The only wooden objects to be seen are the beds.

'Might be best to keep the knife away. Doesn't really give you a good impression in this...' He waves his hand about. '...situation, considering our past.' His lips twitch. I hesitantly toss the knife across the length of the room. It clatters against his table.

Whether I like it or not, he has a point. I can tell he was—if not harrowed—grieving his father, even if he refused to show it.

Out of all the royal families, Desmond and King Thaddeus had the greatest bond. They would never betray each other.

Father had attempted to assassinate King Thaddeus and frame Desmond in hopes of manipulating the crown a few moons before the Tribal War. It failed. But of course, it wasn't enough. Father had to fail masterfully, so he plotted to steal the Blood Crown once more, and look where that got him.

'Where's Xavier?' The words leave my mouth in abundant fear. I didn't intend for it to sound like that. It shouldn't have sounded like that. I breathe heavily. Desmond raises his eyebrows, leaning against the door.

I admire his patience. He's still wearing a suit.

'He's alive. I'm not cold-hearted enough to kill your brother, although he is.'

'What do you mean?' I say, widening my eyes at the confession. He knew of our plan, but why hadn't he stopped it? Desmond ignores me, continuing in a lazy drawl. I bite the inside of my tongue. I hate it when people decide I'm not important enough to be given attention to.

'I hope your father's death didn't shake you as much as it did Xavier.'

I swallow. It hadn't shaken me a bit. 'I could say the same for you,' I murmur.

At that, Desmond chuckles. 'Well, would you be surprised if I told you?'

Breathe in, breathe out. A cold, stinging silence settles between us.

'Why did you want my hand in marriage?' Desmond asks. He tosses his coat aside and comes to sit next to me on our bed. *His* bed. I don't say anything. I don't know what to say. 'Oh, right. Wrong question.' The bedweight shifts as he lies down, right arm under his head. 'Why did you *agree* to the marriage?'

I didn't have a choice.

More silence.

'It was a rushed thing,' I manage to say. I splay my fingers.

'So you would marry the person who attempted to destroy your kingdom and brought your demise?' Desmond scoffs. It was clear he thought of me as low as anyone else would. 'Both faults do burden your shoulders.'

I round on him, clutching the coverlet as heat flushes my cheeks. 'It was not my fault!'

'You were tricked by your own brother?' he drawls on.

'He is my brother! I could trust him,' I punch the pillow next to me, flustered.

'Like father, like daughter,' Desmond chuckles. The realisation hits me straight in the gut. I trusted Xavier, and he left me for the dead to get the throne. Father trusted Xavier, and now he's dead. *Like father, like daughter.*

Desmond claps his hands as my face morphs into shock. 'Xavier killed Father?'

It's not true.

I know it's not.

'Some queen you would make,' he raises an eyebrow, pulling up from the bed.

He begins to unbutton his shirt. Desmond didn't have proof of Xavier doing the deed because he did it himself. He would have shown me if he did have evidence, being the arrogant brat he is. I'm sure of it. I jump off the bed, moving to his table suddenly.

'What are you doing?' Desmond's voice reverberates through the room, brimmed with panic. I shuffle through his papers, trying to find it. 'Since we're... betrothed, I must be allowed to poke my nose into your business.'

'Without my permission?' he gasps, tripping over the bed post as he attempts to stop me from tugging open his drawers.

I thought he didn't talk unless absolutely necessary—which means he is hiding something.

I scoff. 'Since when did people ask for permission to look for evidence?' I hear something clatter against the ground. There it is! I reach for it, but then a hand grabs it before I can.

The bottle slips from his hand, smashing to the floor. We halt, breathing heavily. I look around in alarm as a thick, purple fluid flows out grudgingly, and a stench of wine fills the room.

Wraith Berry.

I step back in a bit of a haze, staring at the liquid. Desmond had killed Father.

'Did you kill your father too?' I choke out.

Trembling, I stagger away from Desmond. He pulls himself up, advancing towards me. He spreads his arms out wide, and I panic. I edge back to the bed, turning when my back meets the rough backboard.

Then two warm hands come around my shoulders.

'Desmond?' I manage to gag.

'I'm sorry, Victoria,' he breathes. 'Our marriage will be sealed in a month, and the very next day, my coronation,' I see him swallow.

He lets go of me, but his hand stuffs a tiny bottle in my mouth. I muffle a gasp, grabbing his arms before—

'Princess?'

'Princess?'

I force my eyes to blink open. Where was I?

'Princess?'

Was that a lady, or was that a man? I mumble and grope blindly before a shrilling screech jerks me awake.

'What happened?' I gasp. My back aches, and I realise I'm lying on the cobblestone floor.

'A poke in the eye is all,' the lady murmurs.

What had happened last night? I recount the events, rubbing my head and hair that is greasy from sweat.

What had happened? Why couldn't I remember? I had been alone in the room, then Desmond had walked in and—

The revelation hits me in the head. *I'm sorry, Victoria.*

I jolt up, pain shooting through my head.

'Where's Desmond?' I look around wildly.

Where is the bloody prince? He poisoned me to sleep! I want to scream.

'Agatha,' the lady says, seeming slightly freaked. She turns to the woman beside her. 'Inform our prince his betrothed has awoken? She seems to be in quite a state.'

I shake my head. 'No, no. Don't tell him.' I heave up from the floor, the lady rooted to the ground. I make my way to the bathroom, slipping a bit.

'My princess,' the lady speaks once more.

'Yes?' I try not to sigh.

'Prince Desmond and the rest of the royal family are in the throne room,' she says. I stop in my tracks, blinking. What? I bite my lower lip and turn reluctantly. She is short for her age, with tiny braids snaking around her skull. She wears a hand-me-down embroidered doublet, its green colours tattered and torn.

'Was this planned?'

'No, it was not,' the lady answers. 'Prince Desmond had urgently scheduled this late at night. He mentioned something about eliminating threats from the Palace immediately.'

'Somethin' about you, m' princess,' Agatha pipes up. Her white hair and accent contrast with her thin demeanour and pale skin. She must be from Fames. 'Said you need not know until mornin', otherwise you woulda' tried to stop him.'

'Stop him from doing what?' I scoff, throwing my hands into the air. Seriously, how would I stop him?

'Why,' Agatha starts, and the lady next to her frantically shakes her head, 'from killin' the King, of course.'

Agatha pours hot water into the tub that has been brought in. The other servant sighs exasperatedly and purses her lips.

Kill the King. My breath catches in my throat.
He may no longer be King.
Xavier is the King.

Victoria Ironhart,
Day 7,

~

Oh woe,
what torment you fill me with,
truly exceptional in thy misery,
no matter how desperate I become,
no matter how ecstatic,
you remain in my heart
like a lover's tortured soul,
forever.

~

I was afraid I would cherish that day forever—and I have—to
the point where my heart convulses in agitation.
'Come on, Victoria,' Xavier called me over.
I could see his behemoth friends giggling like little adolescents
along the cliff. I had watched sceptically, debating whether to follow
him or not.
'Come on, it's fine. Let's go!' Xavier repeated, his insistence forcing
me to my feet. He was only seventeen.
He pulled me by my arm, dragging me towards his friends. 'Sit
down,' he ordered. I did as I was told, an uneasy grin plastered across
my face. 'We're going to test your powers,' Arnold said, one of Xavier's
best friends. He is the son of King Vorin of the Tribe of the Famished.
'Alright,' I answered, bewildered. Test my powers?

Xavier smirked mischievously, pulling out a cloth from behind his back.

The fabric came over my eyes, the sunlight disappeared, and I felt his hands tying the silky material into a tight knot.

'Can you see anything?' he asked, finally removing his hands.

'No,' I replied. It was pitch black, but I recognised something weird. The snickering had increased.

'Good,' Xavier said, 'Stand up.'

His voice had become more demanding.

I rose from the grass, unsure, wobbling.

'Father said he doesn't want you on the throne. He hates you. He said you're just another obstacle in life,' he started matter-of-factly.

What?

Something poked me in the back, and I staggered forwards—no, maybe backwards, I can't tell.

'Father said you're too naive and stupid to be on the throne, that I am the perfect heir,' Xavier continued, enunciating every pronoun.

My heart cracked.

What else had I expected?

I desperately attempted to pull off the cloth, but I couldn't remove it. My heart hammered.

Xavier must have used the binding spell.

I felt hands on my back, and I'm pushed forward. I felt tiny pebbles, large cracks in the grassy stone.

'He told me to kill you.'

I gasped, and then a shrill shriek erupted when I felt the slippery stone beneath me. I frantically flailed my arms in horror.

And then Xavier grabbed my doublet by the collar.

My heart slowed. Maybe he was just telling me that he disagreed with Father. Maybe it was one of those cruel pranks he pulled on Anwen, our servant, to boast his spite.

But then I was jolted forward, and my foot slipped.

The last words I heard were the ones engraved into every nick and crook of my body.

'And I promised him to do so.'

~

'She's in there!' roared a distant voice.

I clutched the ground, trembling.

I could do this. Only a few more, only a few more.

The dirt morphed into sharp crystals, jutting out from the ground all around me. I squeezed my eyes shut, willing for them to rise quicker, faster. If the men passed the curve, I would be doomed, dead for sure.

I heard the soft slice of crystals erupting, first slow, then more rapidly.

An angry bellow echoed.

Stars were forming in my vision when the first blood-curdling scream ripped through the sky. Each slice was deafening, but it didn't leave a single mark on my soul.

Each one of them pierced through the thousands of crystals that jutted out from beneath. I opened my eyes as a flurry of screams echoed, and I tried not to laugh. It was happening. I was so close.

I heard footsteps as blood clawed out from my eyes. I pushed the ground harder. Whoever was behind me would be killed in seconds. I heard something whirl through the air. Just one mo—

The clicking of my heels falls in unison with the bellows echoing from the throne room. I try my best not to get caught in the emerald silk that trails loosely behind.

I hear swords clank and quicken my pace. The raven fur coat I wear sweeps the floor like a broom. Desmond was going to kill Xavier. I should have slowed my pace, but if Desmond realises I know about his little plot, he may try to frame me for treason and have a chance at my throat too.

He would have glory for wiping out the worst royal family in Aetheria.

Chests are lined every few feet across the hallway, each turn leading into a new labyrinth I have yet to discover. The lush green carpet prevents me from slipping when I burst the marble doors open, only to find myself face to face with two gleaming silver swords.

And a dagger that flies straight at my face.

I duck quickly as a scream escapes my throat.

'Lorelei!' gasps Desmond. He knocks it out in a swift movement with his sword, the dagger clattering to the floor. My heart stilled.

One wrong move and I would have been dead.

'You came early,' Lorelei scoffs, lazily lowering her arm.

'Missed by a beat, Lorelei,' Genevieve chuckles, clapping her hands. 'Desmond would've needed a new wife to solidify his rule.'

'I need a new wife regardless,' Desmond bites out. He holds out a hand, and I begrudgingly take it, pulling me up. I immediately snatch my hand away when I'm on my feet.

'What do you mean?' Genevieve raises an eyebrow. Both the sisters stand boisterously on the red carpet, and it seems they are here uninvited—just as I am.

Queen Isolde merely watches from her throne, misery glazing her forest eyes. They are red and puffy from crying, and the tear stains are noticeable over her fixed makeup.

'Where's Elysande?' I speak before Desmond has the chance to answer.

'She needed sleep,' came Xavier's stark reply. I startle. I had barely registered he was present with us because of my near encounter with death. He glares at me, pulling his sword back, sheathing it once more.

'We thought this would go by better if the King would easily confess to his actions in solitude,' Desmond explains.

'And we have been attempting to understand what on Aetheria the *King*,' Lorelei air quotes aggressively, 'has to confess to.'

My eyes flicker from Xavier to Lorelei to Desmond.

Desmond wears nothing but a blue suit.

'Is that why you drugged me?' I ask suddenly.

Desmond glares at me when Genevieve gasps, 'You did what?'

Breathe in, breathe out.

I curl my fingers, heart racketing. 'That's why Elysande's not here,'

What was going on? What meeting did Desmond want to have that could involve getting Elysande and me drugged?

'Maybe you could have cared to inform me what you were to do?' I say to Desmond, trembling. I was being left in the dark all the time.

'You would have tried to stop me,' he shrugs lazily.

'How do you know what I would and would not do? You just met me,' I mutter softly.

Desmond rolls his eyes, not bothering to answer back.

'Can we get to the part of what your brother did that made this unfortunate meeting possible?' Lorelei scowls and points at Xavier, who has remained unusually quiet.

He stares at me weirdly, as if I have been acting bizarre.

'What?' I ask.

Xavier strides forward aggressively, suddenly.

My soul leaves my body as I stagger back at the memory of his hand on my collar.

He grabs my wrist, engraving the metal wound into my flesh as I clamp my mouth shut, blood dribbling from my tongue.

'Remember who you are and why you are here,' he growls quietly.

I nod, attempting to clear my throat.

'Keep using that pretty little face of yours,' Xavier remarks, tightening his grip. 'It's the only thing that should be working.'

My blood boils. How dare he see me as a toy. Xavier yanks his hand away when a crystal pierces his finger.

The words leave my mouth before I can stop myself. 'So you're not going to inform them of Father's stupid plan to steal the Blood Crown?' I raise my voice loud enough for the rest to hear us.

My heart rackets. Why the hell did I say that?

Another gasp escapes Genevieve, and Lorelei rounds on her mother. 'I told you they were to betray us. Kill them all, who knows what trouble they could cause!'

Xavier furiously shoves me backward, Desmond catching me before I fall to the ground. I don't let him pull me up this time. I can still feel the way he jerked the bottle of ivory down my mouth.

'You came here for the crown. You got yours—now leave,' Desmond snarls.

'Oh, I will leave. But I shall return shortly to send blessings upon my sister's marriage,' Xavier smirks wickedly.

He gives me a pointed look—one that says he trusts me to continue acting the doll. I nod once, trying to hide the panic flushing my cheeks. Xavier doesn't have a plan. He doesn't know what to do next—which means I can initiate my own. I swallow the metallic liquid in my mouth, a rush of apprehension dawning once more. Was I sure of the plan?

Because if I wasn't, I was going to live this cruel life for a month more, and then I would be six feet under the ground.

'You may leave *after* Desmond informs us of what you did,' Lorelei scowls, blocking Xavier's path to the door. When did she get there?

'I don't think that is necessary,' Desmond sighs, brushing past me. His hair is an absolute mess. He should at least carry himself like a king.

'No,' she firmly stands her ground.

'Lorelei, you know well this meeting was not meant for any of you; now please, stop being a pain and move.'

Lorelei holds her gaze for a second before shifting to the right sullenly, and Desmond places a hand on Xavier's back as he pushes open the door for him.

Desmond looks as if he's about to play the jester for Queen Isolde when he re-enters a moment later.

He locks eyes with me, cocking a brow. 'Do you feel better?'

My eyes widen. 'Feel better after you drugged me?' Desmond shrugs. 'It was for the best.'

I nearly gag. 'H-how so?'

'I would have killed him if there weren't so many people around,' he says easily.

I go quiet. 'Trying to kill Xavier won't stop him from getting the crown,' I finally say, and Desmond's facade shifts, his voice reaching a dangerous decibel.

'Are you saying I'll have to kill you too?'

I swallow, a garden of fear and anger blooming inside me.

He shoves past. 'All of you, to the Palace Gardens. We have much to discuss.'

The door bangs beside him as Queen Isolde sighs. She plops off the throne, her thin body seeming sickly grey, Lorelei following suit. It is only Genevieve who lingers for a mere moment, casting me a reassuring glance.

A spike of frustration ripples through me. Why did everyone take pity on me?

I wanted power over my own life. That's freedom, right?

And to get that power, the crown, I had to do something. I had to make sacrifices. Father is dead. Desmond was going to kill Xavier, no doubt.

I take a sharp intake of breath, hands twitching as a lone thought crosses my mind. It was time.

I was going to kill Desmond Nathaniel Thorncrest.

CHAPTER VI

'You didn't seem to care that Desmond was going to kill Xavier,' Genevieve whispers. I shudder, the cold wind slapping my cheeks through the open windows. They are patterned with gold leaves across the borders, soft, silky emerald curtains thrashing in the winter air.

I quicken my pace to catch up with Desmond, but Genevieve refuses to leave my side.

'Given Ferrumisle's relations, I don't think you need to question it,' I answer. My voice comes out hoarse.

'I wasn't asking,' came Genevieve's amused reply. 'I'm merely stating. Although, it's not surprising, knowing that he is ascending to the throne and you're not.'

'What's not surprising?' I ask, fidgeting with a feather from my coat. It comes loose and I hesitantly let it sink to the floor.

Lorelei and Queen Isolde begin speaking in hushed tones, and I see Desmond twitch slightly.

'That you would be so nonchalant towards his death,' Genevieve replies simply. Her armour-like suit clanks with every step she takes. Grime is scraped across her face and grass coats her leggings. Genevieve is well known for her steeds. She must have gone riding in the morning and come across the meeting by coincidence. 'He would be out of the way to the throne, then.'

I tilt my head, trying to hide the worry that creases my face. It was pretty obvious what she was implying, but I asked Genevieve anyway to confuse her. 'Y-You think I want Xavier dead to get my throne?' I stutter, staring.

If anyone finds out I was joyous regarding Xavier's death, I was surely going to be killed. I couldn't die with the knowledge that I had not tried to make my life better.

She smirks. 'Your throne?'

I shrug.

Well, it was and would have always been mine.

Genevieve scoffs. 'In your dreams. You're stuck here as the Queen of Briarthorn Atoll.'

I immediately grasp her dismal tone.

Should I say it, or should I not?

The dark room conjures once more in my mind and I cover a shiver that tingles my spine. When she could use my fears against me, why couldn't I?

'At least I'm Queen.' I look down at her slyly, but a small pit forms in my stomach. 'You're not too ecstatic about that, are you? Do I have to be worried about someone killing me as well?'

Genevieve startles for a moment, a fervent fire burning in her deep grey eyes. I shrug, falling in pace with Desmond as she curses behind me.

Did I go too far?

'Here,' comes Desmond's gruff voice.

After what seems like an eternity, we have reached the castle's Palace Gardens. Desmond halts, pulling open the birch door, Queen Isolde turning soft eyes towards me before being dragged in by Lorelei. Genevieve glares, and I feel a soft nudge from Desmond.

I look up at him—he hasn't earned my trust yet, not after what he did last night.

We follow close behind, with Desmond snaking an arm around my waist, steering me to the table in the centre. It is dark, and a putrid stench envelops our surroundings. Everything is musty and ancient, except for the garden we walk upon. We sit on the small mushroom stools, poised in front of each other at the table.

There is silence as Desmond squares his shoulders, standing at the head of the table.

'Our King is dead.'

A murmur of soft agreement rises up from the three women.

'The Blood Crown will now be under my obedience, but so will the vengeful hearts of a thousand others.' He shoots me a pointed look. 'King Xavier is attempting to kill me; thus I shall have to kill him first.'

But didn't he have to sign *Librum Aeternitatis*?

The Scroll of Eternity was to be signed by each new possessor of the Blood Crown, with the keeper vowing and participating in a blood oath to not kill for power. If anyone signed the treaty and continued to be seemingly on the path of killing a hundred thousand innocent souls, the High Prince of Caelumterra, Prince William, would have given them quite a nightmare to remember in the afterlife. Unlocking the complete potential of the Blood Crown was a dire complication that would doom Aetheria.

But Desmond was murdering for power. It was evidently obvious—if you have the world in your grasp, you will steal it for yourself.

'That stupid meeting in the throne room,' Lorelei suddenly says, her voice breaking the tension I didn't realise was there. 'Is that what it was all about? To kill Xavier?'

'Why kill him in private when you can shame him in front of the entirety of Aetheria?' Genevieve cuts in sharply, her steely gaze meeting Desmond's.

'I have suspicions, not evidence. Attempting to lure Xavier

into the open would only make me an easier target.' He sighs. 'The brat would kill in front of thousands to secure the crown.'

I clench my fists. He couldn't have explained Xavier in better words.

'Desmond,' a soft voice says.

We turn to Queen Isolde. 'The papers for my abdication are ready.' She coughs. 'I shall s-sign on the day of your c-c-coro,' she chokes suddenly.

'Mother?' Lorelei turns to Genevieve, fear replacing the wrath in her eyes.

Her eyes dart to Desmond. 'Mother, are you feeling okay?' he asks stupidly.

I stand up, going over to where she sits, attempting to heave her up. Her black hair is thin and flows loosely around her back, the wrinkles under her eyes too evident.

'We need to take her to a nurse,' I say urgently.

Queen Isolde doubles over, retching on the garden floor.

Desmond immediately pulls away from the table, Genevieve coming behind me to hoist her mother up.

'Mother, please. Not you too,' she whispers quietly.

'She won't die,' I say firmly, although the words seem dull on my tongue. She is too sick. Her skin is pure grey, nearly turning to ash. She drags in heaving breaths, clamping my arm so tightly she draws blood.

Queen Isolde gasps, suddenly falling to the floor.

'Mother, Mother!' screams Lorelei.

Her arms wobble, a tortured sob wrenched from her throat.

Desmond hollers out orders, Genevieve shaking her mother desperately as Lorelei bawls her eyes out. Tears claw out of the Queen's eyes, blood spilling from her mouth. I stand, rooted to the spot. Everything is a blur, in slow motion.

The lady from today morning runs in, with Agatha and a few other servants trailing behind like ants.

A stretcher is brought, pulling the Queen to her feet as she repeatedly chokes and staggers, slipping off the stone slab. I hear a bone crunch and wince tightly as Desmond drags me away to a secluded spot.

The last thing I hear before we reach the outside gates and stagger into the afternoon sky is Queen Isolde's final screams, barely heard as she is cut off.

Like someone had stabbed her through the mouth just to shut her up.

Desmond and I stand in silence.

Goosebumps are raised on my skin, and I finally let slip a gasp. I hadn't realised I had been holding in a breath all this time. The sun shines above us, dancing joyfully across the millions of flowers that paint the dirt.

'Are you okay?' I ask Desmond.

He swallows. 'Do you think she'll live?' he asks suddenly. He turns to me, his eyes filled with fear. I instinctively back away.

'Y-yes.' I can't help but eye him suspiciously. Was this an act? *Of course not; his mother is probably dead. Why would he be happy?*

Desmond shakes his head. 'First Father, now her...'

I hesitantly move forward, grasping his shoulders in both my hands. He looks me in the eyes.

'Desmond, it's okay. She'll be fine.'

It's a lie, and we both know it.

'Hold on, alright?' I say softly. 'Even if she doesn't live, you'll be fine. You're going to become King—' I gulp, cutting off.

If Queen Isolde dies, Desmond will automatically be King. Could he have attempted to kill his mother?

'What, you really think—' He breaks off, looking away.

'Desmond, I didn't mean...'

He falls to his knees, placing his head in his hands. His shoulders shake aggressively, a small sob echoing now and then.

He's crying.

Desmond... crying?

I let out a small sigh.

'Come on, Desmond!' I heave, pulling him up.

I hesitantly embrace him, rubbing his back as he weeps into my hair. 'I did not kill my mother,' Desmond pulls away and grasps my hand in his, squeezing it tightly. 'Whatever you know of me, I promise, I would never kill my own family, Victoria. I would not stoop that low, ever.'

His stare lingers on me for a beat longer before he tries to pull away, but I pull him back and squeeze his hand, a bulge stuck in my throat.

We look down at our hands and instinctively drop the other's palm immediately.

I look at his face. The tears still strolled loftily across his pale cheeks.

'Shall we talk about something else?' I ask. Desmond looks up at me, blinking.

'That is not what you are supposed to do when a person dies.' He shakes his head.

I nod my head, feeling oddly clammy as I make my way to sit down, the green dress shimmering in the sunlight. I purse my lips tightly. Desmond follows, grunting as he sits.

'Why did you kill my father?'

Desmond looks at me, his lips twitching.

I clamp my hands together. 'What, you think we're going to be on good terms after what you did last night?'

'You always seem to be on good terms with everyone.' He shrugs, masking the finger that disappears to wipe his eye. 'So kind, so caring. If you had the soul to be wicked, you would not have comforted me.'

He chuckles, a sob wrenching from his throat.

I tilt my head, feeling affronted. 'Affairs of the heart are no laughing matter.'

'Then you know nothing of the cruelty of this world,' spat Desmond, bitterly shaking his head.

I contain the scowl that threatens to reveal itself. 'I do know.'

I had been killed nearly twice by my own brother. Tricked by him. Shunned from the crown. I knew just how much fate could throw at a person.

'Then you have failed to learn.' Desmond laughs wryly, brushing a hand through his hair. My heart drops to my gut, and I shift uncomfortably as the grass grazes my bare arm. 'You should be willing to let free the monster inside of you.'

I start, but he cuts me off.

'And if you repress it, fate will teach you all the ways to untangle the web of lies you so carefully crooned to kill.'

Desmond shrugs, looking to me with a half-smile. 'Fate will gift you all the people to truly unleash the burden buried within you for so long, until not a single morsel of goodness lies in the depths of that pure heart.'

I pull a strand of my hair, playing with my fingers. He was right, in every way possible. 'You're worried—about me?'

'Not worried, simply keeping an eye on your wellbeing so you do not commit to anything stupid. For instance, seeking revenge.'

'I would not do it over such minute reasons. You ought to think better of people,' I reply sarcastically, folding my arms and watching as his features relax.

'Thinking better of people like you is absolutely controversial. You ought not to say stuff like that,' he drawls, a mirthless chuckle escaping his lips. I hold in a gasp.

'A-are you mocking me?'

'Of course not, how could you say that? You ought to think better of people.'

I turn to him, frowning. Something was nagging at the back of my mind. Something he said, but I can't put my finger on it. 'I-I've been wanting to ask you for quite some time, but...' I trail off, pushing my hair back.

Desmond rests on his elbow, watching me closely. 'Wanted to ask me what?'

I take in a deep breath. 'What are you up to? Why have you not called us out for our actions?'

'I see you are beginning the dark confessions first. Continue then, please. You killed my father, and I killed yours in return. It's a win-win.' Desmond suddenly pushes off the ground, hands in his pockets.

'H-how did you know?' I stutter, whipping my head to his standing figure.

'Xavier informed me beforehand. The boy is too gullible.' He shakes his head, a small smile touching his lips. It vanishes in the blink of an eye.

You killed my father, and I killed yours in return. Desmond knew his father was going to die, so why hadn't he saved him? I thought they had been close.

But maybe that had never been the case after all.

'I thought you were a war strategist. Why didn't you call out our entire family and shame us in the faces of the High King himself? Any other smart being would have resolved to that instance. What are you planning?' I argue, hands clenched to my side. Why couldn't he just give a straight answer?

'I'm not planning anything,' he says, prowling around me as if I were his prey.

I swallow, smoothing out my dress. I had every right to know what was happening, right?

I look up to meet his mustard eyes. When they hit the sun, they were an abnormal hue of the flames that erupt around the sun's atmosphere. 'W-what are you and Xavier planning?'

Desmond pauses before speaking. 'It's none of your business.'

'As the soon-to-be King's wife and sister to the King of Ferrumisle, I have every right to know.' I tap my fingers together. Desmond stares at me, a filthy look scrawling over his face.

'As the enemy's daughter, I cannot disclose every matter I have to you.'

'As the enemy's daughter, you should have rejected the proposal, or maybe you were committing to something stupid. For instance, seeking revenge,' I throw his words back at him, and he glowers, shoving his hands deeper into his pockets.

'I want a good relationship where you play the loving wife until I can get rid of you,' Desmond breathes softly, tilting his head. My blood boils, and I pull myself to my feet, the sun batting down on my face. I was always being used by some person or the other. I breathe in shallowly, trying to calm myself before jabbing a finger at his chest. 'Why did you accept the damn proposal?'

'I wanted to help you,' he answers simply.

I hold in a frustrated growl. 'You're not helping me. You never have, and you're the reason my whole life is destroyed!'

'You didn't let me complete my sentence,' he says again. Why was he so calm?

I purse my lips, taking a step back.

'I wanted to help you, and return your throne for what I have done.'

I open my mouth, then shut it.

He wanted me to get my throne back?

'I don't know you. You killed my father, and you may be up to something with my brother. Why in Aetheria would I trust you to get *my* throne back?' I whisper.

'Because we both know that I am the only person capable of doing so,' he murmurs, growing closer, all traces of sorrow scored from his eyes. The heat that emanates from him is uncomfortably consoling, but it does the trick. He pulls his hand out of his pocket and encircles my wrist, stroking the ruby ring that weighs down my fingers.

'How so?' I croak out.

I close my eyes for a brief second. I was playing a dangerous game with a dangerous man, but I had already trapped him. He wanted to eliminate Xavier; I too had the same intentions. But what if I asked for a bit more? My eyes fly open, and I clasp his hand.

'Xavier intends to kill you, which is why you were delighted to have a chat with him, but he was afraid. You poisoned Father and could cut his neck too,' I say, and his grip tightens on my arm.

Desmond laments, 'He'd be stupid to continue with his plan, but he won't because he'll be d—'

'Xavier cannot be killed easily,' I cut in.

Desmond stops, narrowing his eyes. There's a beat of silence before he pulls me closer. His breath cascades across my face, and I hesitantly look away.

'What do you mean?' His voice is low, almost threatening.

'Prove you're trustworthy, and I'll tell you more,' I say, gasping when he interlocks our hands.

Return my throne, and I'll help you.

His eyes are a steely ombre, and it seems as if the life has been sucked out of them.

'Know that I can slit your pretty little neck with my sword. I expect the information to be revealed to me soon.' He lets go of me, and I stagger away from his grip. He runs a hand through his hair, beckoning towards me.

'Do you have anything to tell me, Victoria?'

My heart sinks. Was I that poor at holding secrets?

'Do you think I will trust you after drugging me last night, killing my father and attempting to kill my brother?'

'Yes.'

I stay silent. He was right.

Desmond cocks an eyebrow. 'Every good relationship must

have trust; it is the core. Without it, every other matter is destroyed. If it can be created, it can also be destroyed. If we never had trust in the first place, did I ruin anything?'

He tilts his head in an almost comforting gesture. Desmond was right—again. Our families had a long history of animosity.

'We both know you want your brother out of the way. If you had not roused from the drug, none could have blamed you for his death.'

My jaw drops in disbelief, and I feel as if a wave has crashed and knocked me over.

If Elysande had not been there and I had not, Xavier would be dead, and I would have assumed the throne.

Desmond places a hand on my cheek.

He had been attempting to *help* me, and I had destroyed it all.

He smirks when the realisation dawns on my face. 'Do I have your trust now?'

I watch him brush past me toward the exit of the Garden, pride etched in his every step. I understood what he was playing at. Confessing Xavier's plans had been a grave mistake, but trusting him would be an even greater one.

'I'm going to see if mother is well,' he calls gruffly from behind.

And then the thought nagging at me slaps me in the face.

We don't know if his mother is dead.

But had he not said one was not supposed to distract a grieving person when another dies?

CHAPTER VII

'I regret to inform you of Her Majesty's death.'

General MacQuoid sighs, the nurse who announced the news departing the room. Desmond's complexion crumples, and I place a hand on his shoulder. His reaction doesn't appear fake.

Maybe he had mixed up his words—or he had been acting cynical for the best.

And maybe I shouldn't delve into wondering if he is right or wrong, for I would have to kill him anyway.

A sob bursts from behind, and I see Lorelei weeping in Genevieve's arms. Her white gown drifts about, clad in raven feathers at the shoulders. Slowly, they begin to shake off with every shudder of her head.

Resentment tugs at my heart.

I knew what it was like to lose my parents. I lost my mother, after all. But none knew if she was dead or alive. I shake my head, a rash spasm splintering through my soul.

This was not the time to brood over such things. I needed to kill Desmond, but if I did, everyone would know.

I should wait—allow Desmond to kill Xavier first, then take the crown.

Elysande would never allow that to happen, though. My tongue runs dry. The only choice left to do then would be—

'My goodness! What has happened?' Elysande tumbles out from the corridor, where we stand in a large expanse near the staircase overlooking the throne room. The dark circles under her eyes are apparent, and the rugged pitch of her voice reveals she has just awakened.

I had been wondering how long it would take for the effect of the drug to wear off.

How had I roused so early—because there had been a racket?

'Forgive us, Elysande,' I start. Her unkempt snowy hair falls around her lean body in an unladylike fashion. It seems as if someone combed through her braids. 'Her Majesty just passed away; I was offering my condolences to the Thorncrest family.'

Elysande's mouth hangs agape. 'Oh, my. I am deeply sorry for your loss.' She did not sound pitiful in the least.

'My condolences.' She bows low, the wicked glint in her eyes hardly coveted. Desmond winces at her lack of theatrics.

'How on Aetheria could such a wonderful queen be taken to the afterlife?'

'Thank you, Your Majesty,' Desmond replies softly, his jaw tightening. 'We cannot comprehend the reason, but we believe she may have been poisoned.'

'The way she doubled over, and—and her vomit,' Lorelei cries, trailing off.

Genevieve pats her shoulder, her own face stained with strikes of marred kohl. 'Her vomit was sickly green, tinged with red.'

'It could have been arsenic,' I offer.

'Arsenic is rare in Briarthorn Atoll.' Desmond shakes his head.

'Xavier visited Fames a few days before our arrival,' I say again. Desmond frowns.

I recall vividly when Xavier had sworn to return with an

ally. King Vorin of Fames was an effortless man to bring around, yet it took my step-brother multiple nights to return home.

Lorelei takes low, shallow gasps. 'You're saying...'

'If Xavier killed King Thaddeus, then he surely killed Queen Isolde,' I say, shrugging.

Elysande gawks at me, stupefied. 'How dare you accuse my son!'

It couldn't have been Desmond... Right?

I smile up at Elysande as she scowls, glaring. *I'm going to have a little talk with you later,* her eyes say.

As much as I wish she had not woken up so that I could avoid performing the deed, I would much prefer to kill Elysande now.

Genevieve stifles a wry chuckle. 'Now that I think about it, Xavier offered Mother a glass of water today morning.'

Lorelei sniffs. 'She did say she had been feeling quite nauseous for the past few days.'

Genevieve clamps her hands together furiously. 'Arsenic is an odourless and tasteless powder! It could have easily been dissolved in the water, and inflamed Mother's gastric distress!'

Desmond claps his hands together, all traces of grief replaced with fury. His voice is cold, and I feel like I'm back in the throne room all over again. 'Not only has the King of Ferrumisle killed our Father, but he has also killed our Mother, our *Queen*, and attempted to kill me as well.'

A small smirk plays at his lips. His reactions were too real. Maybe he hadn't meant what he said before. It was probably a slip of words.

'Please escort Elysande to a bathroom,' I say to General MacQuoid, relishing the little bit of power I have. It tastes weird on my tongue, commanding someone. But I want it more.

'She is in quite a state. Xavier must have drugged her a bit more than intended.'

Elysande gasps, bringing a delicate hand to her mouth. The

shock in her eyes is clear, but she is adamant not to believe any of the things being said about her son.

'Come, Your Majesty,' General MacQuoid says, placing an arm on her back, guiding her away from the rest of us.

'My son would dare not try such foul measures to achieve his desires!' she bursts, trying to fight off the general.

'Your Majesty, I would appreciate it if you would observe the royal family's distress.'

You are not wanted here, was what the general meant to imply, and Elysande gasps again, her voice echoing through the fifteen-foot-high hall.

General Steelborne guides her behind the oak chester, their voices fading as they disappear around the corner.

As soon as she leaves, Lorelei lets out a string of curses.

'Damn your brother!' she seethes at me.

I take a few steps back, crystals raising on the chandelier above me.

Fury boils my blood. I was connected to by far the most murderous and failed family in all of Aetheria. If not for myself, maybe I could raise the reputation for us all.

'How much of the drug did you feed the both of them?' Genevieve interrupts.

I turn to her, but the question is directed to Desmond.

'Only a vial, which is what I'm confused about,' Desmond answers stiffly.

'What do you mean?' Lorelei asks, dabbing her eyes with a forest green leaf. They help with soothing and nourishing the skin, so she must be using it to reduce swelling and puffiness around her eyes.

'The ivory should have knocked Victoria out for a good seven hours, but only lasted about five.' He turns to me, and the already ready-made prediction I had conceived churns my stomach. I had hoped it was not true.

'You gave Xavier the exact same vial?' I ask, rubbing

my palms together. The chills here had increased, and now
goosebumps were forming. The hairs on my back rise.

'Yes, I did. Had the same amount; I made sure of it myself.'

'Did he have the vial alone with him?' I question again.

Desmond shakes his head. 'I made sure I was holding the
both of them so that he wouldn't try to add more to the other.'

'You're saying Xavier purposefully added more ivory to
the vial to knock Elysande out for a longer period of time?'
Genevieve says slowly.

Lorelei looks blank. The deaths must have gotten to that
petty woman.

'Xavier tried to kill Elysande?' she gasps suddenly, and
I look down.

'If Queen Isolde's death had not made such a huge fuss, she
would've stayed in a slumber.'

'But how? Where in Inferis did he get more ivory from?'
Genevieve spits.

Lorelei gasps aggressively again.

'What, Lorelei?' Genevieve finally bursts. Gosh, that woman.

'I remember decorating Elysande's room! There were ivory
leaves strung across the black curtains. If Elysande had been
sleeping, Xavier could have easily squeezed the sap and poured
more into the bottle.'

'And pure ivory is worse than contaminated ivory,' I say,
swallowing.

A disgusting thought crawls its way into my mind, and I
can't help but agree with it. If Father had not been dead, he
would have surely encouraged Xavier to do worse. Kill not only
Elysande, but me. And I bet that is Xavier's ultimatum, but I
know he would not stop there.

His eyes were on the Blood Crown, and he would stop at
nothing to have it in his clutches.

My eyes train on Desmond, who looks onwards towards the
path Elysande left through, deep in thought.

He mops a hand over his face, frowning. 'We have to contact Queen Nyx.'

Genevieve curses. 'What the hell?'

'Queen Nyx? You're in contact with that devil?' I burst, aghast.

Desmond nods.

'We are not meeting her!' Lorelei shrieks, flinging her arms up into the air, dropping the forest leaf.

'Are any of the other lands in contact?' I ask. I can't breathe. I can't. This plan that is forming in my head is going to kill me.

'Yes,' Desmond answers simply.

'We are not meeting the Queen of the Underworld, a blood and power-thirsty nixie who threatened to tear off your neck and devour it until the crown rested on her dainty little head!' snarls Genevieve.

'You've met her before?' I shake my head. This day is full of surprises.

'Regrettably, I have.' But Desmond doesn't explain more. 'Why?' I press, edging closer to him.

He lets his head hang between his arms on the polished wooden table against the wall. A window in front, with its clear glass, shows his mustard eyes to be alight with an infuriating and indescribable fire. A hungry fire.

'I'd prefer not to tell,' Desmond murmurs, pushing off the table. I fidget with the beads on my dress and nod, biting the inside of my mouth.

'We'll leave in about a day's time,' he turns to me. 'And make sure you stay with someone at all costs. By the look of your step-mother's face, she doesn't want someone to be alive for too long.'

Victoria Ironhart,
Day 6,

~

Woe shall always live by thy side,
remind you of its constricting power,
making sure you pay heed to those who never witness your sorrow,
playing with your heart until you see,
until you finally understand,
you are not who you are meant to be,
but instead who you were moulded to be.

~

The day I had been thrown off a cliff was the day I finally decided to pave my own life and not let the essence of being a pitiful princess everyone thought—and taught—me to be reside in my thoughts. Or so I thought. It's not as easy as it looks, is it?

Remaining silent, acting the dutiful princess and allowing others to walk over me like I was nothing but dirt broke something in me. Maybe it was a piece of my heart, although I'm not sure. I was told it was made of crystal. Likewise, Xavier's of metal. No wonder he and Father were so cold.

The Hart's Thaw was built in the dungeons of Ferrumisle, snaking under the castle with not even a ray of sunshine breaking through the earth.

When a Missilian is born, the family is demanded to bring their child to the Hart's Thaw. The Soul Reaper has been there for centuries, legends say. His hair aged from jet to snow and muscle to bones, few whispering that mortality was growing on him with each soul he tore from a child, replacing it with one that fits their power.

Enough of the sad talk; I had to figure out how I would break free of this prison.

What shall I do?

Trust was a luxury I couldn't afford, not in a world where every land sought power, where kings and queens would stop at nothing to claim dominance.

But then a crazy idea formed. Mad, it was. Not as mad as when Desmond first mentioned it, however. Truly, I was taken aback. I could have strolled right into her abode, yet I didn't in fear. And there Desmond was, walking straight into the land of hell, Inferis. He was a prince of power; of course she would listen to what he had to say—and offer.

I, on the other hand, could be used as a vulnerable back-up plan.

If I went to Nyx, she would surely use me to get the Blood Crown.

But maybe that is what I sought out to do, that day in Briarthorn Atoll.

Trick her.

Say I want to help her get the crown, and in turn I'll eliminate all her rivals. All I would ever need from her is the reputation that would come with stealing the crown, being the naive princess I was.

Victoria Drakewell Ironhart: The Fallen Queen once more.

If I could join alliances with Queen Nyx, then stealing the Blood Crown would be effortless.

She is a corrupted soul searching for power. Nyx Darkryn would do anything to achieve her desires.

The Blood Crown has many qualities, but one reason remains superior. It has the power to control all of Aetheria—if the heir is killed, or a hundred thousand innocent souls.

All I had to do was play innocent until proven guilty. If Nyx agreed, we both knew the first step.

Eliminate everyone who was a threat, which means Desmond and King Avalorian, no matter what. Well, I didn't need to kill Father anymore; Desmond had done that for me.

Xavier would be next, and it seemed like I didn't have to worry about him either.

Elysande was a petty pawn, yet she was just as formidable as the rest. It is always better to be safe than sorry.

If the alliance with Nyx held, I would become her prime target once she discovered the betrayal.

So what shall I do then?

Blame her; the witch, blame the villain.

Never had I ever had bloody hands, so if I ever did, the world should never know.

~

I saw them out of the corner of my eye.

The bomb in my hand felt heavy. What if I missed? What if I didn't kill them all?

They were approaching my way—where I was hidden at the entrance of the cave.

Sixty-three thousand four hundred and fifty-seven people in his whole army.

Dead.

My palms were clammy, sweat dripping off and coating the bomb. I heard the distinct chatter, their worrisome words filling the air. I was still drenched from the water and had hidden inside a lair. The ships had docked on the other side, and I knew they would return to hunting for me.

I sucked in a breath. I could do this. Just throw the bomb. It was twice the size of my head, and I had a few more lined up next to me. One wrong move and I would be thrust back into the obsidian water. The whispers grew closer, and I exhaled.

I rushed out from the cave, shoving away brambles and tripping over rocks before I witnessed the huge army before me. They were spread as far as my eyes could see, specks of stony-eyed soldiers.

I acted on instinct.

I hurled the bomb and ran back to get more.

A thunderous explosion ripped through the air, the screams of terrified souls creating a cacophony of fear.

I hurriedly grabbed another one of the bombs, and when I turned, I saw him next to the trees.

Saw them. Saw the thousands of soldiers that came rushing at me.

I didn't know what to do. I heaved and threw. Before it could hit solid ground, I grabbed another and struck it onto the earth I stood upon.

A deafening crash reverberated through my bones, and I staggered back in horror. I could feel my dress on fire, but I darted into the cave, and the flap of cloth erupted dust that ceased the fire. Breathe in, breathe out. I crumpled to my knees, cradling my chest.

A few more days, and it would all be over.

A few more days, and they'd all be at my mercy.

I never contacted Queen Nyx.

I never tried; it was just a few minutes of my hot-headedness where I thought I should, and then I returned to normal.

But now an opportunity presents itself to me once more.

Desmond is willingly taking us to meet Queen Nyx tomorrow. All I had to do was ask her. Ask her what I was to do to get the Blood Crown. I feel my eyes droop, and I resist the urge to collapse onto the floor.

She would help me; the woman is as good as her word—but there's always a catch. One that I am ready to betray to get the crown.

We ascend the stairs leading to the dining room. It is time for lunch.

Desmond holds the door open as I enter, Genevieve and Lorelei following close behind.

Vast chandeliers hang from the ceiling, and pillars rise in all four corners. Compared to the throne room, the dining area is relatively small, and shards of mirrors, which must reflect the sunlight in various ways, have been draped across with a thick layer of green cloth. The wool must have been expensive.

Crimson baubles hang from the ivory leaves knit through the wall. It is a weird sight. I've never seen anything like it before. We take a seat at the large mahogany table, delicate iron chairs scraping as the rest settle down. I find one drowned in cushions and take a seat there. Desmond is seated next to me, and the two sisters opposite us. I pull up a dusty napkin from the table, which is white and embroidered with a delicate draconia symbol, and shake it. Lorelei sneezes, placing an arm over her face.

She scowls.

'How long has this place been unused?' I ask, resisting the urge to clog my nose at the smell that stinks through. I notice cobwebs on the wall and wince. This place seemed ancient already.

'A few years,' Desmond shrugs. My eyes widen in shock.

Just then, a soft bell tingles, and a waiter arrives with a cloth in hand. His black hair is tied into a half pony, and I notice the little bob of his head. I recognise him as one of the waiters from last night, Hemsworth.

There is a soft clatter as he picks up our plates and replaces them with new, freshly carved stone. For me, he places down a pottery fork and spoon, and the rest earn iron utensils.

We wait until he leaves.

'Much has occurred over the past two days,' Genevieve says, clasping her ringed hands in front of her.

'You think? 'Much' seems like an understatement for murder,' Lorelei sneers, pushing back her hair. Her eyes are red but not puffy. The forest tree leaves must have helped.

Desmond plays with his fork as Genevieve continues. 'I understand we all want to grieve properly, but there's no use crying over spilled milk.'

'Blood,' Lorelei corrects.

'Shut up, Lorelei,' Genevieve hisses, batting a hand at her sister. 'Not all of us have an addiction to metal-tasting liquid.'

She nods at me, and Lorelei rolls her eyes. 'Get to the point.' Desmond raps on the table, his voice low.

Genevieve shoots him a look, but I can feel the tension increasing. I search for something to say. Something that will take their minds off me being a traitor and aid me at the same time. 'What was Desmond like as a child?' I ask randomly.

The three siblings exchange glances, and a small blush creeps onto his cheeks.

'Perfect question!' Genevieve claps her hands in glee. Desmond lets his hair fall over his eyes, covering his face with his hands.

'Why are you so interested to learn about his past? Lorelei halts Genevieve before she can continue.

My eyes narrow. 'I'm trying to be helpful. It's the first question I could think of.'

'Doesn't help that you're from a family of traitors,' she retorts, folding her arms over her chest.

I clench my fists. It was and would always be clear I wasn't welcome here.

'I didn't ask to be stuck in this family, nor for my own parents to be killed,' I bite out. Were they always this paranoid?

'Elysande's still here,' Lorelei answers without thinking. My heart stops. What the hell?

Genevieve lets out a small gasp, dainty hands over her mouth. 'Lorelei, sto—'

'I can stand up for myself,' I spit, my fingernails digging into my palm.

'Enough.' Desmond's voice echoes through the room.

I didn't realise I was standing. Desmond pulls an arm around my shoulders, helping me back into my seat.

The doors swing open once more, and five waiters enter with silver dishes. I feel my mouth water, but I resist the urge to let this go.

I would not tolerate being disrespected any more. I wasn't someone to walk over.

'We're done here. You two will eat in silence; it would help all of us.' Desmond shoots them a warning glower, pointing a fork at the both of them. He takes a nonchalant bite from the meat on the utensil he brandished, his hair nearly dipping into the gravy.

Genevieve bites her lip, but Lorelei dabs a napkin to her eye. 'I want Mother back,' she suddenly sniffs.

Irritation claws at my back. Why are they so worked up over their mother's death? Genevieve embraces Lorelei, shooting me a glare.

Maybe because she actually loved her children. Maybe because you're a lunatic for not feeling remorse over your own father's death.

I push the thoughts aside. Who cares anymore?

Desmond sighs and pulls his head down. That's when I realise something—abnormal.

Genevieve and Lorelei are close, but when all three are together, a bizarre tension wraps over the both of them. It's unlike with me and Desmond. He's calm around me; sure he ignores, which makes me want to strike a knife across his throat, but with his sisters? It's like they think that if they make one wrong move, they're dead for sure.

I pour myself a bit of gravy onto the smooth stone and cut myself a slice of meat. I take a bite, trying to savour the herbs, but I don't taste any.

'You wanted to know how my life was as a child?' Desmond asks suddenly, looking at me.

I startle at the squint in his eyes. I try to chew quickly, heat flooding my cheeks before I finally swallow. 'I—I mean, sure,' I stutter, trying to smile. I hope this doesn't stretch too long.

'I was three when my father forced me to wield a sword,' Desmond starts, and I blink. That young? I nod, setting down my fork as he watches me, a grateful smile creeping onto his lips.

'It was hard,' he shrugs, looking down at his hands. 'The sword was twice my size, and when I would try to hold it, I would topple over into the dirt.'

I shake my head, aghast. 'Why would your father do that?'

'You learn life through pain,' Desmond clicks his tongue.

I tilt my head.

'That's what Father told me. The earth doesn't crumble when, after all of nature's hard work, a flower is plucked; it regrows. But it can only rise once more with the help of a flicker of fire from within you—hope. Hope to redeem, hope to avenge, and hope to rebirth.'

I swallow.

King Thaddeus was right; all it took for a fire to burn was a flicker of anger—or hope—and you had the power to wield the world in your hands. It was a powerful emotion and had the power to corrupt the very individual that rendered it unfaithfully.

'When I was five, I could hold the sword without falling over. I thought that was it.' Desmond chuckles wryly, and I flinch at his mocking tone.

'Father told me we would spar when I was ready, and I thought it meant that when I could finally hold the sword, he would teach me to fight.'

I hold in a breath. They never fought. They never did, so what happened?

Desmond purses his lips. 'Every single day from dawn to dusk, when I would hold that gemmed sword in my hand —' I bring a hand to my mouth. A gemmed sword—the sword that Desmond held when he brandished it during the Tribal War and when he was in the throne room with Xavier. The sword was at least half his height and twice his strength.

'Yes,' Desmond murmurs. He sighs softly. 'My father pushed me. Over and over until I sat on the dirt covered in blood from the slashes of my own sword.'

All I can do is stare at him. What on Aetheria? That was outrageous, considering Desmond was his own son!

'He'd make me sit there and cry my lungs out before he left,' he murmurs, rubbing a hand over his face. Is that why he was so nonchalant all the time, because he had learned life too young?

'It was hard, coming from my own father, but it taught me all the same. There are always obstacles after obstacles, and you can only grow if you choose to fight back.'

A beat of silence passes between us, and Genevieve and Lorelei's hushed whispers dominate the room once more. I can barely make out what they're saying; all I can think about is Desmond.

You learn life through pain.

It hurt in so many ways.

'I-It's kind of weird,' he says quietly, playing with his food.

I look at him, frowning. 'What is?' I try not to breathe too loudly. Whatever he wanted to say seemed important.

'That you seem to ask me the smallest things nobody ever bothered to question.' Desmond shrugs, but I see the hint of embarrassment that crosses his eyes and tinges his cheeks a pale red.

'Oh,' is all I can manage to say. He nods, taking in a deep breath.

'You learnt about life at a young age, and that's something you should be grateful for,' I murmur, taking another bite.

'It hurt,' he admits, his eyes still on me. I wince a bit, wiping the stupid grin off my face. Why was he staring at me so aggressively?

'I would've done anything to learn young,' I say quietly, trying to distract myself from his gaze. He looked as if he had found a rose in a garden of tulips, lips set apart and eyes wide in fascination.

'Why so?' he answers back quietly. A small smile touches my lips at his thoughtfulness. He respected my privacy—something not many bothered to do. After all, what privacy should I, a fallen queen, have? What more defeat did I need to obscure from the world?

I shake my head a bit, trying to get the thought out of my head, and a frown touches Desmond's features.

'You would know how life responds to all your wishes,' I breathe out shakily. 'When you're young and naive, everybody greets your mistakes as learning. When you're older and naive, everybody greets your faults as idiocy—like it was my fault for not being educated young, for being spared from the world's harsh realities, when all it took was just a little push.'

We approach the large, brazen door. Claw marks are slashed across, scratches like wounds splintering the wood. A stuffed lion head sits atop the door, its eyes gauged out. I squirm before entering behind Desmond into his room. He merely ignores my presence. I curl my fingers.

Again, even after giving him my undivided attention?

The lunch was absolutely horrible. Both the food and atmosphere.

'Why the sudden plan to meet Nyx?' I try asking when the silence gets too loud. I stifle a yawn.

He pulls off his coat and tosses it across the room, ending on the floor in a heap of clothes, picking a pen from his table and scraping the chair back to sit in it.

'I don't think Xavier is going to be easy to kill,' he answers simply. 'We need all the help we can get, so I was thinking you could draf-' Desmond cuts off.

He clatters off the table and pulls a cloth over his eyes. 'What the hell are you doing?'

I tug off my dress, leaving a shirt and pants on. Agatha had insisted I wear them under my dress. I shake my hair free, face planting into the bed. It creaks. I turn, pulling the covers over me and murmur loud enough for him to hear. 'I need sleep, and not a drugged one.'

He yanks the cloth away.

'No! You need to help me draft a plan of action so that we can ask Nyx to help us,' Desmond groans.

'Fine.' I huff. 'I'm not getting out of bed, though. What do you need me to do?'

'I need information.'

I rub a hand over my eyes.

'Xavier is coming back next week, so I will kill him upon his arrival.'

'Why don't you just execute him in front of all the lands now that we have evidence to frame him?' I ask. For what all the lands know, it could be the King's own son who killed him to get the Blood Crown. A cold breeze sweeps in through the windows. It is evening, and the sun is blanching into darkness. The crystal lights above us flicker.

I bring my hand forward, focusing my strength on the stone ceiling as an amethyst crystal cracks out.

'If I do so, he will exploit me killing your father,' he replies, running a hand through his black hair. It comes through even more messy.

'That doesn't matter; you did it for revenge. Anyone would understand,' I argue.

Desmond ignores me, waving a dismissive hand in the air. I try not to suck in an audible breath. This man was getting on my nerves—and in the way of my plan.

'However, Xavier knows I want to kill him, and will at his utmost discretion attempt to avoid me.'

'How will Nyx help us kill him?'

'She will give me a sword, or something of that sort, to help me destroy his soul,' he replies.

I bite my lip. He had proven to be trustworthy, but as I utter the words, my gut sinks all the same.

'His heart is birthed of metal. If two clash together, they would form a stronger bond,' I point out. 'He could possibly be resurrected even if killed.'

'No one has ever been resurrected in all of Aetheria's history,' Desmond scoffs.

'Wherever you stab him, the metal will connect with his veins and will absorb the power from the weapon. He will die for seven minutes, and then shall he be resurrected,' I explain, my heart sinking at that thought.

Our brain replays the best moments of our lives when it dies. I wonder what he would see sometimes, but then I hope he dreams of nothing at all.

'You're telling me that murderer gets to repeat the best moments of his life then be reincarnated?' Desmond spits, turning to me in frustration.

I shrug. 'You have the blood of more than sixty thousand innocent people on your hands.'

He cocks an eyebrow. There was no way he could argue with that.

'I could ask for poison?' Desmond tries.

'Metallures are immune. They cannot absorb poisons.' He opens his mouth to argue, but I don't need to hear his question to answer him.

'Father is half metallure and half stollar. That's the only reason the wraith berry worked. It's deeply rooted to the earth, so even a morsel could cause a person to die if they have a heart made of Aetheria herself. May I add that he attempted to steal the Blood Crown as well, therefore easily being poisoned?'

'I remember as clear as day,' Desmond murmurs. 'So even crystallites are affected?'

'Even crystallites,' I nod. I pull deeper into the covers. It is cold.

Desmond shakes his head, pursing his lips. 'Then I'll somehow have to convince Nyx to give up Eclipses,' he concludes.

I suck in a breath.

'The sword used to banish Nyx?' I sit up suddenly, kicking off the coverlet. 'Why does she have it? How does she have it?'

'Came as a gift of pity. When the Blood Crown chose Caspian, they gave Eclipses to Nyx hoping she would forgive them for their —' he pauses to choose the right word. '*Unwariness.*'

I shake my head. 'How will that help?'

'It's made of crystal. It will be easy to kill Xavier then,' Desmond answers, splaying his hands.

I nod.

There's a beat of silence.

'Are you scared?' he asks suddenly.

'Of what?' I realise what he's trying to say. 'Oh, Nyx?' I wave a mildly dismissive hand in the air.

'A bloodthirsty nixie who tried to bring Aetheria to her knees, and nearly succeeded?' I add sarcastically.

He laughs. 'Nearly, being the key word. Besides, it has been five thousand years. She is weakened, relying on other souls to aid.'

'She could easily kill a hundred thousand souls,' I argue. 'Her reputation still remains. People still fear her to this day.'

'I doubt it would be easy for her to battle at such an age, and times have changed. We have more defences, multiple tactics. For now, the lands have a mutual bond. We do not have a reason to fight with one another, so even if Nyx does show herself, all the lands will reunite and end her for good.'

I nod. What he has said is true. The only way Nyx would be able to destroy us is if we turned against each other. A lone thought surfaces, and a chill runs down my spine. If I wanted her help, I would need to act as if I did not care about anything or anyone.

It wouldn't be too difficult.

There is a brief silence before Desmond says, 'I was asking about your fear of the dark.'

I stare onwards, having lost the ability to move momentarily.

'Are you going to answer me or not?' His voice is low.

I shift nervously in the bed, swallowing. 'What led you to that conclusion?' I ask him warily.

'The way you brandished the dagger yesterday when I entered my room,' Desmond says, trying to meet my eyes.

I dodge them.

'Two people died. Of course I was going to act on instinct,' I laugh.

'If you insist.' He makes his way to stand up, clutching the edge of the table. 'Then I'll just turn off the li —'

I nearly jump off the bed in fright. 'Don't!'

I don't feel completely safe with him. In the light, you know what is to come next. Everything unexpected occurs at twilight, always.

'Why not?' He stands.

'Because I said so,' I say, trying not to stutter.

Desmond, however, seems amused. 'It's alright, I'll protect you from the monsters,' he croons, a small grin perking at his lips.

I resist the urge to spit a *shut up* in his face.

We sit in silence once more. I lower my arms, my heart beating erratically. This isn't how he acts around his sisters. What was he playing at?

'You should get some sleep. It's been a long two days, and we have to leave early tomorrow,' I tell his slouching figure. His eyes meet mine, a mixture of suspicion and softness in his mustard eyes.

'Don't get ahead of yourself,' I snap.

'As you say, my Queen.'

He grins, pushing off the chair.

My Queen. *My* Queen. 'I'm not a Queen, and you're not a King,' I bite out, but I feel bad even as the words leave my mouth, my heart heavy in my chest as if it is a burden upon my body.

Desmond flinches.

Sure you will, my little Queen.

I feel the world spiral. Everything is in slow motion. Mother. Mother used to call me that. My gut clenches. My heart beats faster. I swallow bile. I feel a burning sensation in my stomach. Mother had left me. Where to, no one ever found out.

Another bed has been set adjacent to mine, and it creaks as Desmond climbs into it, bringing me back to Aetheria.

He kicks off his shoes and brushes a hand through his hair, his locks falling over his ears. The tattoo of the wolf burns, its intricate outline on his neck flaring with heat.

He catches me watching and grins.

Why was I looking? Why the hell was I looking?

I hesitantly turn away, lying down and pulling the covers over my head. All I can see is white with a tinge of orange illuminating my surroundings.

'You're not going to turn off the lights?' My voice comes out muffled.

'Oh, I thought you might want to keep the nightlight on to keep the monsters away,' Desmond teases, his voice low and warm. 'Seeing as you don't trust me.'

I don't miss the beat of grit in his voice as he says the last sentence. But I don't really care. I'm not sure what being with the Thorncrest family is doing to me, but it isn't anything good.

CHAPTER VIII

'Rise and shine, King and Queen!' Genevieve hollers. I groan, shutting my eyes as soon as I open them when the sunlight bursts in blinding rays. I yank up a pillow and stuff myself under it, scratching my jaw against the rough coverlet.

That ought to leave a bruise. Stars form in my vision.

'A Queen—' I feel my blanket being ripped off me. I slump in the bed, not bothering to pull the coverlet back. I hear Desmond groan, cursing,

'How did you even get in?'

'A magician never reveals their secrets.' She chuckles, producing a key.

Desmond starts, but Lorelei muffles him with a pillow.

I manage to open my eyes, blinking to get used to the sun. I see him kick his legs about in the coverlet, but her strength is no match for his human form.

'As I was saying,' Genevieve continues. 'A Queen should most certainly not sleep in. It is undutiful and beneath her! Now get up, both of you. We have work to do,' she says firmly.

'But sleep is vital for a healthy lifestyle,' comes Desmond's muffled voice. I shift in my sheets, rubbing my eyes as the black stars recede.

I swallow, getting off the bed, feet on the floor. I gasp lightly. The stone is burning today.

'Forget lifestyle,' Genevieve says, flinging her hands about in the air. 'A real Queen should not be kept waiting.' Emphasis on the *real* as she shoots me a glare. My stomach flips.

'Especially if she is awaiting your arrival,' Lorelei murmurs. Desmond sits up straight.

'You sent the letter? How?' he asks, shocked.

'Always two steps ahead of you, brother,' Genevieve answers with an air of pride. She straightens her back, greyish-black hair flowing with a braid meticulously created to form a crown. Today, she wears a deep emerald dress with a white corset and golden string sewn through at the chest. Her white boots clank with every footstep. 'We sent one of the soldiers. Sure, he came back with a few torn limbs, but he got the work done.'

I stiffen.

'And she replied already?' Desmond asks again, aghast.

'Yes, brother. She did.' Genevieve sighs, impatiently tapping her foot on the ground. 'Alright, I've had enough.'

She pulls off Desmond's blanket, who gasps at the heat of the sun on his bare feet, pulling them away from the sun's grasp.

'Stop acting like a child,' Genevieve says, smacking his arm.

He winces. So much for being a bloodthirsty war strategist. I didn't have to worry about him killing me; I had to worry about Genevieve stabbing a knife through my gut—at her kindest.

'What are you staring for?' she suddenly hisses at me. I jump.

'Get to the bathroom already!'

I nod quickly, coughing out a bubble of laughter that threatens to burst from my throat.

'Sorry, Mother,' I murmur.

Desmond laughs, a low rumble that reverberates through the room.

'What did you say?' Genevieve snaps, hands on her waist. She perks up an eyebrow, lips pursed.

'Nothing,' I say hurriedly.

Genevieve scoffs and turns to Desmond.

'You too,' she snarls, ruffling his hair.

'Not the hair,' he stops her hand, and for a moment, I see something dark cross his eyes, but then it disappears.

I blink. Maybe I had imagined it all.

A smile slips across his face. 'Lorelei, go ask General MacQuoid if the carriage is ready.'

A sudden thought enters my head. 'What about Elysande? We can't just leave her alone in the palace.'

'She's being dealt with,' Desmond answers, swiping off the blanket. It falls to the ground, and he sighs before picking it up.

I stare at him. 'Did you drug her again?'

'This one asks too many questions,' Lorelei groans, placing a hand to her temples. 'Yes, we drugged her.'

'Nothing you should be too worried about; it helps in your master plan to kill all of them,' Desmond says, brushing messy jet hair out of his eyes.

The sun hits his eyes differently. They're a hazel brown in the light, and his cheekbones stand out, sharper than my dagger could ever be. It's hardly noticeable, but for the first time, I see the brush of freckles that sprinkle over his nose.

I didn't realise the room was quiet until Desmond grins up at me.

'You think Nyx will be as interested in me if I go like this?'

'She might be if she's looking for a jester,' I retort, raising an eyebrow.

Desmond's lips perk in amusement.

'I'll be going then,' Lorelei purses her lips and pulls up her dress, which is identical to Genevieve's.

I don't miss the small smile as she turns around. 'Be ready in a good half hour.'

General MacQuoid leads us out to the back of the palace, where the Queen's Forest lies. The trees rise up to the sky, casing the sun. Anyone who dares step foot inside would be lost amongst the willowy branches and dark green arrowheads that wither away every other day.

The Queen's Forest overlooked Thorncrest, named after King Caspian's wife, Fallon Thorncrest. She was buried there during the Aetherian War, a reminder of the power Briarthorn Atoll possessed. Being a warrior, she aided in fighting Nyx along with the other Kingdoms, but her reign was put to an end when a sword cut her in half.

'Better be careful,' the General says, pointing to my dress.

I look down.

Desmond and I wore matching fits, just like Genevieve and Lorelei. His is a fitted white jacket with silver embroidery along the lapels and cuffs, mirroring the patterns on my gown. There's a crisp white dress shirt with a high collar and a matching white vest underneath. The pants are white too. It is an unusual colour on him, one that I don't think anyone would be fond of.

I pull the delicate lace veil that trails behind me. I wear an off-shoulder gown adorned with intricate silver embroidery and pearls in slight curves around my bodice. I try not to itch at my sleeves. I don't like the fact that they're netted and have lace cuffs.

'Where will we meet?' Lorelei asks. She descends with Genevieve behind us. General MacQuoid swings open the carriage doors for us. The coach blends in with the surroundings. The gleaming jewels are the only objects that betray its identity.

'She has agreed to meet us outside her cave,' Genevieve answers. 'Did you not read the letter, Lorelei?'

'I did,' Lorelei folds an arm over her chest. 'There's something called forgetting.'

She brandishes her black umbrella overhead, shielding herself from the sun.

'Vampires are among the smartest creatures out there,' Genevieve remarks.

'Are you implying that I'm dumb?' shoots Lorelei.

'You simply inferred, so it must be true if that's the first thought that entered your mind,' Genevieve replies smoothly.

The bickering continues, their voices dissolving as we enter the first carriage. Desmond holds out a hand when he enters, but I ignore it.

Something tells me Desmond has created a plan with Nyx to steal the Blood Crown. It would arguably be the most logical solution for a dashing reputation, yet obviously, Nyx would never allow that. She wanted the crown for herself, so even if she did aid, she had another trick up her sleeve.

Was he trying to challenge her, attempting to earn a higher rank amongst the Aetherians by ending the one entity billions are afraid of?

My pulse quickens.

Breathe in, breathe out.

Remember your plan, Victoria.

Desmond is nothing but an ally, and allies can betray. I had to keep him at arm's length.

I keep in mind to look out the window and mark the landscapes. Maybe I could come back some other day, say I wanted to explore the Land a bit more so I could talk to Nyx.

I take a seat opposite Desmond. He was so eager to help me—he must have an ulterior motive. Betray me?

I shift in my seat, placing my hands over my legs. Desmond closes his eyes, leaning back as the carriage rumbles forward, General MacQuoid thundering an order.

'Since Lorelei has remained at the Palace, Genevieve will

undoubtedly be an unnecessary blabbermouth. Let me do the talking when we reach there,' Desmond's voice is gruff and harsh. My palms begin to sweat, and I rub my fingers together.

'I wasn't planning on speaking either way.'

Desmond's eyes fly open and he grins. 'Good.'

Anger spikes through my heart, singing the crystal. If I sit down and listen, it's good?

'I'll fill Nyx in on my plan, to help you eliminate Xavier,' he continues. *What about Elysande?*

'We must hope she agrees; otherwise, we shall have to figure out another way to kill him.'

He bites his lip. 'I'll need an army of ten thousand, too,' Desmond adds, tapping the wooden slab we are seated upon rhythmically.

I resist the urge to roll my eyes. I knew why. He was probably going to attack another land and achieve the hundred thousand kills he needs to completely claim the Blood Crown as his own, so that even if someone did manage to steal the coronet in the future, he could earn it back.

'Why are you so eager to help me out?' I tilt my head in confusion.

He raises an eyebrow. 'You can be queen, go back to your kingdom and rule. The faster you're out of the way, the better for me.'

I open my mouth, then shut it.

He'd said the same thing twice, and there seemed to be no way to change his mind.

A rumble against the rocky earth nearly jerks me out of my seat.

'We're here!' calls out General MacQuoid. Desmond grasps my arm before I can fall off the slab. I snatch my hand back. What he had said before was outrageous.

Does everyone here see me nothing more than a pawn?

At least he's helping me become queen.

If he helps me get my crown, it'll just make it easier to kill him, won't it? He'll probably cut off the marriage, but I'll do something.

Oh, he shouldn't worry at all. I'd say I couldn't rule the Kingdom alone, I needed some help. Then when he realises he could take both lands, that's when my sword will be at his neck; I won't be the only one pleading for a better life.

General MacQuoid's soles crunch on the gravelly earth. It has a fearful rhythm to it.

A lilting voice whispers through the air, and then I realise why the general is in such a hurry. 'Please, let them out quickly. I have work to do.'

My heart reaches my mouth.

The wind shifts, and the branches rustle. The leaves crinkle, as if air were walking over them. Light as a feather.

'I'll go,' Desmond says, taking one look at my face and then deciding it would be better to leave me in the carriage.

'In your dreams,' I hiss back. He eyes me weirdly before pushing off the slab. He fixes his shirt, brushing a speck of dirt, before General MacQuoid holds the door open. He keeps his eyes firmly on the dirt, the gleam in his eyes extinguishing for the first time in the last three days.

Breathe in, breathe out.

'Really, it would be better to go alone,' Desmond says again.

'No,' I glare at him. 'I did not come on a five-hour drive just to sit in the carriage alone.'

'Xavier was right—you really do talk too much now.' Desmond's voice comes out cold, and I feel something crack inside me. He couldn't just say that—he doesn't know me all that well. It's only been three days.

It was true, though.

I'd noticed it myself. I had become more free with the way I spoke—and the way my thoughts spiralled. But the fact that he knows I have something against Xavier is even worse.

I resist the urge to sigh. I am trapped in my own bloody plan. He knows that I loathe Xavier and could use it against me if I ever betrayed him. But if this meeting with Nyx goes well, then I could very well expose him.

I chuckle to myself—perfect.

He squares his shoulders.

'I need you to trust me, Victoria,' he sighs. 'This is not a game. It's a matter of life and death. From our perspectives, it would be crazy to trust each other, but please. One wrong move, and this could all go wrong.'

'If you're not out in another second, it'll be no move and we're all dead,' I point out, not bothering to listen to his wise talk. I have no interest, like he has none in me.

Desmond purses his lips. 'Very well,' he says. 'Stay close, and don't speak unless you're spoken to.'

Just like the pretty princess always played.

We step out into the sun. It must be early in the afternoon now. I shield my eyes. Solthren—the sun of Inferis. Sun of wind, and sun of night.

I expected the wind to be warm, but the gale that slaps me is cold and remorseless, sending chills down my spine.

I look up from under my hand and nearly startle myself into reality.

She stands before us, back straight, shockingly pale skin and light blue eyes, dressed in a shimmering black gown that smokes its way around her.

Wait, not blue eyes. It's hard to tell in the sun. She looks sick. Her cheekbones are sharp, almost as if carved from ice. I notice Genevieve is already here, bowing before Queen Nyx. Desmond shoots his sister a scathing look.

I suppose she is that desperate to become Queen.

Nyx pulls her chin up, eyes landing on Desmond's bowing

figure, then on me. Desmond was smart to bring us in the morning. Fewer chances of our bodies being mutilated.

Rumours have it that Nyx loves to strike at night.

The hairs at the back of my neck rise, and I hesitantly pull back my dress and bow as low as I can. After years of practice, it should be unusual to forget how to balance, yet it somehow happens to me. I pinch my white dress from both sides and sink into a deep bow, quivering at the ankles.

The long grass tickles the bottom of my chin.

She too, bows low. We close our eyes, and I grit my teeth. My back is beginning to ache. How long have we been down for?

'Rise,' Nyx whispers.

We do as she says, and I keep my eyes in check. I want to look at anything and everything but her.

'Prince Des-mond,' she hisses, gliding forward slowly. She raises a hand, and we are suddenly enveloped in darkness.

I grab my head, swaying.

Her long shadow halts, flickering in the lights of the amethyst crystals. An eerie silence settles, only the clanking of her heels against stone. I realise she has teleported us to another place entirely.

A crystal cave.

We're all going to die.

She looks at me meaningfully, her eyes narrowing. 'Please, tell me what brings you and your traitorous blood-wife to my humble—' she gasps lightly, smirking. 'Abode.'

Traitorous blood-wife.

I halt in my shoes, not like I was moving about in the first place. I hope she meant that my bloodline was traitorous, and not me. Desmond would kill me on the spot if he found out I wanted to kill him.

'She has a name,' Desmond points out calmly.

'I would care—' Nyx spits violently on the floor. 'But I have no taste for fallen Queens.'

I will not remain a fallen Queen! I want to scream at her, pull her hair, thrash and stab her until she's nothing but a pile of bones.

To my surprise, Desmond speaks.

'There wouldn't be much of a difference between the two of you, then.'

I nearly trip on air. I stare at him with wide eyes as Nyx purses her lips, glowering daggers at Desmond. 'Hold your mouth, young man,' she snarls.

'I did not come here to bicker like children,' he says again with a steely glare, jabbing his hands into his pockets, holding his head high.

I resist the urge to wipe my clammy palms on my dress.

Nyx shakes her head, her black hair draping over her face before she parts the ebony fringes. 'Then what did you come here for?' she asks with an air of sarcasm.

'I want Eclipses,' he answers, hands now regally clamped behind his back. I observe the nervous ticks in his jaw.

'Ah,' Nyx tilts her head, scoffing. 'And why would you want my prized possession?'

'To eliminate adversaries.' Desmond pulls out a hand and gestures towards me. 'I'm sure you heard of King Xavier's ascension to the throne?'

'Yes, not formally King, but King anyway.' A small frown forms between her eyes. 'You say—he is an adversary?' She practically exhales the sentence.

'He is attempting to get the Blood Crown. Poor girl got wrapped in the plan, so I'm sending her back after doing her a favour.' Desmond replies smoothly.

Poor girl?

He straightens his back more, aware of the amethyst eyes that bore straight into him. If eyes could kill, Nyx's would.

The crystals in the cave quiver uneasily, and I try to control the anger that agitates them. The amount here is overwhelming, describing my every emotion. I suck in a breath. No wonder Nyx brought us here. Being too close to the power that is buried in my chest could make me burst. She wanted to keep an eye on me, especially since she had no reason to believe my motives. One wrong move and I would be sliced to pieces.

'Killing her brother—is a favour?' She pouts, confusion glazing her eyes.

'Yes,' Genevieve says.

Nyx ignores her. 'What guarantee do I have that you shall bring back Eclipses?' She blinks her eyes. 'I'm quite fond of her.'

'An army of ten thousand men, ready at your feet upon your arrival.' Desmond's reply is hurried, like he has been eager to say it. He holds his breath as Nyx grows closer, thin, bony fingers caressing his jaw. I try not to wince. I can feel his discomfort and a pang of guilt hits me.

Was he really going through so much to get rid of me?

A smile slips onto Nyx's bauble face. 'Per-fect.' She rolls her 'r's majestically.

'You knew what I came here for, didn't you?' Desmond asks. He runs a hand through his hair as Nyx turns on her heel.

'Of course I did. But I had to take precautions, did I not?' Her devilish grin grows wider. 'Fol-low me.' Her lilting voice is like a trance, one that I'm dragged into.

My feet find the guts to move forward, and Genevieve, Desmond and I walk in sync, passing the shards of rocks that jut out from the ground. Glow worms are stuck stubbornly to the wall, upside down. I try to stay close to Desmond. If something happened, at least he would try to protect me. Smoke clogs my lungs and I try not to gag. Genevieve stifles a cough, as Nyx disappears around the corner. Desmond bursts into hacking wheezes, doubling over. He sighs, pulling back up. I hold his arm for support. Dust allergy must be common in their family.

We continue, turning around a curve draped in flowing

shadow, and when we do, we are met with furious purple eyes. They're blinding.

I blink rapidly, clasping onto Desmond for footing. My eyes are still getting used to the dim light, and now I have to readjust to the neon blue that bursts from behind Nyx like two planets colliding.

'I would rather not be kept waiting,' she hisses, addressing Desmond. 'It would not be good for either of us.'

She turns pointedly, her heels clicking. They're white, an odd contrast to her dress. I wonder what led her to wear this. Maybe she doesn't have a sense of aesthetics, or they help navigate the dark land.

Nyx pauses in front of the neon light, and I crane my neck to peek a look behind her. I nearly gasp at the sight. The blue chest before her stood tall, its surface adorned with intricate carvings of Latin patterns that seemed to shimmer and shift in the light. The chest responded to Nyx's presence, unlocking with a flick of her hands. A soft hum rumbled through the cave as the lid began to rise, a gentle breeze stirring and blowing her hair out of her face.

The lid lifted smoothly, revealing velvet fabric in the deepest shade of midnight blue, nearly indistinguishable from the dark that enveloped us. Nestled within, on a pedestal of swirling mist, lays Eclipses.

'No wonder she keeps it locked away so safely,' breathes Genevieve. 'She's beautiful.'

Nyx grabs the hilt, her fingers seemingly used to the odd curve of the sword, the hundreds of tiny jewels that could blind the opponent if placed at a certain angle in the light. Its blade was a flawless, translucent crystal, refracting light into a mesmerising kaleidoscope of colours onto the cave walls.

There was a reason it was called Eclipses. It could render an adversary sightless in every way possible.

'Come, Desmond,' Nyx whispers. I feel a shiver run down

my spine. Desmond looks down at me, and I nod. He swallows, pushing up from the wall.

'Walk faster, prince. How many times do I have to repeat myself? I do not like to be kept waiting,' Nyx bites out.

She resumes observing Eclipses, breathing in the weapon that was once wielded against her. Nyx brandishes the sword in the air like the many times she must have done before, and Desmond yelps, dodging only by a millimetre. 'Sorry, dear. It's been quite some time since I held her.'

Desmond staggers back as Nyx swiftly flings the sword wildly around, slashing the air as if it were a human. She grunts, her dress flowing around her. She comes to a sudden halt, roaring as she shoves it down into the hard stone.

I hold my breath.

Nyx tuts and ushers Desmond to pull the sword out.

With a slight movement of his hand hovering above the hilt, another rhythmic hum wracks the cave, and the crystals around us clatter onto the ground. He grabs it.

'Come on, then, pull it out!' Nyx cackles, watching the power surge into Desmond. He heaves, dragging Eclipses out slowly into the air. The tip of the crystal slips to the floor, refusing to let Desmond carry it.

'Strength will come, Prince. Come, girl,' Nyx hisses, beckoning me over.

I break free from behind the stone, my legs like jelly. 'A crystallite, are you not?'

I nod, gulping. 'Faster!' she shrills.

My pace quickens, and I nearly stumble over the pebbles across the floor.

I come to a halt beside Desmond, and she snatches the sword from him.

He staggers back, breathing raggedly, bending over with his hands on his knees.

She pushes the sword into my hands. 'Carry it.'

'Desmond!' cries Genevieve. She runs over to him, who shrugs her off aggressively.

'Go!' Nyx thunders to the both of them. 'Des-mond, your request has been fulfilled. Now let me have a talk—' she drags out the last few words. 'with this helpless morsel.'

I stop in my tracks. The sword is in my hands, and it feels unusually light. It glows luminescent blue in the dark, and I see Desmond and Genevieve nod their heads hesitantly, bowing and tripping over each other as they make their way out. The echoes that bounced around decrease to nothingness, and silence fills the cave. I slant the sword, moving a step to the right, frowning.

I see Genevieve's figure panic and slip across the stone.

Nyx squeals in delight. 'Smart girl!'

With a wave of her hand, I hear a splat.

No, no.

I pivot to Nyx with wide eyes.

'Y-you k-killed her?' I croak out.

Nyx waves her hands about in the air and tsks. 'Merely a small scratch. Carry her on the way out, will you?'

I blanch.

'Desmond?' I manage to gasp out, rooted to the spot. 'Oh, he knows he would not have a head for the crown if he lingered behind.' Nyx smirks in amusement at my shock. My hands are so sweaty that Eclipses slips from my hand. It nearly clatters to the floor, but I catch it by the hilt and swing it up around my head.

An intense warmth courses through my veins. The sword feels alive in my hands—I can almost hear the hum of its energy resonating with my heartbeat.

The crystals in the cave begin to crack, quaking the cave wildly as one—two—three—smash the earth in agony.

My pulse quickens.

Nyx cackles. 'Perfect, perfect!'

I swallow, pulling Eclipses down from the air, letting it scrape the cobblestone earth.

Her laugh reverberates through the cave, never-ending and vile. 'W-what did you hold m-me back for?' I manage to choke out, my voice hoarse.

Nyx sighs, tilting her head as her teary-eyed face morphs into a little frown. She shakes her head. 'Traitorous bloodwife.'

I suck in a breath, shuffling my feet. 'Tell me, what—' she advances toward me, taking a stride with every word uttered. 'Is—' footstep. 'your—' footstep. 'name?'

I can feel her ashen breath on my cheeks. She is much taller than me, or any man I have ever met.

'Victoria,' I breathe, clenching my hands, gulping.

'Ah.' Nyx brings up her hand, and the hairs on my back rise. I feel chills tingle on my cheek as she traces a delicate, frigid finger across my jaw.

'The fallen Queen,' she inhales, as if breathing the very essence of me in. 'The fallen Queen,' she repeats, 'out for redemption.'

I try not to give in to my thoughts to turn and run. I can barely breathe without gagging. 'Yes, Vic-toria,' she drawls, snatching her hand back. 'I know what you are up to. You wish to get your crown.'

I nod, unable to speak. I can't. It's like my mouth has been glued shut by force.

'Desmond is kind enough to help you, but no,' Nyx's eyes narrow, sharpening as a dark cloud fogs them, tinging them nearly black. 'Your hunger was not quenched. You wished for more to prove yourself, since your prince charming is aiding you.'

'What another has done for you is a job incomplete,' I manage to croak out.

I shriek and shrink back as she grabs my arm, holding

it in place. I hold my head back, my chest rising and falling aggressively.

Nyx chuckles. 'Yes, yes. But let us talk about why you really came along. You want that crown, do you not?'

'What crown?' I rasp back, my hands balling into fists. I refuse to meet her eyes.

'The Blood Crown, of course.' Nyx places a finger to my lips before I can say anything more. 'The only way to get the crown is to kill Desmond, and you want him dead, do you not, Vic-toria?' she hisses.

'Yes,' I wheeze weakly. My surroundings are beginning to blur.

'Tell me,' I feel Nyx breathe down my neck, inching closer with every passing second. 'If I help you, what do you promise me?'

'An alliance,' I whisper, attempting to pull away.

Nyx tugs me closer, revelling in my fear, breathing in wildly. 'The world, in exchange for the crown? You can rule, Vic-toria, but under your Queen,' she murmurs.

Anyone would be stupid to agree to that plan. But I do anyway. I can betray her; that is alright. I'll figure it out as I go—after all, every chance not taken is a lost opportunity.

'Answer me!' Nyx barks.

I nod feverishly.

'Not like you could achieve much,' Nyx tuts, before gripping me tighter. My blood boils. 'Very well. What do you need?'

'To kill Desmond,' I choke out, finally meeting her eyes. They are a steely mauve.

'That's all?' She cocks an eyebrow. Confusion flashes across her face.

'Yes,' I say. Nyx eyes me closely, then suddenly pushes me away. I scream, falling to the floor. Half moons are printed across my arm.

'I will help you,' Nyx hisses. 'When the time comes.'

She rounds on me, and the crystals in the cave begin to crack. Burst in place.

'Now leave, go!' she thunders.

I stagger to my feet, my legs shaking uncontrollably. My breath comes in short, ragged gasps as I turn and stumble towards the cave entrance.

The walls around me seem to close in, the fractured crystals casting jagged shadows that make my skin crawl. I clutch Eclipses tightly, its weight grounding me as I push forward.

I foolishly look back, and Nyx remains rooted to the spot. I feel like I have not moved a single step forward.

The ground beneath me is uneven, and I trip over a loose rock, falling hard onto my knees. Pain shoots through me, but I force myself up, adrenaline numbing the worst of it.

I can feel Nyx's gaze burning into my back, urging me to move faster. I round the corner, desperate to put as much distance between us as possible.

Then I spot red hair on the dirty earth, connected to ashen skin, and pale, lifeless eyes staring blankly at the ceiling. I step closer, splashing in her hair. 'What—' I murmur blankly. I feel dizzy as I hear Nyx's lilting voice sing in the background.

'Vic-toria! Leave now, or you shall discover just how much pain a Queen can endure,' another menacing cackle echoes through the cave.

I step closer to the body, frantic.

Blood trickles from a wound on the woman's temple, pooling around her head. It's with a sickening thought that I realise that I'm not stepping on hair.

That's blood.

Genevieve's blood.

CHAPTER IX

'You let her die!' screams Lorelei.

Desmond stood by, his gaze glossy with unshed tears, allowing Lorelei to batter his chest with useless, flailing punches. Tears streamed down her cheeks, glistening in the firelight.

When we had escaped, Genevieve was in Desmond's arms, blood dripping from her head and spewing from her mouth. The carriage rumbled through the branches and hurtled against the wind while we sat silent, eyeing her limp body in stupefied shock.

I shiver in a corner of the nursing room, a blanket draped around my shoulders. Desmond had tried to ask what Nyx had held me back for, but one look at Genevieve's motionless body shook his curiosity out of him.

'S-she's not d-dead,' I chatter out.

I hope she's not—or maybe I do.

She was plotting to kill me, wasn't she? I pull the coverlet closer, snuggling. It's light in here, torches spitting fire in every corner as evening dawns. The mood, however, is a stark contrast. Another death lingers over our heads.

Bottles of potions line the wall adjacent to the entrance, wooden slabs used to stabilise them. Wooden boxes with knitted wool draped over them stand two metres apart from each other against the wall.

I had considered leaving Genevieve behind in the cave, making a run for it instead of saving her. But I did anyway, and maybe I do regret it just a little bit.

Genevieve lay on one of the seven beds, her arms over her stomach, her eyes shut peacefully. Deep scars line her face, with cotton wrapped around her forearms and legs. A metal clangs every five minutes to reassure that her pulse is beating.

It hasn't made a single sound for the last ten minutes.

'It's broken,' Desmond murmurs.

'Your heart?' Lorelei spits. 'You don't have one to break!'

'I meant the pulley.' Desmond walks over to Genevieve, bending down, pressing a thumb to her wrist. Lorelei swallows hard, her eyes wide with fear and hope.

'It's beating,' his breathless voice breaks the tense silence.

'What?' Lorelei whispers, clutching her hands.

'It's beating!' Desmond suddenly yells, his voice filled with relief.

I startle, my heart rate spiking.

As if on cue, Genevieve coughs and jerks from the bed. Only then do I let out a long, shaky sigh I hadn't realised I was holding, the stone on my chest lifting, allowing my organs to suffice back to where they had once been.

Lorelei laughs tremulously, grabbing onto the wall. Desmond clutches Genevieve's hand as she pulls up into a sitting position.

Her eyes are bleary, and her hair... her hair is chopped off. I don't remember that ever happening.

The weight is lifted off my shoulders. My eyelids grow heavy, fluttering shut despite my attempts to keep them open. Each breath I take deepens, slowing as my body sinks further into the bed. The joyous laughter around me blurs into a soft, distant hum.

I saved her in time.

But what would have happened if I hadn't?
Wouldn't it have been better for me?

'Your Highness, the coronation must take place in a month,' Lord Clyde croaks out, watching as Desmond crashes a flower vase onto the floor, sending the pieces soaring into the air.

'Clyde, I am quite well aware, but what about the memorial of my Mother?'

'Have a chat with your civilians, then.' Prince Rhysand chuckles, flicking ebony strands of hair from his face.

Desmond grumbles, straightening his back and fixing his shirt cuff. 'What are you doing out here, anyway?' he asks, stepping behind his table to a cupboard.

The Prince of Caelumterra eyes him closely, and I flinch at the sound of glass scratching the cobblestone floor. 'William wants to know where the Librum Aeternitatis disappeared to,' Rhysand answers, leaning against the emerald leather chair. His grey eyes twinkle in the orange crystal that grows a millimetre every second in my presence.

We were in the Chief Commander's Office, and out of the corner of my eye, I spied the Blood Crown under slabs of wood, a glass box protecting it from being crushed. But on further inspection, it was an illusion. A mirror that led the power thirsty individual to fall into a trapdoor and into a pit of slithering serpents. The real crown was obscured under the labyrinth of stones the prince stood upon.

Desmond cocks an eyebrow, glaring at Rhysand.

'I have signed the scroll.' He digs in the cupboard, pulling out a solid black book with three words scrawled across in gold.

The Blood Crown.

'Then show it,' Rhysand says, shrugging. His voice was

deathly, and the chandelier above was beginning to quiver. 'It's as simple as that.'

'I would, but it appears to have taken a quest. When it reappears, I shall inform you and your dear brother,' Desmond replies, smacking the book on the table.

Dust flies and I choke in a cough. Rhysand looks to me, his eyes narrowing.

'How lucky to be married to a fallen Queen,' he sneers.

I will get my throne back.

'I don't know about her being a fallen Queen, but I do know she's still strong enough to silence fools like you,' Desmond spits, pulling out a sword from under the table.

I swallow, watching Lord Clyde brush white curly hair out of his face, nearly tripping in his own forest green robes.

I flush when a crystal erupts from the ceiling, but Rhysand smirks. 'I'd like to see her try,' yet he instinctively places a hand on the hilt of his gemmed sword all the same. I don't miss the way his eyes dart to the crystal looming overhead.

'If you were dethroned, you shouldn't be Queen on another's throne.' Rhysand's grin grows wider, making his way to place a cold hand on my cheek.

A sword cuts his hand and I bring a horrified hand to my mouth.

Rhysand gasps, huffing as he pulls back a bloodied finger. I could see the chopped white bone peeking from underneath, and the string of flesh that bled in pattering droplets.

Desmond pulls back his sword, coming to stand in front of me. 'Touch her again and I'll make sure the hand you swear your oath to the throne with is chopped off.'

Lord Clyde hesitantly pulls a handkerchief from his robe, offering it to Rhysand.

'William wants the scroll by the end of the month,' he growls, seething when his finger limps deeper.

My hands go numb, a feeling of detachment tearing them from the rest of my body.

'Kind one, he is. If it were up to me, I would've forced you to hunt for the scroll in front of my own eyes.'

'But it's not,' Desmond drawls, crossing his leg and balancing himself with his sword. 'There's a reason you were chosen as Crown Prince, and William as High King.'

A splutter escapes one of the servants, and Rhysand's pinky plops to the floor. I gag, turning to find the waiter, Hemsworth, peeking his head in through the door, and watch as Desmond purses his lips in irritation.

'Best if you went along, Rhysand. My floor is getting dirty.' Desmond waves his hand about, and Rhysand grabs his sword, glaring as he shoves Hemsworth aside and stalks away.

'Hemsworth,'

'Yes, my King?'

'You're fired.' Desmond throws his sword across the room, and it clatters against the wall. Hemsworth whimpers before scurrying away like a lost bunny, his hair bounding behind him. My heart pounds in my chest, and a crystal drops out from the ceiling to the ground, crashing against the sword.

'I-I thought Caelumterra was your closest ally,' I murmur, watching as he thumps open his book, shaking the wooden table.

'Times change,' Desmond bites out, chewing his nail. 'Clyde, what did the council say?'

'The country is afraid of an upheaval against the current monarch, and they wish for you to not extend the coronation any further than it already is,' Clyde answers, hands behind his back.

I flinch. The council—Prince William and High King Cassius—were afraid Ferrumisle were planning something bigger.

They weren't wrong. I needed that crown. It would shut up all those who dare think I was weak and unworthy of the throne.

Desmond sighs, mopping a hand over his face. 'Then be it.'

I watch him as I meet his steely glare. 'You may leave,' he gestures his hand to the door.

'Why did you protect me?' The words leave my mouth, bitter on my tongue.

Desmond looks up at me, his eyes softening. I pull at the thin lace on my dress.

'Why?' I croak out. 'If we're going to leave each other anyway, why? What's the point? At times you act like you hate me, and then later—

I cut off.

Desmond opens his mouth, then shuts it. Like a goldfish breathing underwater in the depths of the navy sea that pools around the islands in a satisfying illusion of grass quivering gently against the wheezy breeze.

He pulls up from his chair and makes his way around the table. I stagger back a bit, meeting the rough stone as he grabs a hold of my shoulders.

'This world is too cruel for an innocent soul like you,' he breathes, and for the first time, I see pain flicker through his eyes. 'Take advantage of the people around you before you lose your worth and yourself. You are worth it, and when you get your throne back, you will prove it.'

CHAPTER X

I don't understand if he hates or cares for me.

I lean deeper into his arms, feeling his warmth spread through my body.

Every time I attempt to convince myself that he is untrustworthy, I fall deeper into a rabbit hole I am incapable of escaping.

I have to kill him.

I cannot afford to trust anyone any longer.

Sunniva dances high, a still explosion in the sky with a beam of light that slices through the clouds in a circle around her.

'Did you find the Scroll of Eternity?' I murmur softly.

'I hope I do so soon. William will have my neck if I do not present it to him on the day of our wedding,' Desmond sighs.

His hair splashes over his face, illuminating it like a magnificent pearl, eyes gleaming a furious gold.

We sit under the shade of a tree in the palace gardens, the autumn leaves tickling my bare arms as they gently float with the breeze.

'How did you lose it, anyway?'

Desmond chuckles. 'I gave it to Genevieve to store in the Commander's Office.'

I turn to him slowly. 'She tried to sign it?'

Desmond shrugs, plucking grass from the earth.'You understand she desires nothing more than my throne.'

I nod, and uneasiness creeps into my heart once more.

'Do you trust me?' Desmond asks suddenly, as if he had read my mind.

I stay silent, my heart thundering in my ears.

'Why do you not?' he asks again, his voice soft.

'I—I don't know,' I croak out, unable to swallow the lump in my throat.

'Is it because you think of me as ruthless?' he whispers, brushing a strand of my hair to the side.

I suck in a breath.

'Is it because you believe I will betray and destroy every ounce of your strength until you crumble in my arms, begging me to slit open your throat?'

He pauses, locking our gaze.

'Or is it because you fear to die alongside me as your equal, when none can hurt you except me?'

As your equal.

I feel my heart convulse, choking on its own blood.

I clutch his coat tighter around my neck as his arms stiffen.

'I want to trust you,' I barely manage to whisper.

'You need to trust me,' his voice is raw. 'Because if you don't, only one will be able to destroy the other, and I don't want to go down that path.'

The rest of the weeks passed by in a blur.

The coronation was to take place in just two days, with preparations having been done by Lorelei. She had a knack for strings and baubles, and the green chiffon curtains and golden hoop chandeliers hanging from the sky said it all.

Elysande was most certainly not happy. She and Lorelei would have tea together, discussing matters related to those who fiendishly dressed or corrupted the rule of aesthetics.

Otherwise, she would lock herself in her room, and not a single soul would know her acts.

Xavier was probably consuming every nerve in her brain.

I nearly stop in my tracks.

Xavier was to arrive today.

I swear I feel a part of my heart crack and shake my head aggressively.

Not him. I should not think about him.

I continue down the staircase, nearly slipping over the side. After our meeting with Nyx, I'd spend my time alone in the palace gardens, and Desmond would join me at times. Breathing in the faint scent of flowers was better than the musty cave. It was strange that, despite spending nearly every evening in the gardens, I only remembered that one night where death hung by a single, thin rope, ready to slip from the heavens and conquer the dead body.

Genevieve's wounds were being treated, and whatever pain she might have been in was erased when I invited her to teach me archery three weeks after her injury.

'Really?' she gawks, nearly jumping off the bed. The nurse who had been with Agatha in my room the other day frantically pulls her back down.

'Yes,' I say.

I do not know why I asked such a thing.

Maybe because I felt bad.

Stop feeling. Just stop. It's going to get you nowhere.

But I couldn't help it—not even after she tried to eavesdrop on what I was saying in the cave.

Nyx's voice marred with Genevieve's laughter as she gently plucked the needle connected to the pulley from her arm. I flinch, squirming.

'I'll get ready,' she says firmly to the nurse, who panics.

'My princess, I don't think—'

Genevieve waves a dismissive hand. 'Think whatever you wish, Edna. I need to reconnect with nature after this month's occurrence.'

She pointedly bounces off the bed, a white cloth wrapped around her head and a clean, snowy robe draped over her.

'What if I had said no?' Genevieve gestures to my clothes.

I was wearing a sleek black leather jacket with silver accents, a fitted charcoal-grey tunic, and dark trousers.

I flex my hands where I wore fingerless gloves, playing with the arrow in my palm. A slim silver circlet keeps my hair in place when I shrug. 'I would have dragged you out anyway.'

She grins, brushing past me.

I hear Desmond yell in pain as she trips over him on her way out.

He curses, and Genevieve chortles before the palace settles back into silence.

Desmond. Nyx said she would help me kill him. I clutch the arrow and place it in the bow bag slung across my back. I wasn't sure I wanted to kill him anymore.

Maybe I should just settle in my own kingdom. But what if he hurt me after that? *Why would he hurt you after protecting you—and after all that he has said?*

Then I would just have to do it alone. I breathe shakily. The meeting with Nyx had shaken me. Maybe that's why I was so reluctant.

She's helping both Desmond and me.

'Why though?' I murmur aloud.

'What?'

I startle at Desmond's voice. 'Mind moving?' he says, cocking his head to one side. I hesitantly move, realising I had been standing awkwardly in the middle of the nursing room entrance, letting him pass.

'What's been on your mind?'

Other than those evenings in the garden?

He seems unusually relaxed. Not a tick in his jaw, not a frown on his face, not the lazy drawl he usually addresses me with.

I rub the back of my head, noticing the velvet midnight case he held. The outdoor conversations did wonders.

'Eclipses?' I ask.

He nods. 'You didn't answer my question.' He gives me a playful bump on the shoulder. 'Not scared after the meeting, are you?'

You could hardly call it simply a meeting.

I shake my head.

'I just—' I sigh. 'Why did Nyx not kill us—or you—when we got there? I mean, she nearly killed Genevieve, but...' my voice trails off.

Desmond places a hand on my shoulder, balancing the case in his other. 'Because I can help her return to Aetheria, stronger than before. I gave her a reason to not kill me. Not yet, at least.'

He looks me straight in the eyes, and I place my hand on his, making way to remove it.

'But the real question is,' his voice is quiet, nearly crooning. 'what did you offer her that made her not kill you?'

There was something about the way Desmond always asked that question. He had not eavesdropped on Nyx and me, and he even stopped her from lashing out at me like a hungry mongrel. Nyx wouldn't have ended him, because he was more powerful than I was, and would inevitably provide more for Nyx's return than I ever could.

He never ever pushed forward if I didn't answer. He was curious, of course he was. But he never overwhelmed me with the night's happenings any more than twice these two weeks.

He knew exactly what to say at the right times.

I push his hand down, hearing a thud on the staircase behind us. I shake my head. I could not look him in the eye and lie. I could not. Not after that night, which happened a mere week ago.

An out-of-breath Genevieve rushes down the stairs, bumping into me from behind. I yelp, grabbing onto Desmond. He manages to grasp me in time before I fall to the ground. The case clatters on the floor.

'Victoria, let's go,' she pants, breathless. Her cheeks are tinged a deep red, hands on her black knee-high boots before pulling herself upright.

'Where are you guys going?' he asks, squinting his eyes and eyeing Genevieve up and down. She wears a deep emerald velvet jacket with gold embroidery, a cream silk blouse with a pearl brooch, and matching leather trousers.

'Archery,' Genevieve answers.

Desmond pulls me up, and I straighten my back. 'Mind if I tag along?'

Victoria Ironhart,
Day 5,

~

Oh, woe.
I call upon you,
more and more,
seeking refuge in the solace of your deplorable lore,
unable to romanticise anything other than gore.
If I continue with my indecisive prospect,
I fear I will become a mere, lifeless object.

~

To kill, or not to kill?

What a terrible life decision to make; one that desperate people ponder over in desperate times. I was going to be sent to my Kingdom, alone, without anyone—maybe Elysande. But I had to kill her, didn't I?

I had to kill Desmond, too.

The thought burst forth in my mind once more.

To kill, or not to kill?

He was only trying to help, after all. And the week we spent together, oh, it felt as if we had a mutual understanding. The times in the garden were one to behold. He was usually quiet, charming, cold, oblivious to another's existence at times. But in the garden, he was... changed.

Somebody new.

I sat alone, the evening sun settling behind the grassy hills, tinging the sky a fiery orange and deep purple.

The shadows lengthened, dancing over the rolling landscape as a cool breeze whispered through the tall grass, carrying the scent of wildflowers. The horizon seemed to blur where the earth met the sky.

The world was quiet, save for the distant call of a nightbird, echoing the loneliness that wrapped around me like a shroud. This was the only night I could ever recall so vividly. It is etched into my being, burnt and singed.

A crunch of leaves made me suck in a breath. It was time.

'May I?' *Desmond asked. When I didn't reply, he promptly invited himself to take a seat beside me.*

'You know, I've been thinking,' *he said, rubbing his chin.*

'Thinking about what?' *I asked, noticing how he went strangely quiet. Sometimes, silence stretches so long that it forces words to fill the void.*

'I'll miss you when you finally go back to your Kingdom.'

'I've only been with you for—what,' *I said,* 'barely two weeks?'

'There's this... fire, inside of you,' *Desmond answered, splaying his arm out into the open, dragging it across from left to right in slow motion.*

I squinted in confusion. 'I like it,' he said, grinning down at me.

I raised an eyebrow. 'And where have I shown this,' I waved my hand around. 'Fire?'

'Aiding in killing your own brother should be enough.' Desmond chuckled. 'They practically controlled you, but when you arrived here—you changed.'

'Step-brother,' I corrected, plucking the grass. I hadn't bothered giving much thought to the rest of his reply. I was too busy hiding the dagger under my dress.

I really shouldn't do this.

'Your kin is your blood. Step-sibling or not, he's still family.' Desmond shrugged. I bit the inside of my lip.

That was true. 'W-will you actually miss me?' I stuttered shakily, swallowing.

'Why wouldn't I?' Desmond shot back. I felt a shiver tingle down my spine, and the words spilled out of my mouth before I could stop them.

'I'll be dead then; it makes sense you'll miss loathing me.'

Desmond's eyes widened. 'Victoria, no, no.' He had laughed. 'Are you saying I would betray you? Why the hell would I do that?'

How many times would I have that conversation with him? How much longer before I could let go of the fear inside me?

I looked down, not daring to meet his eyes. My teeth chattered. I felt warmth suddenly envelop me, and I sat rooted to the spot in shock.

'Even after all that my family has done, you're just going to let me go?' I said, pulling his coat over me tightly.

'I have no reason to hurt someone like you, who has not done anything. I am not that vile, Venefica.' That stupid nickname. Desmond pulled me closer, laying me down on his lap. 'And even if you tried to kill me, I would push the dagger through my heart myself. You shouldn't be asking me to take revenge on your family. I should be asking you that. I destroyed your life. I owe you your Kingdom back if that's the last thing I ever do.'

'You finally came to your senses.' I let out a hoarse chuckle.

'I'm always in my senses. Wise people don't kill without a reason.'

Must I do this?

Kill him! Kill him! Kill him! Kill him! Kill him!

I pull myself up a bit, sharply tearing the dagger out of the coat before—

'Victoria,' Desmond's sharp voice rang out in the night. I felt my eyes narrow, become slits. I was so close. The dagger was at his heart. If I could just push it in, it would all be over. The crown, mine. The world—mine. Mine, all mine.

But I couldn't.

'Do it,' he breathed. His hand enveloped mine, and I looked up to meet his eyes. The world is blurry. 'Do it, Venefica.' His voice was cold. His command was remorseless. 'I-' I cut off abruptly. The dagger was sinking in. It was going inside. It was going into his chest straight into his heart.

'I didn't expect such cowardice from you.' His voice dropped to a low decibel, eyes fluttering shut. His fingers were rigid and pushing, slowly and painfully. His face was masked in peace. I felt the dagger drowning lower. I felt the way it cut through his skin, peeling slowly to flesh, a sickening glob sounding.

'Stop!' I gasped.

His eyes clawed open.

His downcast eyes. The little tilt to his head. It looked like... disappointment. I had disappointed someone else, again. Really, what was my worth in this world?

I threw the dagger aside like it was spit, drawing blood. I grasped onto him harder, breath hitched and a sob escaping my lips. Desmond brought down two hands and cupped my face gently, pulling me against him as I wracked in his arms.

'I'm sorry,' I cried.

I'm sorry—I'm sorry—I'm sorry!

Is that all I was to say in my pitiful life?

Apologise for every little thing I did for myself?

I felt my chest heave with each gasp, the weight of his words cutting deeper than the blade that dug through his heart. I owe you your kingdom back, if that's the last thing I ever do. *Then did the tears stream down my cheeks uncontrollably, leaving me trembling in his grasp.*

I twisted.

I turned.

I tossed.

I screamed.

I cried.

There he was, trying to protect me. Trying to help me. And look what I had done. Betray him. And look at what he did all the time I lay in his arms like a helpless child.

He held me until my sobs subsided.

He held me until I screamed my lungs hoarse and bled my lips.

He held me until I was grasping so tight to his neck I could choke him.

And what had I given him?

The sweet taste of being on the brink of death.

'Are you sure you can do this, Victoria?' Desmond asks, wincing as I send another flying arrow plummeting into the earth. I missed a target by five metres—again. He leans against a tree, eyebrows raised in mock anticipation.

'Of course I can,' I answer for the tenth time, more stubborn than ever. 'I just need practice.'

'Practice—' Desmond plucks an arrow from his bag and pulls the bowstring. He stands only a few feet away, but the distance between us seems to stretch for miles. He turns slowly, aiming for the target I had failed to strike. 'Looks like this.' Desmond pivots suddenly, letting the arrow soar through the air and strike the apple on the top of my head.

I stand still as juice leaks over my hair.

He did this all without looking. I scowl when he laughs.

'Really, Victoria. I asked you to use that apple to balance and straighten your back, not play lovey dovey trust games.'

I startle, pivoting. Genevieve stands with her hands on her hips, seeming every bit the angry Mother.

'Come on, Genevieve. Give her a break,' Desmond calls, dropping his bag to take a seat against the birch tree.

'Alright.' Genevieve sighs. 'So much for trying to teach you archery.'

'We'll come back to it.' I smile, giving her arm a reassuring squeeze. We both make our way over to Desmond, and I collapse down onto the earth beside him. He pulls out a sandwich from the cross-stitched wood picnic basket and hands it over to me. I take a bite. Oh, sweet oblivion.

'Waiting for the time Victoria leaves so my lovely brother can give us some attention too,' Genevieve mutters angrily when Desmond resumes eating his own sandwich, not bothering to offer her any.

I stop chewing. *I was going to leave for Ferrumisle. As Queen.* That should have been a reassuring thought, but it wasn't. I take another bite, my gaze far away, until Desmond's next words pull me back to the Queen's Forest.

'Oh, she's not going anywhere.' He takes a huge bite of what seems to be his third sandwich already. 'She'll be Queen by my side.' I blink at him.

'What about your plan to overthrow Nyx?'

After all that had happened, I remember Desmond and I sat in the Keep, alone. We had been discussing the future a mere four days after visiting Nyx.

Why did you offer ten thousand soldiers to a devil who's going to kill you the moment she enters this land? I could hear my own voice warped in disbelief.

I'm going to kill her first, once I have exactly a hundred thousand deaths. Desmond had answered.

Just as I had suspected. He was going to use The Blood Crown to his advantage.

You think she's stupid enough to not figure it out? I had bit out.

I made sure word of my killings was not leaked. She still thinks I'm a pawn. I didn't ask how. Desmond had his ways. *Why are you sending me away, then? I can help you.*

His next words had left me in a pool of warmth. *Because I believe you need to be protected. I need to have an ally to rely on, don't I?*

Then, his motives had been different, but in the garden, he'd sworn to sacrifice himself for me.

'You can stay in Briarthorn Atoll as Queen of Ferrumisle and help me defeat Nyx.'

'What about Ferrumisle?' I asked, shocked. I don't think I've processed this information quite well yet.

'You can visit it once in a while, but not too many times,' Desmond answered, inhaling the last chunk of his sandwich.

I scoff, crossing one arm over my chest. 'Why? It'll be my land.'

Desmond opens his mouth, then quickly shuts it.

'Lorelei said you would be here,' a voice spoke from behind. I stiffen. That voice has cracked every bit of my universe.

'Oh, Xavier,' Desmond says, pushing off the grass. I pull the sandwich away from my mouth, turning to see my brother. 'You're here early.'

Xavier stands tall, hair unruffled. A silver coronet enwrapped in mercury holds a shining ruby at the lone spike in the centre. He wears a deep crimson doublet with intricate gold embroidery along the edges, pulling forward his flowing black cloak, draped over his shoulders and fastened with a jewelled clasp to hide his belt. I tilt my head a bit as the breeze slightly lifts the fur coat.

I spot the gleam of an ornate sword sheath hanging by his side. Why would he want to hide his sword?

'Why, yes. I've been looking forward to the marriage,' he speaks to Genevieve next.

'Are you alright?' He bends down, pushing her hair out of her face. I swear I see a blush creep across her cheeks.

'Just a little accident.' Genevieve pulls out an arrow. 'A crow decided it would be fun to peck at the apple over my head.'

'The crow must have missed brutally,' Xavier replies, not in the least believing her crafty lie.

'Say, could you teach me how to shoot a target?' He nods over to one of the blue and white boards with a red centre.

'S-sure,' Genevieve stutters.

Desmond and Xavier shake hands, nodding to each other with stony faces. It's laughable, the way they both try so hard to seem like great entities. Genevieve stands up, leading Xavier a few metres away from us.

'Shall we leave?' I say, turning to Desmond.

Desmond bites his lower lip and nods down at me. 'We shall.'

We make our way to the Armory Chamber.

'Genevieve and Lorelei know about all your plans?' I ask. Desmond pushes open the door. Not even a single stream of light sneaks through the locked windows, and the room stinks of moss.

'They have to, otherwise they could abdicate me for plotting against the monarch—my father's—decision.'

I nod.

'In case you're wondering, I'm here to play dress-up with my men. They need to look pretty for Nyx,' Desmond adds, pulling at a rope. Dozens of torches lined up on the wall erupt with fire, illuminating the mass of brass armour that stands tall on wooden stick-men, glistening like pearls under the warm light.

The fires flicker, casting an eerie shadow across the cobblestone-bricked walls. They are lined with rough wooden bows, and poison-tipped arrows, and iron spears. Bludgeons sat helplessly in crates at the end of the vast room, some a perfect sphere while others a moulded muddle.

I laugh. 'She'll be pleased to know that those in Aetheria are easily enticed by beautiful men.'

The thought hits me suddenly once more, and I feel my smile vanish.

Desmond shakes his head, grinning. 'You can go if you want. It'll take some time here,'

'Alright.' I answer, squeezing his hand, my facade wobbling. I let go, beginning a short walk to the fork.

'Get ready for tomorrow, it's going to be quite a day,' he calls, his voice a distant echo as the great emerald doors bang shut.

I take a left to our chamber. Nyx. How was I to tell Nyx I no longer wanted to kill Desmond?

Somehow, the lights were dim, and an eerie shadow cast across the walls. Strange, it was only the afternoon.

'Hello, sister.' A voice catches me off guard. Wasn't he supposed to be outside with Genevieve? Desmond and I had hardly been gone for ten minutes. I don't bother turning and instead make my way forward.

'I am not your sister,' I bite out.

'Blood is blood.' An arm drapes over my shoulder, and his ring burns my cheek. It sends a jolt of agitation through my body, and I feel my bones weaken, like I cannot walk anymore.

'How can metal sting that bad?' Xavier murmurs, more to himself than me. I feel his breath on me as he brings his hand once more to my cheek, attempting to rub the ring again.

My heart thrashes in my chest as I cover his hand, the metal burning through. My palm would be purple and blue tomorrow. Xavier chuckles, ruffling my hair aggressively.

'Where's Genevieve?' I ask, an irritation scratching my head.

'Her head began hurting. Said it happens on and off these days, so I took her to the nurse,' Xavier answers, pulling me closer as we near the narrow hallway. My chamber is just a few metres away.

'How was it with the Thorncrests while I was away?' Xavier asks, his hand at his sword. I hope he doesn't decide to kill me. I attempt to pull away from his grasp, pushing his arm off my shoulder.

'As good as home,' I reply lightly. It wasn't a lie.

'Good to hear that.' He turns to an open window where the sun beams through delightfully when we reach my chamber. 'I'll best be going. Genevieve awaits my arrival.'

He bows his head, smirking before pivoting away.

Breathe in, breathe out.

I gasp when Xavier disappears around the corner, tugging at my chest, everything suddenly crashing down on me.

Tomorrow is my marriage.

Tomorrow Xavier dies.

Tomorrow I become Queen.

CHAPTER XI

Last night's sleep had been horrific.

I tossed and turned, hidden under the covers. Desmond had not yet arrived. He should have specified that gathering an army of ten thousand men would take nearly the whole day. I swallowed. How would I tell Nyx I didn't want to kill Desmond any longer?

But I couldn't think about that now—no, I could not.

The chattering of the crowd decreases to an echo, bounding off the walls and pounding my brain as I step onto the red carpet. I was late, but others would assume I was acting to look my best. I had been.

After I had left for the bathroom, Edna immediately got to work, providing me with a warm bath. Agatha returned with a stunning snowy ball gown that flowed from the bottom like water, coveted with green swirls at the sleeves and emeralds at the hem. They had put my hair up into a crown, allowing the rest of my locks to float around, and placed me in glittering, glassy heels.

Normally, I would have raised my head high and walked the carpet with as much revolt as possible—but now, I could not bear to stare into the gawking eyes.

I fear them. They remind me of a shadow. It will keep on chasing you, and when it finally catches up, it devours you whole. These creatures are searching for a flaw, another fault of mine to prove themselves right.

You don't need to prove yourself to anyone, Mother had said.

She had seen the pain in my eyes, heard the cries from my mouth, touched the wounds of my heart—something no one else bothered to do.

But as I try to grasp for her voice now, another comes in. My own. Father's distancing and Xavier's insulting—they have achieved their goal; to make me feel lowly and unworthy. Now I no longer need to prove myself to anyone else. I need to prove myself—to me.

I flash a smile as I take a step forward, my palms clammy and my legs jelly. Xavier is at my side, locking arms and forcing me forward.

I see Desmond in an emerald fur coat and white suit, the Blood Crown shining in a glass box, hovering out of reach from the creatures. Nixies, centaurs, faes, vampires, and sorceresses and sorcerers of all kinds swarm the crowd, eyeing me inquisitively.

My blood begins to chill as we grow closer to the dais. It would have been an honour to any other royalty to be married off to the heir of the Blood Crown. But this unsettling news had taken me aback. Visiting Thorncrest had been part of the plan, killing Desmond had been a part of the plan, but Father had been, as usual, two steps ahead of me. Now that we were going to be married, if I killed Desmond, I would be the first suspect.

Kingdoms and tribes would be against me. The whole world would be against me.

But I didn't need to kill Desmond. I would have my own kingdom, a part of Briarthorn Atoll, and a reputation. I would defeat Queen Nyx with Desmond.

'My princess.'

Xavier lets go of my arm, handing me over to Desmond and eyeing me with a fury in his eyes I cannot decipher.

'My prince,' I say, bile filling my throat. I want to throw up. Never in my life have I thought I would be saying these words.

General MacQuoid takes a step back from the dais, allowing us to stand side by side, facing the crowd. I let a shuddery breath escape, the sudden cool of Desmond's hands intertwining with mine catching me off guard. Were we not going to make the vows?

'Creatures of Aetheria, I have a confession to bring forward,' Desmond's voice booms in the throne room, a small sigh punctuating his sentence. The crowd rings with gasps of shock and I blink. Confession? What confession?

'I regret to say, my love for Victoria surpassed me.'

Amused chittering erupts, forcing me to smile and rub Desmond's hand.

He grimaces but doesn't say a word, continuing, 'I pledged to her my vows in the darkest night, pleading to forever be by her side. Our marriage was sealed at midnight, on the seventeenth of Aprilis, Dies Mercurii. She will now accompany me in my reign over Briarthorn Atoll!'

We never made any vows last night.

Cheers succumb the hall and shake the earth beneath us. I see the kings and queens of the Tribe of the Famished shake their heads uncertainly.

The lords and ladies of Inferis, Ferrumisle, and Briarthorn Atoll flinch as if someone had slapped them. They knew something was up. This was the third 'love' marriage Aetheria had witnessed, and they were prepared for this one to crumble, just like the other two. Some of their gazes linger upon me, and I know why.

It was because Calypso and Avalorian Ironhart's love marriage had been doomed.

And they expected as much once more.

'Congratulations!' Nixies, dwarves, and vampires rotate, as one by one they congratulate Desmond and me in the delighting revel. It is awful.

We were not actually married. Engaged, but not by heart. No soul besides the two of us knew. Or maybe Genevieve and Lorelei did.

I cast a sideways glance at Desmond, swallowing. Why did he lie?

We nod heads, strolling along the crowds, greeting and thanking the revellers. When would this night end? I shudder, the cold wind slapping my cheeks. Desmond opens his mouth, then closes it.

'Why did you lie about the vows?' I croak out. I let go of his arm, but he pulls me back.

'They don't know that we've been together for only a month.'

'Then this should have been done later,' I say.

I wanted him to leave me.

'The council forced me to; you were there. I had to arrange the marriage for today and the coronation tomorrow.' Desmond pulls up my chin.

'Do you think I'm lying?' There was a soft undertone of a threat to his words. I try to look away; but he pulls me closer to him. 'Answer my question, Venefica. Do you think I'm lying?'

'I don't think you're lying, Desmond.'

My voice said otherwise.

Desmond blinks, letting go of me. I gasp and trip over the carpet that's been curled up. He catches me before I can fall, hurt flickering across his eyes.

'I expected more than suspicion, Victoria,' he only ever used my name when he wanted to make a point.

'Desmond,' I say, trying to grab his arm.

'I'm sacrificing everything for you,' he mutters, turning and attempting to walk away.

'Y-you have every right to. You're the one who destroyed my life.' I burst, splaying my hands.

'So you're going to keep chasing me and not your stupid brother?' Desmond pivots, eyes ablaze.

I stagger back, heaving.

'I could kill you right here, and right now, Victoria. I could have killed you at any time before. But I didn't, because all I have been trying to show you is that you have worth.' He pauses, his eyes boring into mine. My chest tightens, and I feel as though my heart is made of burnt coal. Even the slightest touch of a feather could turn it to ash.

'I saw the cracks in your soul and wanted to mend them, even if it wasn't my place. I didn't want to play good and kill for you; heck, I didn't even know you.'

Desmond rubs a hand over his face, shaking his head. 'But I still helped you, and that's the difference between you and me,' he spits.

I feel a hot tear rush down my cheek.

'I give a damn about others, even when I shouldn't. You, Victoria, only care about yourself.'

His words slapped me in the face with brutal force. I feel a wave of stinging pain wash over me, each word cutting sharply into my heart, each slice deeper than the last. Tears brimmed my eyes, threatening to spill.

With that, he brushed past me and walked straight into the revelling crowd.

Victoria Ironhart,
Day 4,

~

Woe looks down upon me
as screams echo through the night's oblivion,
every being deaf and blind to the aching soul,
with only the creatures of the night
hunting and prowling,
devouring my worthless fervour,
with glee and droll.

~

Living was a task. Harder than most, easier than some.

I sank deeper into the water, the waves dragging me under and blurring my vision. A shadow hovered over where I sank, and I felt my body go limp. I tried to move my hand, pushing it back and forth as I swayed, the water thrashing down my throat like a waterfall.

I can't drown, though, and eventually, I began to feel my legs. I kicked, watching as figures emerged. The deed was done, but not completely. I still had a lot more to do. I noticed the crumbling dirt around me and realised the land must have been blown to smithereens. Inferis must have been somewhere around there.

More shadows dove in from above.

The silhouette must have been a boat. I closed my hand before stretching my fingers and feeling a hum of power from my left. I breathed, the water clogging my throat, and pulled closer to the energy. It thrummed in my body and soon, I allowed it to drag me to the depths of the undersea, the water transitioning to a murky green from a starry blue hue. I heard bellows from above and watched as the men following me started to close in.

I sank lower. I felt mostly numb, but I could still stretch my fingers. The water and I felt like one, morphed to create an entity powerful enough to drag lands. The current began to slow, and I heard a distant whistle wrack my ears.

We were close, and the men could sense it too.

Some of them paused, attempting to swim back to the top, but they coughed in water and choked, grabbing their necks as I watched the soul of each and every one of them blink in the darkness of the ocean. I bumped my head against something solid and raised my hand a bit, propelling the energy to carry me to the mainland. I lifted up, and then they arrived.

A flurry of whispers sighed a song when the sirens appeared, their pale skins gleaming like the moonlit waves, while their hair seemed to cascade like black silk, but it was their eyes—those fathomless, obsidian pools—that held me. The desire, the urge to control their victims and slowly destroy them bit by bit, ripping away their flesh, made my mouth water. How I wished I could lure innocent victims into seemingly harmless traps in seconds.

Oh, wait. I was.

I burbled a laugh, and bubbles burst forth.

I felt the pull of their melody seeping into my bones, but it could not possibly fuel me with more desire. I was already overflowing.

The men who dropped like fish into the ocean swam towards me. I looked up. I was nearly there. I could make out the rift in the sky that led to the other worlds, a melanoid, starry sky painting life black and blue. The pitch of the sirens' melody grew higher as the men were drawn in, their eyes glassy, as if in a trance.

Oh, how stupid they were to send so many after me.

Did those fools never realise that the more you give, the more is taken?

I gasped for air when I reached the top, puking the water out of my lungs. I scrambled to the charcoal land, away from the ships that plagued the ocean. My hands trembled, and I groped the ashes that stained my clothes, crawling through the dirt and grime that stuck in my fingernails.

I flipped over onto my back.

The clear blue water was now a deep red, and I could hardly make out the sirens tearing the flesh from the men below.

A horn bellowed, and I noticed the ships were inching closer. I staggered up, clutching my chest where a scar dragged from my neck to where my heart was.

A burnt patch lay stamped across where the phoenix tattoo used to be. The flame I had ignited had worked well to obscure all traces of who I had once been.

Victoria had been the past, and now Venefica will be the present.

Desmond was right.

He was so damn right.

I sat at the lunch table beside him. I could feel the way his jaw constricted and his face morphed into stone when I followed him. I had to apologise, but how? I opened my mouth, but then Elysande appeared, and I clamped it shut.

I had to kill Elysande, right? Desmond had never mentioned killing her, though.

She would never let me ascend the throne, so the only way for me to become Queen would be to end her. Desmond would take that as an apology in itself, right? It was something I was doing for myself, but at the same time, I was taking action and taking weight off Desmond's shoulders if I told him about how big an obstacle she was.

I nodded, breathing in as Xavier plopped down beside me. The table was long, and at least ten duplicates stretched out in the hall to manage the large crowd.

'Well, you are finally to be Queen, Victoria,' Elysande said, pulling a napkin and flapping it in the air before tying it around her neck. I smile tightly.

'Not that there was ever any doubt about it,' I say.

'I wish Avalorian were here to witness this beautiful

moment.' She wiped at her eyes. 'He would be utterly,' Elysande paused a midget to shoot a look at Xavier. 'Ecstatic.'

'I have no doubt.' Xavier picks up his goblet of wine. 'Where's Genevieve, by the way?' he asks Desmond, taking a delicate sip.

'The information should not concern you,' Desmond bites out, picking up a knife and fork, cutting through his full chicken.

'Why not, brother-in-law? We're supposed to be as close as creatures can get,' Xavier says, digging his elbow into Desmond's ribs.

'As close as creatures are in their graves.'

I suck in a quiet breath.

But Xavier was right. Genevieve was nowhere to be seen, and nor was Lorelei. It would not be like her to miss an event she prepared, even if it was half-heartedly.

'No need to be so dejected, brother,' Xavier coos.

I see Desmond visibly flinch at the label.

'You'll visit your parents in their grave, too.' Xavier finishes sweetly. The fork in my mouth pauses, and I feel my heartbeat quicken.

What the hell was he doing? I slowly pull it out.

'If I go down, she comes with me too,' Desmond murmurs, nodding to me.

I drop the fork. It clatters, and Desmond stares at me with something like sadness blurring his eyes. I try not to look too closely into them. It would make me feel that same gut-wrenching guilt all over again.

'Victoria.' Desmond suddenly grabs my arm, his voice cold and dark.

Xavier wipes his mouth, pushing out of the chair. 'I have to have a little chat with General Steelborne. I shall be back.'

He accidentally drops his plate and feverishly looks around before turning directly to me. 'I would say it was a pleasure to know you, but then I would just be lying.'

My cheeks flush. That little—

'Xavier!' Elysande gasps, looking hesitantly towards Desmond, who merely pulls me back into my seat.

The velvet covering the chairs cushioned my fall.

'I—I shall have a drink,' she stutters, leaving the table, only Desmond and I left of the royal family, the crowd's chatter suddenly music to my ears.

I feel his breath on my cheek. 'I think you owe me something.'

My stomach pools. 'An apology dressed as murder?' I try, meeting his mustard eyes, breathing in softly. Something flickers across them. Amusement.

'I won't ask,' he muses. Desmond takes a bite of his caviar. I try not to retch. 'I never knew.'

I fail to muffle the sigh of relief that escapes my lips.

A beat of silence passes between us before he says, 'Genevieve had a concussion and went to the nurse. She said she'd be out by night. Lorelei...' he inhales sharply.

'What?' I say, squinting my eyes. My heart thrums softly.

'She found a prince.' His hands are balled into fists.

'Oh, that is a surprising change of events.' I bite my lip. Should I ask, or should I not? It was an invasion of privacy.

'Who is the lucky prince?' I finally ask.

Desmond scoffs.

Lucky was the last word anyone would use to describe a relationship between Lorelei and another.

'Prince Arnold the Third.' He rolls his tongue around his mouth.

I blink.

Prince Arnold? Xavier's best friend? My heart stills as I begin to recollect the reminiscents of that day, Arnold chortling as I went over the cliff, their laughter bounding off the sky in great waves crashing in my ears. I quickly shake my head, willing these thoughts to dissipate in thin air.

'That is absolutely outrageous, considering what you said earlier about taking me down with you!'

'Not sorry for that.

I roll my eyes.

'By the way, where were you the whole night?' I ask grabbing a stone fork.

'I sent the army to Nyx last night as there was word of Fames prowling about.'

'You didn't tell them they arrived a bit too early for the wedding?' I murmur, pulling a pot of gravy towards us.

Desmond chuckles. 'I wish I could've, but they would have tried to kill me.'

I wave my hand dismissively. 'Why stay in your study, though?'

'It was the safest place to be. MacQuoid stood outside, and no one else would have been targeted. Fames only know of the location of my study, as that is where the crown is safeguarded.'

I nod.

'If the army was ambushed, I would have been able to make amends briskly. I didn't have to worry about anything, though. The army got to Nyx by daytime, and I decided it was too late to sleep.'

'Sleep would have given some light to your face.' I raise an eyebrow at his baggy under-eyes. Who thinks it's too late to sleep in the morning?

'I agree.' He grabs a loaf of bread. 'But I thought of spending some time with Genevieve, since she is usually awake that early.'

'Xavier said she was at the nurse's last night,' I point out, grabbing a clear goblet filled with water.

'They let her go at night, said it would be better after drinking some crystal gel.' I make a face.

Crystal gels were the most disgusting edible orbs, after caviar.

'We rode around the horses for a while, but she nearly fainted.' His eyes glaze for a moment. 'I-I don't understand how that happened.'

Crystal gels always healed. How did Genevieve succumb to a concussion later?

'They could be frauds?' I suggest.

'Maybe.'

Desmond turns.

I trail his gaze, watching the couples holding hands and twirling to the lilting music that now plays.

He grins at me, abruptly standing. 'Would you like a dance, my Princess?'

I hesitantly take his outstretched hand. 'Are you sure you won't spin me to death?'

His grin widens. 'No promises.'

Desmond pulls me up, placing his right hand on my waist and his left in my hand. It is an uncomfortably close range. We join the crowd as a flurry of whispers descends upon us, growing by the minute as the music intensifies. I take a spin, revelling in the air before his foot hits mine. I gasp, grasping onto his shoulders before I can go tumbling down.

'You don't know how to dance, do you?' I murmur.

'I may have forgotten,' Desmond says unsurely, trying to find his footing.

I laugh. 'Here,' I take his hand in mine and his other back around my waist. 'Now, move your right foot forward and your left a smidge back. It will be like gliding across the floor.'

Desmond does what I tell him, and I see the tinge of delight that crosses his eyes when he gets his footing right.

Silence stretches out, and Desmond attempts a conversation. 'So, what's your favourite type of sword?'

I stare at him, blank. 'P-people have favourite swords?' I sputter, blinking.

Desmond leaves my hand, scratching the back of his head before taking me for a spin.

'I don't know, but there's the longsword, katana, rapier, scimitar, claymore, all that stuff.'

'Do I have to learn the sword language now?' I say, laughing when he blushes.

'Maybe you do, maybe you don't.' He grins, pulling me back in. I hold his hand tighter.

'What sword do you think would suit me best?' I ask softly, looking up to meet his gaze.

He stares at me thoughtfully before slowly answering.

'The rapier.'

'Why so?' I ask, twirling again, the distance between Desmond and me digging a tiny hole in my heart.

'Rapiers are elegant, and might I add—deadly. There's a sharpness to you that makes one wary.' Desmond murmurs, his voice nearly breathless.

Heat rises in my cheeks. 'I—'

Desmond's smirk is wiped off his face as he nearly trips over my dress.

'Why isn't this working?' he growls, his grip on my waist growing tighter. 'Patience,' I say.

'Princess Victoria,' a voice calls from behind. Desmond hesitantly looks back, rubbing his eyes.

'I think we are done here,' he murmurs quietly.

I gawk. 'Don't tell me you still didn't find the Scroll of Eternity. I'd never expect a man with high intelligence to lose such an important thing.'

'Distract him,' Desmond orders, eyes narrowing. I purse my lips, spotting Prince William of Caelumterra from afar.

I am a bit sad—I was enjoying the compliments.

Desmond follows my trail, a frown on his face.

'I'll have a dance with him, then.'

'I don't mind.' Desmond pretends to cover a yawn. 'If anyone questions, just say I'm killing time with my brother-in-law.'

He makes way to leave just as Prince William shoves past the last of the crowd, bowing low. 'My Princess.'

I bite my lip before imitating his action. 'My King,'

We both straighten ourselves, and he attempts to help me up.

'Really, there's no need for that.' Prince William grins, brushing back blonde hair near the colour of snow.

He tugs at his black suit, looking around. 'Where is King Nathaniel?'

Prince William is a few years younger than Desmond and refuses to refer to him by his first name. 'Xavier was interested in spending time with his brother,' I say.

My heart thumps dully. The lie had come so easily.

'Ah,' Prince William shakes his head, his emerald eyes narrowing. 'Please do let me know when you meet him.' He fixes his tie, tightening it at the throat. 'We have much to catch up on.'

'Could you perhaps tell me what it is, so that I could inform Desmond?' I ask helpfully, smiling.

Prince William chuckles hesitantly. 'It's something between the two of us, my Princess. You would be better off not knowing.'

You don't need to know. It's a matter between the rightful heirs.

Just like that, he wipes the smile right off my face. I perk an eyebrow, nodding as my blood boils. I clutch my hands tightly to ease the power that thrums in my veins.

'Oh,' I bow my head. 'I wish you luck in your search for him.'

I straighten, a sly grin curling on my lips as I turn sharply on my heel. Behind me, realisation dawns on Prince William's face—he knows now that his message will never reach Desmond. His intentions are always pure, that one. But I would not stand for being seen as less than all the others.

I made a mistake, but did I need to be seen as one too?

Damn Desmond's sleep. I needed sleep.

I give a damn about others, even when I shouldn't. You, Victoria, only care about yourself.

I feel my insides ache all over again. It was alright though. Elysande was handling it, General MacQuoid too. The guests were leaving already. It was fine. I stumble across the carpet, the lit torches casting eerie shadows across the hallway.

I'd done what Desmond said.

Each reveller that passed by wondered why my *husband* wasn't with me. I'd just say he was building relations with Xavier. Exactly what Desmond said. I hope. Oh, God, I feel like puking.

I gratefully near our chamber, but then I hear muffled voices.

'Why did you kill my father?' a low voice growled. I'd know it from anywhere. Desmond.

My breath hitches. The door to his chamber is bolted shut. I clutch my stomach, nearing to hear what is being said. Was he going to kill Xavier now?

'I didn't! I stuck to the plan. I would've cut your neck first, wouldn't I?' Xavier bursts.

'No excuse, King,'

'Victoria's after the crown, you —'

My heart creates a racket so loud I feel like it is echoing through the hall. How did Xavier know? It was obvious, but how was he so sure?

'Fool, do not try to switch the subject. You think I am not aware?' Desmond booms.

'I didn't kill your father! We're on the same side—' Xavier breathes.

'Then why did you accuse me of harbouring the Wraith Berries?'

Silence stretches out. Then a small gasp from Xavier reverberates.

'I thought it wou-'

'It would what? Demolish suspicions about you?'

'Desmond, please-'

I edge closer. Desmond was going to kill him. Any loving sister should protect her siblings, but Xavier hadn't done anything either, had he?

He had willingly pushed me off the cliff.

'You think I'm going to let you roam the castle exposing more secrets about me?'

'Victoria killed hi-'

'Whether she killed or did not, I will attend to her later.'

My eyes widen in shock. That little liar.

'Then why kill me? Please, Desmond, you do not understand,'

My hand reaches for the door, and I realise it is not bolted. I knock it open a bit, ready to run in. Some part of me wanted to make the kill, but Desmond wouldn't be happy about my eavesdropping, and I had already upset him.

'I am afraid it is you who lacks understanding. Power doesn't take sides. It is either for, or it is against. And you, my King, chose to play against.'

I watch as Desmond unravels Eclipses—curled brutally at the top, heart in my throat.

I watch as Xavier inhales his last breath, his pathetic and puny face morphed into pure fear. I have never seen him like this before. I watch as Desmond holds his neck in place, the glowering sword plunders into his gut, my soul reaching my mouth, a scream ricocheting the silence.

I can only stand rooted to the spot, hunched behind the door. Xavier's dead. He's gone.

'My, my, to what do I owe the honour, Your Highness?'

The rough, guttural voice reaches my ears, and it takes me a minute to register what had just happened. Desmond lets go of Xavier's throat and walks over to me, grabbing hold of my arm and yanking me away from the door.

I see Xavier's body slump, gasping as his limbs settle in a position an acrobat could never attempt.

The question leaves my mouth unbidden, although its answer sings in the air. 'How did you see me?'

Desmond steers me away from a massive trunk, and I can feel his grin before I can see it, 'It was not the Banshee wailing, my princess—or should I say, my *Queen?*'

'Why did you leave the throne room?' Desmond's voice is low and heated. A cold gust of wind slaps me in the face, earning a strangled gasp from me. Being pushed off a balcony was the worst way to die.

It's fine. Desmond wasn't going to kill me. I wasn't going to die.

'I came to our chamber because I was tired,' I answer simply.

Another scream echoes in my mind, and I grasp my head. Xavier. Xavier's dead.

I am a Queen.

I'm the Queen of Ferrumisle, but not entirely. Something was still missing.

I shake my head, turning to stare into the horizon. A void paints the night sky, not a single star to be seen.

'How did you see me?' I reiterate again, looking at Desmond.

'I caught your scent long before you hid behind the door,' he answers, and I flinch. How could I have forgotten?

An awkward silence settles between us, then Desmond finally speaks: 'You heard, didn't you?'

'Heard what?' I ask.

'My conversation with Xavier, before he so willingly begged for death.' His voice had become sombre, and my heart began to thunder.

'Oh, no. I only came in time to see his dead body slump across the floor. Devastating, it was.' I sigh. I feel the sweat in my hands, twisting and playing with my fingers.

He wants me to play along, right?

Desmond flexes his arms, pushing against the railings. 'Father's murder was deeply disturbing to me. I understand the pain you are going through.'

'Yes, of course.'

Another beat of silence.

'Where's the sword?' I ask suddenly, wildly looking around for it.

Desmond watches me, a small smile on his lips. 'It's still stuck in your brother.'

I flinch, shivering at the thought. 'You didn't need to tell me that,'

'You asked.' Desmond replies matter-of-factly, shrugging. 'What will we do when Elysande questions tomorrow?' I ask again, feeling absurdly dumb for not having a single ounce of knowledge of what was to happen.

'Say I've buried him.' He waves a dismissive hand in the air. 'But let's talk about what you'll do.' Desmond leans against the wall.

'I thought you were not supposed to know about anything.' I fire back, cocking an eyebrow.

'Very well.' Desmond holds his hands up in surrender, looking away. 'Best be prepared for whatever you have to do, though. If you really want your throne back, we need to be as slick as possible.'

Desmond Nathaniel Thorncrest, the man that you are.

CHAPTER XII

'Oh, my baby boy!'

I rub Elysande's shoulders as she bawls her eyes out. It had not taken long for Xavier's body to be discovered or for her to renew her place on the throne. Father never trusted me and nor did she. I couldn't complain, though—I expected it and greeted the option wholeheartedly.

We were in the throne room, and Genevieve and Lorelei were yet to arrive.

'Condolences, my Queen. I fear his father's death got to him,' Desmond says from beside me.

Elysande bats her eyes with a tissue, sniffing delicately. 'Please, Desmond, call me Elysande. It is not like Xavier to kill himself. Why would he ever do that, especially when he has earned his role as King? My boy was so strong and...' A soft sob is snatched from her throat.

Desmond and I glance at each other. Xavier was certainly not strong, and most certainly did not kill himself.

'Victoria, I will have to return to Ferrumisle. You must stay here with Desmond; it is too dangerous.' Elysande sighs melodramatically, placing a hand on her forehead.

My heart rises in my throat. No, no, no.

I stutter. 'N-No! Elysande, I must come with you! As Queen, you will have higher chances of being killed. If I go with you, I can protect you!'

Elysande shakes her head, enunciating every word. 'Victoria, I said no.'

I hold back a scowl. People had an unfortunate habit of disrupting my plans.

I sigh. 'I'll be out for the day, then.'

I was wearing the crimson wrap dress borrowed from Lorelei's cupboard. 'I'm going to visit the Queen's Forest.'

'My coronation is today at night,' Desmond reminds me. 'I'd like for you to be there.'

'Why wouldn't I be there?' I tilt my head, a smile tugging at my lips.

'Mother and Father aren't here. Genevieve and Lorelei, well,' he sighs, shrugging. 'At least I'll have you there by my side.'

I feel my heart crack a little. Sure, I was happy about Father and Xavier's murder. The two most torturous people in my life had been wiped out, so I was happy about Father and Xavier being murdered, but Desmond hadn't planned his own parents' deaths. My smile slips. 'It'll be fine,' I whisper, rubbing his shoulder.

Desmond nods, hesitantly turning to Elysande. 'My Queen, please follow me.' He helps Elysande up, and she trips a bit before managing to stand upright. 'You will need to pack your things. I shall lead you to your chamber.'

'Thank you, Desmond.' Elysande takes his hand as he pulls her up, and they make their way outside through the right exit, the brazen doors thud echoing through the hall.

The moment they disappear, I rush to the left exit of the throne room.

I am not taking anything with me to the Queen's Forest, but of course I had to have an alibi if a murder were to take place, so I grab a sunhat and an empty basket, perching it behind the curtains of the window where no one would see.

If anyone asks—I was plucking strawberries.

I walk down the bright hallway, burning in the sun. Elysande's chamber is down the staircases and to the left. By the time I reach, Desmond will be gone, and Elysande—all alone in her chamber.

Really, who knew I could be capable of murder?

The thought chases a fresh chill down my spine.

I take the staircases two at a time, my heels pattering like rain as I make my way to turn left when I hear voices. I grasp onto the railing in time, heart in my throat.

Breathe in, breathe out.

I look around and spy the trunk of a pillar and immediately dash behind it.

'Keep an eye on Victoria, will you, Desmond? She can be a bit... difficult,' I hear Elysande say.

I bite my tongue, bawling my hands into tight fists.

'Of course I will. I've had a taste of that difficulty,' Desmond answers, letting out a soft chuckle. I hear the door scrape open and then creak shut. *Go away.* I think. *Go away.*

'I'll be waiting for you,' Desmond says to no one in particular.

I see his figure, the emerald and white suit a stark contrast from the pool of gold the hall drowns in.

Desmond sighs. I hear his hands slap his legs in frustration, a soft grunt echoing through the hall. His footsteps faint away, and I slip out from behind the pillar.

Elysande's door is shut, but not locked. Perfect.

I venture toward it, quietly turning the handle and knocking the door open.

The room was glassy, an absence of light where the darkness was reflected in every corner. Jet curtains where the devils would reside, ebony sheets where one could be buried, and a moonlit balcony, shaded from the sun for the stollar Queen.

I dive deeper into the void, watching the snaking ivory draped over the open balcony doors.

Elysande stood beyond, holding onto the railings. She was shivering, her veins an unholy blue. Her skin glittered in the fake night sky, and the snowy bun of hair added an angelic touch.

I inch closer, breathing in the scent of wine for the last time before I stand behind her, eyeing each movement she makes.

The flick of her elbow, the stomp of my heels against the hard floor, the way she freezes, realising her fate.

'Who is this?'

'The fallen Queen,' I sigh softly, chuckling. 'And you're about to join me too.'

'V-Victoria y-you don't have t-to do this—' she stammers, turning around, backing against the railing.

Her creased features cry for help.

I understand.

Being attached to such a dramatic persona must be tiring.

'I'm sorry, Elysande, I truly am.'

Her eyes flicker shut, gulping softly.

'You never called me Mother,' she finally says, opening them.

I notice her arms come behind her. She was going to push me away at any moment and make a run for it. I step forward, blocking her path, locking eyes with her.

'You never called me daughter.' I counter flatly, and sadness envelopes her features.

'Please, Victoria—'

I step closer, the wind slapping my naked arms, goosebumps sprinkling over me.

I take the last tiny step forward, Elysande's breath ragged and confused. We were just a kiss apart.

I whisper softly, my heart pummelling in my chest—begging to be the one to push her off.

'I truly wish I had more time to revel in your absence,' I

murmur as Elysande attempts to push me away, but I grab her arms tightly. 'But I have a coronation to attend to.'

I summon all my strength and shove Elysande off the railing. 'Victoria!'

Her body buckles, face into legs and arms behind her back as she falls.

Another strangled yelp echoes. 'Help! Stop me!'

And then she just keeps falling.

'Victoria, please!'

My name echoes in the sky, and then a thundering crash deafens me. I watch as the rocks splinter into Elysande, the stones failing to protect her. The blood seeps the colour back into her body, but her eyes remain dull.

I feel her last breath down my neck, standing over the railing.

Then, I turn and leave the balcony, shutting the marble doors behind.

Would one call me a psychopath if I admit that killing could be refreshing?

I walk in the Queen's Forest, undoubtedly knowing Elysande's disappearance would be discovered any moment. It is cold despite the sunny air, and I blame the murder I committed. The royal family of Ferrumisle had fallen. The only rightful heir to the throne remained—me. Xavier would be rolling in his grave.

I sigh, slumping against a brazen birch trunk. Xavier would never have made a great king, but he would have certainly been a commendable jester. At least I would have had someone to laugh with despite our rocky past.

I remember how my fall felt. How I had noticed Elysande watching us before Xavier placed a cloth around my eyes and sent me to my doom. The rocks below the cliff were as jagged and crooked as a werewolf's tooth, and if I hadn't summoned a crystal floor, I would have been scored through, just like Elysande had today.

I admit, I do feel bad.

But she wasn't my kin; therefore, I am not hurt by her loss, and what doesn't hurt can't break you.

I shake all thoughts of her out of my head.

Desmond would be proud. I imagine the smile that would reach his mustard eyes, setting them alight.

The basket I had hidden behind the curtains swings in my arms, and I'm about to pluck a fern when a nearby bush rustles.

I jerk up, looking for any sign of a behemoth creature.

It was probably just the wind.

I bend down, grasping for the stalk when a shrilling shriek echoes.

I jump up, splaying my hands and using the basket as a shield, ready to fight.

But no one came.

I place my hand over my chest and breathe. Five seconds in, five seconds out. Five seconds in, five seconds ou—

'My Queen!'

I stagger back as General MacQuoid comes rushing toward me.

'Please accept my graciou- oh, there is no time for apologies! Your kin has been decapitated!'

I gasp, feigning shock. 'Pardon, why are you addressing me as Queen? And what kin?'

'Why, Queen Elysande! It seems the poor lady fell ill thinking about her son's death and walked right off the balcony!'

Instinctively, my eyes sharpen at his words. I am begging myself not to correct him or say anything out of the ordinary.

'What horror! Why, it has only been a month in Briarthorn Atoll, and the entire Ferrumisle lineage has been butchered!' I cry. 'You must tell my Prince he ought to search for the killer!'

Oh, how the lies came too easy.

General MacQuoid fumbles with his coat as I stalk past him, seeming determined to exploit the killer.

'What?' I ask.

'My Queen, it's just that—

'What?' I say again, rounding on him. 'General would you care to speak your thoughts?'

'I think you are unaware. I believed King Desmond would have previously informed you of his coronation to be held in the aftern—

'King Desmond?'

My footsteps thunder against the carpet, the brazen doors in view.

I hear General MacQuoid behind me, panting for all his life. 'My Queen, not from—

I shove the doors open, ignoring his blatant warning, and the horror I see before me is too lethal to describe. Every folk has arrived, chattering over one another. No one notices my entrance, but it seems someone has, for the lights dim and wrought iron is struck.

Desmond.

I was late. I should be standing beside him.

But he'd never told me it was held in the afternoon. He'd said the coronation was to occur at night.

A tiny arrow pierces my heart.

He is clad all in white, a furry red coat cuddling his shoulders and a crown looming over his head.

The Blood Crown.

General MacQuoid sighs, shaking his head. He brushes past me as Desmond meets my eyes, a soft demonic glint in them.

I do not understand him.

I recognise the soft whispers from the day of our wedding

and notice secret glances thrown at me from here and there. I wrap a protective arm around myself. I do not understand anything that is happening.

Desmond stands in front of the throne on the dais, his voice echoing through the grand hall and sending shivers down the spines of those gathered. 'My dear subjects, esteemed creatures of Aetheria. Today marks a special moment in our history,' he begins. 'As you all have undoubtedly heard, the sudden and tragic demise of my father, King Thaddeus, has left us all in shock and mourning. His life was cut short in a way none of us could have foreseen, a tragedy that has brought us all here together.'

He pauses, letting his words sink in, his eyes sweeping across the diverse assembly of beings before him. Then the mustard eyes land on me.

The Blood Crown floats down, and Desmond grasps it so majestically there seems to be no trace of the murderous monster under those luscious curls.

I feel my heart sink, trying to focus.

'But amidst this darkness, there is a glimmer of hope,' Desmond continues, his arms in the air. 'As you all know, the Blood Crown is possessed by the killer of the heir. Unfortunately, Father's death was caused by a rare illness. The Crown yielded to me, allowing me to bear it.'

Liar, liar, liar.

The crowd stirs, murmurs of curiosity and anticipation rippling through the hall.

Desmond's gaze narrows, his expression solemn: 'It is true that Queen Elysande of Ferrumisle has too met an untimely end. Her loss is a tragedy that cannot be understated. However, we must face the reality that our world is fraught with danger and treachery. It pains me to utter these words, but evidence has surfaced suggesting that the Princess fell victim to a plot meant to seize this very crown. *My* Princess.'

My legs buckle.

Then only does the shock engulf me, realisation slamming into me like ferocious waves crashing against the razor-blade rocks, attempts to scream useless because of the thundering storm.

No, it cannot be.

Gasps erupt, and I feel the eyes of the crowd shifting towards me.

'Fortunately, her plan failed. The Crown entrusted me with Briarthorn Atoll. But then began her devious plot to claim right over their land, killing her brother, father, and step-mother to ensure no individual stood in her way to achieve absolute dominance over the position of Queen.'

This is what he had been planning all along. This is what he had been planning all along, probably for days or months before we arrived.

It was not Xavier who had killed Father. It was not Xavier who had killed King Thaddeus.

It had been Desmond.

It had always been him.

The small talk, the flirting, the hugs, the garden, everything.

Everything had been fake, and I have waltzed straight into his game.

But he is a killer! I want to scream. But then I realise nobody will believe me because Victoria Ironhart is the daughter of a dead king bent on attention and an unhealthy obsession with power.

And what better way to silence a person who could potentially exploit their plans than by killing them? The dead cannot speak.

That's the plan Xavier had been talking about. That's the reason Desmond wanted to rid of Xavier so badly.

I was right. I had always been right. Desmond was a murderer.

The piercing glares of those around me shoot through my body like a million arrows.

I have no reason to hurt someone like you, who has not done anything. I am not that vile, Venefica.

He's not vile.

He's a goddamn monster.

You shouldn't be asking me to take revenge on your family. I should be asking you that. I destroyed your life. I owe you your kingdom back, if that's the last thing I ever do.

He had given me my kingdom back.

You can stay in Briarthorn Atoll as Queen of Ferrumisle.

Dead. I would be dead.

That filthy scoundrel.

But my rage is dimmed with fear. My heart rackets against my chest in frantic beats, failing to escape out of its prison.

All my family killed by the hands of this murderer. If this were a village, hands would have been thrown at anyone and everyone, but lo and behold, when it comes to royalty, it's always one of the family.

Desmond sighs. But his gaze is steadily locked on mine.

His smirk widens.

'As it is my duty as King, I vow to protect this land from the shadows that seek to undermine it. From this day onwards, all delinquents shall be shackled in Carcerem Regum Mortuorum, and all deceivers shall be promised death!'

No.

I collapse to the ground.

Desmond wasn't doing this.

I trusted him.

My fate had always been the same, whether I plotted to kill Desmond or not.

He had always been two steps ahead of me.

I had trusted him.

I shift back on the ground as there is an upheaval of cheers from the crowd when Desmond flourishes his arms in the air, a devilish gleam in his mustard eyes. I need to leave. I was not going to be chained in the dungeon, now or ev-

Two guards grab a hold of me, and I feel the heaviness of iron weighing my legs down.

There is an echoing thud, and I look up, gasping for air.

The guard pulls me down, slumping my shoulders. I tug against their stiff hands, glimpsing up to see the crowd parting for their King to come through.

Desmond bends down on one knee, the red cloak obscures his body, a white puff at the collar.

The Blood Crown is settled arrogantly at the top of his head, as if chortling me for my defenceless demeanour.

His hand meets my chin, and I yank myself away, panting.

He chuckles, hoarse and full of spite.

'Until next time, my Queen.'

Victoria Ironhart,
Day 3,

~

Oh woe,
I don't really know what to say anymore.

~

Oh, look.
He wrote down all his plans.
How foolish.
I pulled the book from the crumbling ashes. I think it's been three days. I had been roaming around mindlessly where anyone could capture and put me to death. I made out the faint words scrawled

across in gold, brushing the grey flakes that marred the black cover with my own ashen hands: Corona Sanguinis.

The Blood Crown.

My blood boiled. I clenched my hands, debating whether to open the book or not. Oh, whatever. How disdainful that I still had traces of the good princess I was when I had been betrayed over and over again.

I trusted him. I trusted Desmond to put things right.

My teeth chattered amongst the rocky shards. Sparks from dead fire shot up like fireworks, and despite the heat that surrounded me, I felt strangely cold. Not from the outside, but the inside. If someone was to dig out my heart, there would be a crack running through from the top to bottom.

Like a knife being dragged through my veins.

That is how bad it hurt. No, not hurt.

I had felt harrowed, tormented. I ached and burned in their foolish plans. I was deceived, denounced, destroyed to a mere pebble in a garden of rocks. I was shaking. Shaking so uncontrollably the book slipped from my hand, and a shiver ran through my spine. I heard voices from above.

I must not be found.

'She must be down there!' I heard a forlorn voice call. Desmond.

He called me a witch; I call him my equal. The devil.

'Throw down a rope!' Desmond called again, his voice more frantic. Victoria!

I groaned, clutching my head. I heard his voice. I still heard it.

I clutched the book close to me and staggered over to hide behind a ragged rock. The putrid stench of metal stuffed my nose. Blood.

I touched the rock gingerly. My blood. Slowly, I broght my mouth closer. I felt the rock emanating heat, but I pressed the tip of my tongue against the crimson liquid regardless.

The voices decreased to screaming. Chanting. Bawling.

I couldn't care less.

I snapped open the book, knowing no one would be able to observe me from any angle. My heart clenched while I read. Not read, skim. I *didn't have the mental capacity to read. My eyes were dodging words like bullets, my hands quivering, causing the book to slip from my gasp a dozen more times.*

I began to whisper the words slowly, hoping they would embed into my mind forever. Stitch itself, so I could remind myself who made me the witch I am.

'M-must wait p-patiently,' I breathed out shakily. I flipped another page. 'K-kill M-Mother a-a-nd F-Father. K-k-ill G-gen–' I cut off abruptly, trying to focus my breathing. Genevieve and Lorelei.

I swallowed hard, my throat sandy and nose dry. 'V-Victoria w-will t-t-trus-st y-you. K-kill X-xavier, b-b-but,' I broke off coughing. I should never have thought to mess with a war strategist. I didn't need to read the next lines aloud though. It stuck. It sewed itself into my being.

Victoria will trust you. Kill Xavier—but let Victoria kill Elysande.

The understanding dawned on me a week or two too late.

If Desmond had killed me, he would have two Kingdoms to rule and claim glory for wiping off the worst royal monarch in Aetheria. When Nyx would arrive, Desmond would have killed exactly a hundred thousand souls, and would have easily defeated Nyx.

Eternal glory once more.

I clenched my fists together.

Xavier and Avalorian had been against Desmond. Elysande had never done anything. She was innocent.

Desmond was no murderer. Not unless you counted killing his own family, which none knew about. He put Elysande's death on my head.

I killed an innocent woman.

Desmond killed those who had wronged him and his family.

So if I kill Desmond—I would be doing the right thing.

Am I wrong?

I dropped the book.

'Help!' I screamed. My voice came out hoarse, bounding off the canyon walls.

'Get her, you fools!' someone called. It was a familiar voice, but I didn't recognise it. I saw the ropes drop, whipping the lumpy boulders that decorated the partition.

'She's down there!' the voice bellowed again, harsh and rough. I clambered up a vast rock that gave me a bird's eye view of most of the guards. I saw them climbing down, grunting as they did. I took a deep breath, spreading my arms wide open in the air, gathering all my strength.

I shut my eyes, pooling myself in a void.

You are no Queen!

My eyes flew open, and I staggered a bit in front of the stars that lined my vision. I blinked once, then twice, and then did the canyon walls unfurl.

They split open from the middle like lightning ripping the air, cracking and rising as crevices appeared, jagged rocks splitting the ropes, each crack a deafening whip that tears the sky in two.

The men screamed, dangling against the frayed rope. They crashed against the walls, trying to find a grip as they crawled into the darkness that the crevices provided, others dropping to the rubble like dead birds, bones cracking on impact and flesh splattering everywhere. I looked down. What a waste of life.

I heard panicked clamours from above and smirked.

They had all made a grave mistake.

Hollers rang in my ears and screams flooded the sky as crystals sliced the remaining ropes—and maybe a few bodies—in half.

I inspected the ground hungrily, watching the fallen bodies of thousands, and then to the gaping hole that ran through the canyon.

I clasped my hands shut, and the last thing I heard was the thunder clap that crumbled the very land I stood upon.

CHAPTER XIII

'I trusted you!' I scream, throwing a flailing punch at one of the guards, but I am no match for their strength. Vampires. They confine me in place when Desmond catches hold of my cheek, smirking down at me.

My muscles stretch.

'That wasn't my fault, Venefica.'

I had trusted him. I had trusted him, and he had failed me.

He shoves me into the cell. I scream again, the iron shackles shoving me to the floor. I bounce against the bumpy floor, trying to find a footing in deep holes that could make way for vile creatures to slither up and devour the victim. I feel hot liquid ooze down my face.

Blood. I gasp, mustering all my strength to pull up from the floor, my legs failing to hold my weight as I shiver, collapsing once more.

'You know, I was waiting for you to pull out the dagger, that night in the garden,' Desmond says, leaning against the metal bars. He spits on the floor. 'It would have damned my plans if it had gone any further than the artery.'

Blood patters onto the ground. I had been so close. Desmond would have died. The crown would have been mine.

Two kingdoms, mine. Aetheria, mine—all mine. I reach out a hand to strike him across the face, but I meet metal instead and yank my arm back in a blood-curdling scream.

I stagger onto my stomach.

'Next time we meet, it shall be in the afterlife.' Desmond chuckles. The silver bars clink shut. One of the burly guards pulls out a spray and the sound of an engine whistle rattles my ears as a purple mist engulfs the murky room.

My head feels dim.

The last thing I see is Desmond jabbing a sceptre through the hole of the lock.

'Get your filthy hands off me!'

I groan, blinking.

A hazy figure trips over me. 'Watch your feet!' I spit, instinctively pulling out a hand. Everything is hazy, a distant light blinding what I can barely make out.

My hand is pushed away. Gently.

'Aye, no need to get physical.' I hear a gruff voice grunt. 'Any more nonsense from ya' and the King will have yr' head a day ter' early.'

The weight lifts off me, and I shake my head.

Breathe in, breathe out.

Desmond was going to kill me. Tomorrow. In front of all of Aetheria, no doubt.

I heave, clutching my chest and turn to lie on my back. It aches from my stiff posture. I watch as the vampire shoves a young woman about my age into my cell, dressed in the same attire as me: mucky green pants and shirt.

They're rough and grind against my skin unpleasantly.

'We'll be shifting ya' out once another cell's empty. Don't give no trouble,' the vampire with ebony hair growls. His locks dance over his face, his bared teeth abnormally larger than the rest of his species, tugging at his chin instead of just over his lip. I'm surprised he's here at all. Too much silver could burn a vampire to the ground.

'Vampires,' the lady mutters, brushing her sandy clothes. 'So brutal yet so sentimental.'

The gate shuts with a bang. It was dull outside, with small torches of fire blazing the way to what could possibly be an exit. If only I could—

The outside world is shut in less than a minute, the rectangular block of obsidian sliding down with ease, continuing to keep the promise of darkness. Tiny holes are created for sunlight to peer through, but it's as much help as a snail pushing a turtle.

'What'd you get in for?' scoffs the woman, sprawling across my bed in a most unladylike manner. I scowl. I was not answering her.

I make out her figure sit up straight on the bed. 'I asked you a question.'

'I was framed,' I bite out, covering my eyes. My stomach aches, grumbling wildly.

'That's what they all say. Name's Dorphne.'

'Victoria,' I say.

Dorphne gasps, 'Princess Victoria? As in killed-her-family-to-get-their-land-and-become-Queen Victoria?'

I stare at her in the darkness. I don't know why it surprises me, but it had only been an hour and the news had spread like wildfire.

'As I said, I was framed,' I repeat, tilting to face Dorphne completely. I make out the climbing ivy behind her that would have added a touch of reverence in the torch light, never mind the sinister spider webs hanging on the walls.

Silence claws out, and Dorphne rubs her knees nervously.

'What did you get in for?' I quietly ask.

'Oh, me?' she tosses back her hair. It seemed to be auburn in the tinge of sunlight that speared through.

'All I asked was for a bit of gold to survive in this land, but I was thrown in for demanding from the King when I should be grateful, and being *below royalty,'* she huffs.

'I'm from Fames,' Dorphne adds with a knowing growl, as if it explains everything.

It does.

Briarthorn Atoll was not always an independent land. Long before Inferis came to be, Fames and Briarthorn Atoll were one: a unity.

Terra Thronorum et Thorns: the Land of Thrones and Thorns, was their name.

It made sense why the Blood Crown chose Briarthorn Atoll, the Land of Thrones. Their independence sparked a revolution and gave Nyx the perfect time to strike.

'All Desmond desires is power.' I punch the floor, hauling myself up.

It was something I should have realised sooner. My spine throbs in pain.

'Oh, how I would love to wipe off that stupid smirk from his conceited little face!' I slam my fists together and kick the bedpost.

The torn shoes are too large for my feet, and they slip off at impact. Dorphne catches me before I can fall.

'So you really haven't done anything?' Dorphne asks, looking at me in a way that seems as if she's sizing me up. Her narrowed blue eyes glitter in the dark, and they tell me she's wondering whether to trust me or not, and right now, I need all the trust I can get.

'Of course not,' I lie, waving my hand dismissively and sitting on the bed instead.

She nods her head and comes to take a seat beside me.

'The marriage, was it a love one?' she asks.

I shake my head. 'Nothing more than what it looked like.'

I play with the stones on the ground, and my rear finds some comfort in the soft mattress after the cold, solid rock. I don't bother lying down in fear of falling asleep.

'So you like him?'

I nearly stumble off the bed. I stare at her in shock.

A smirk tugs at the corner of her mouth, but as quick as it came, it disappears.

'W-what?' I splutter.

Dorphne raises an eyebrow.

'He drugged me, then used and betrayed me! If anything, a man who breaks his promise is a man vile enough to corrupt and destroy not only others but himself too,' I spit.

Dorphne shrugs, a small smile pasted on her round, chubby cheeks. 'Just seeing whether your priorities are set straight.'

She thumps her feet together in sync with my heartbeat. It had been erratic not only a few minutes ago, but for some reason, it had dulled.

'You really trust me?' I ask her. My knuckles go white as I pressure it against the wood of the bed.

'You haven't done anything except show the King for who he really is, so yes,' Dorphne replies. Show the King for who he is?

'What do you mean?' I turn to look at her, confused. I hadn't shown the 'King' for who he is—in fact, it had been quite the opposite.

'You told me that you haven't killed anyone, and that he did.' Guilt pools in my stomach as I force myself not to correct her. She was too trusting. Maybe that was good. 'But if I manage to convince our allies when we escape, then everyone will be on your side.'

My heart jerks as a smile spreads across her face. How is she so confident that we will escape? I sigh, not wanting to tell her the truth.

'We aren't escaping anytime soon, Dorphne,' I tell her

quietly. She looks up at me, and the glint in her eyes washes away, the tide taking her smile with it. We lapse into silence, and I can only kick my legs frantically.

Why was she trusting me so readily? She couldn't be that stupid.

'Aren't you from a line of sorcerers?' Dorphne suddenly asks.

'Magic will not work; the entire dungeon is barricaded with charms.' I smile pathetically at her.

'Why don't we wait until the guards come to shift me, and then we escape?' she suggests.

'I'm sorry, we?' I turn to her, and Dorphne stares back with raised eyebrows.

'You're a Queen; you have dominance over your own people. Surely someone in Ferrumisle will—'

I shake my head in frustration. 'No one is going to believe a rejected Queen over the King of the Blood Crown, let alone trust me after what they heard.'

'Single-handedly, no. But with others, yes,' Dorphne says quietly. 'You can't do everything alone.'

I sigh. 'Believe me, a job best done is a job best done alone.'

I hear a resounding thud, and my heart drops to my gut. Heavy boots clunk in the distance.

'That was quick,' I murmur, aghast.

We didn't even have a plan. How the hell were we to do this?

'They won't let two prison mates stay long together. You're a queen; I thought you would have some sense.' A tiny arrow shoots into my heart, and I feel the crack widen.

'Dorphne, how are we suppo—'

Dorphne presses a finger to my lips. 'When they come, we run.'

I clamp my mouth shut. Something was nagging at me, clawing the depths of my brain, fighting the tiny voice that grew louder by the second.

Why was I letting a random stranger hold the reins of my life?

Why did she get the freedom to save me?

Their laugh echoes, hollow and rough. Dorphne jumps up and leans against the bars immediately, shooting me a wry smile. She pastes a tired face and tries to act annoyed while I remain seated on the crumpled bed, scowling at her. I guess we were going along with her plan.

The obsidian doors wrack open, the earth crumbling above us. A guard with sea-blue hair, a torn murky jacket, green shirt and pants with the odour of gutter opens the lock, while another guard brushes his hands through his golden locks, shuffling in the oversized uniform.

He seems half-dazed, not caring when Dorphne yanks the blue haired guard into a head-butt, and I stagger off the bed, dashing for the exit.

The golden guard suddenly snaps into action, swinging his fist at me.

Dorphne takes the blow, stumbling back in a bloody mess. 'Run!' she screams. But I don't. The other guard is unconscious, lying on the floor—and I should run because Dorphne will only slow me down.

Just as the guard goes in for another blow, a string of crystals erupt beneath the soles of his shoes, and he falls in pain as Dorphne throws a kick under his waist.

I turn and notice a green goblin staring at me, panicked. He turns quickly, scampering off, and without a second thought, I make a run for it.

'Dorphne, we have to be quick!' I holler across the dungeon.

There are thousands of creatures locked up, gnawing at the metal bars and whimpering when it stings them. Out of the corner of my eye, I see a glint of grey hair. I nearly stop, slowing my pace and turning to see who it really is. Genevieve lies in mid-air behind bars, long hair sweeping the floor. Next to her, Lorelei makes a failed attempt to gnaw at the metal in front of her. She hisses when she catches me staring, and a scream from Dorphne ricochets in the dungeon.

In panic, I turn my heel as she rushes into me from behind.

Desmond is a maniac.

Desmond is a killer.

Desmond is mental, and if we don't find a way out soon enough, Desmond is soon to be aware of my escape, and he will stop at nothing to silence me.

Dorphne gasps for air. 'If we get caught, I swear on my mother's grave I will kill you.'

She pants heavily, footsteps slowing then racing every few seconds.

'Then you should have thought twice before convincing me,' I snap.

I grab Dorphne's arm, pulling her behind a cobblestone wall at the intersection of the exit.

'Wh-' I cut her off, shoving a hand over her mouth. I had removed my shoes so the escape would be easier, but it didn't stop the sharp stones from digging into my feet. I raise a finger to my lips.

I heave.

There was pin-drop silence, save for the grunts of the fallen guards. The creatures had too been silenced.

Then voices emerge.

'Gunter, I understand one escaped delinquent, but two? Do you realise how much damage she can do to me?' growls one. A familiar foreign accent. Desmond.

'You should have listened to Prince Xavier before killing him,' murmurs another—supposedly Gunter.

Dorphne's eyes widen, staring at me in shock. I glower. I guess she didn't trust me completely, but given what she just heard, she does now. Good. I wasn't taking any chances with more traitors.

'Moreover, Queen Victoria is from a lineage of sorcerers. She is a witch.' I resist the urge to stalk up to Desmond and strike him across the face.

And his little goblin too. I was a crystalline sorceress, but most certainly not a witch.

Welcome to the family, Venefica. Desmond's words sent shivers through me, and I almost don't register Gunter's next words.

'You, my King, defy others. If you had just used the charms—'

'Werewolves can't do magic!' Desmond hit a sceptre hard to the ground.

So the dungeon had not been charmed. Embarrassment washes over me.

A gasp escapes Dorphne, and I curse. The dungeon drowns in silence once more.

'Who is it?' Desmond's voice cuts sharply through the dungeon. I swear I hear the crack of his bones.

I shut my eyes, anticipation flooding me. If we get caught, Desmond will not only put me to death, but Dorphne. My heart races as I hold my breath, crouching behind the wall. I take one look at the red-headed girl and I know we need to run.

With a wave of my hands, the torches lining the dungeon corridor flicker and dim, crystals erupting in place, casting eerie shadows that dance across the walls.

A low rumble reverberates through the ground, and Desmond's voice echoes once more, wavering, 'Show yourself, or face the consequences!'

Coward.

And with that, we run.

Behind us, crystals begin to grow and jut out sharply, creating a cacophony of thundering stone cracking from the depths.

The lined torches are burnt out, but it seems that the crystals have taken on the shape of the smoke, clinking furiously as they make impact with the ground.

Our footsteps reverberate in the narrow passageway as we sprint through the winding corridors, heartbeats pounding in rhythm with our hurried breaths.

We turn a corner, only to be met with an abrupt dead end. I pant, heaving, panic surging through me like fire snaking along a dry wick. I scan the walls, searching desperately for an escape. And then I see it—a small crawl space, hidden behind a tattered tapestry.

I grab Dorphne's arm roughly. I can tell by the way she is gasping for air that she's nearly on the verge of losing consciousness, but I pray that she does not fall limp through the tunnel.

'Just a bit more,' I urge, my own breath coming out in heavy pants.

With a heave, I push her through the opening, and Desmond makes his appearance a few feet behind us. I stumble forward behind Dorphne, pushing her and myself, clawing at the stones as the soles of my feet cry in agony.

The space was tight, claustrophobic. I hear a sceptre bang and Desmond's desperate command to Gunter. 'Well, follow her! That tunnel was made for goblins, not witches like her!'

The words send wild fury through my blood, and Dorphne screams as a crystal obstructs her path. I yelp in pain as one digs through my palm, a deep slice bleeding red.

'Move faster!' I yell.

'You're a crystalline sorceress,' she screams, looking back at me, 'you're blessed with the power to see in the dar—'Her response is cut off as her head whips back to the front with a gasp. I turn my head to see what had caused her such fear, and wish I hadn't.

A pimple-bursting goblin with slimy frog skin and wig-like hair grins grimly behind me, a dagger in hand as his dwarf figure casually saunters through the tunnel, as if he were taking a leisurely stroll through the gardens rather than attempting to kill his King's escaped prisoners.

I pivot, seeing Dorphne has left quite a space between us. I follow her desperately, slipping against stones and hitting my head against the bumpy wall. My vision begins to blur, the sound of crystals cracking through the rubble and Dorphne's screams rendering me deaf.

I cannot hear. I cannot see. I cannot do anything except move and hope. Hope I will survive, because if I don't, everything I killed for will be proffered useless.

'Victoria!' a shrilling shriek rings out, and I look up in expected horror and panic that I almost miss the sunlight peering through the hole at the end. I double over in pain. Not now. I can't fall now.

My palms sweat feverishly as I try to get a footing. I push and crawl and I can feel my fingers scraped and shredded, as if I had led a razor through the tips. My feet hurt, and I have no doubt I cracked a few nails along the way. But I still push forward, and then suddenly, there is no one in front of me.

Dorphne.

Had she left without me? Had she? Did she jump through the sunlight and leave me to die? Di—

Dorphne plunges through the hole and out with a whoop of joy, and I see her bloody and scarred features coming into view. She lends me a hand, and I grab it without a second thought, letting out a small relieved breath.

'Gunter!'

The shock of his voice so close makes every fear climb and seep into my veins. My hand slips from Dorphne's, but she catches my arm and hauls me out. I stagger onto the fresh grass, my hair a terrible nest.

I turn to stare back into the hole, falling into Dorphne's arms as Desmond's face comes into view. 'Victoria! Do something!' Dorphne shakes me wildly, but I can't think straight.

What do I do? He's there. He's going to grab my neck and chop it off, then all my plans of reclaiming my throne will be ruined. And Nyx will prevail. Nyx will doom the entirety of Aetheria, and everyone will be walking dead.

I didn't want to rule under the eye of another any longer. I wanted to be free. To command the power I rightfully deserved.

So I do the only thing I know how to. I push away Dorphne, scrambling to the ground as I dig my fingers into the earth.

The crystals burst forth and draw a curtain of bars around Desmond and Gunter. He growls viciously as he forces an arm out, as if daring me to move.

Dorphne sighs, falling to the ground, taking me with her. We thump against each other on the cold, wet grass, but I quickly scamper to my feet, pulling a breathless Dorphne behind me. I can feel her heart beating, but she has fainted.

I can't do anything except run, dragging her behind me.

But Desmond's next words echo through the Queen's Forest, his voice never dying. Not now, not ever.

'Victoria Drakewell Ironhart! Mark my words—I will find you, and when I do, you will die! You will die a lonely and sorry princess, and that—' He bangs his sceptre on the glassy crystals, unable to shatter it.'Is—' Bang. 'A—' Crack. 'Promise!'

'Your Majesty?'

I sit under a mangrove tree, possibly miles away from Briarthorn Atoll. My knees are scraped, my clothes are tattered and torn, my legs aching and begging for peace. I look up to see General Steelborne staring into my eyes with his own anxious ones. Dorphne groans beside me, tears streaming down her face.

What have I done?

What have I gotten her into? What have I gotten myself into?

'We left for Ferrumisle as soon as we heard of your escape,' he explains, bending toward me, taking my hand in his. I take it away. This is all just a dream. I am miles away from both Briarthorn Atoll and Ferrumisle, and no one can be here to save me.

'How long has it been?' I croak out, my voice barely a whisper.

General Steelborne shakes his head. 'Nearly four days since your escape. King Desmond is unaware of our departure, but I'm sure he must have figured out as much.'

Again, his hand is outstretched, and I take it, allowing him to pull me to my feet.

'Did you...' his voice is hesitant.

'Did I what?' I demand.

Four days. Four days of no food and water. Only greenery surrounding us and creating an illusion, forcing us to go in circles again and again.

'Did you really kill everyone?' he finally asks. For a second, I stare at him blankly. Then all the plans suddenly burst forth in my mind, the ones I plotted with Queen Nyx, my own, and the damning schemes I committed that even the General could demand my execution himself.

I know there is no way out, so I reply with what I find to be the partial truth. 'Not really.' I shake my head vigorously, nearly collapsing once more. 'But I assure you Desmond has a hand in the murders.'

General Steelborne nods. 'We'll discuss more once we are in the palace,' he finishes for me.

I point a shaky finger at Dorphne, who looks up dazed. 'We need to get her to the castle immediately.'

General Steelborne makes no movement and does not hide his disregard. 'Do you think she can be trusted?'

'Yes,' I answer without hesitation, the lie coming easily. I don't trust her completely. There is something off about her. Something I can't quite put my finger on, but maybe that's my problem. I either trust people too much or don't trust them at all. In each case, both lead to my downfall.

The General sighs. 'As you wish, my Queen.'

CHAPTER XIV

The castle was the same as before. Wrought iron doors loom over us as we enter, the Missilians sneaking glances from behind their windows as we halt for the gates to be opened.

'On whose command?' demands one of the soldiers. I recognise him as Admiral Lancelot.

I remember Elysande would on occasion call him Lancy, irritating him very much. Sweat prickles over me, and I immediately feel nauseous. The picture of Elysande's bloody body no longer looks as appealing as I once thought it would.

I notice another guard, younger than the others. His blonde hair is neatly slicked back, and a lopsided grin slips to the verge of laughter. Felicio. He was one of Father's strongest men.

I step out of the carriage, General Steelborne and Dorphne following suit.

'On the command of your Queen,' I echo back, waiting for the comment of disapproval.

'Murderers are not Queens,' another soldier says. A tuft of his hair is slick against his forehead beading with sweat, and I recognise him as Sergeant Cormac.

'Funny for you to think Father was a King,' I retort back.

I can practically feel the fear of the villagers, wondering

how on Aetheria I could be Queen. My hair, although combed as much as it could be, was still filled with leaves and specks of dirt, with thorns digging into my sides and bruises across my head that desperately need medical attention.

Besides the fact they think I killed the whole royal family and I was imprisoned by my own 'husband' for doing so.

Cormac remains silent, but Lancelot seems to think better.

'Pleasure to have you back, my Queen,' he smiles at me before yelling out an order, and the gates creak back, spiralling until they are completely open.

The soldiers bow graciously as we enter, and Dorphne tugs at my arm. 'There's something off about the sweaty guy,' she murmurs.

'What do you mean?' I say, shrugging. 'Cormac's always like that.'

'No, it just seems like—

'Get down!' hollers a voice. My heart spikes. I instinctively turn, imagining Desmond running at me with a knife, but instead I see someone else: Cormac.

I stagger back as he spits out foul words, running at me with a sword. I'm rooted in place, and when he comes to slice me in half, I'm ready for it.

But then a hand shoves me aside, toppling onto the ground with me. Shrieks and squeals echo from the villagers, and I see General Steelborne and Admiral Lancelot holding Cormac in place. He writhes and roars and fights for all his life, but two men are stronger than one.

I push to my feet, Dorphne beside me for support.

'My Queen,' grunts Lancelot.

'You killed my sister, bastard!' roars Cormac, baring his teeth, blood drooling out his mouth.

He stands tall in front of me, towering over us all.

'What—' Lancelot tugs at his shirt to keep Cormac in place, 'shall—' another kick from Cormac sends a growl of pain through General Steelborne, before Lancelot slams Cormac to his knees.

'What shall we do with him?' Lancelot finally hisses.

A crowd of guards and soldiers has formed around us, Felicio coming to stand behind Cormac, and a sense of unease washes over me. I never loved Elysande, or liked her for that matter. But Cormac had. And Cormac had always been there for her, a loving brother ready to shower his sister with more affection than any man ever could.

With a shuddering breath, failing to stare into his deep red eyes, I say the words.

I didn't expect them to come out readily.

'Sergeant Cormac. You will be hanged tomorrow at sunrise in the presence of the people, lords, and ladies you swore to protect for attempting to kill your Queen. You may go silent, or be put to death here. The choice is yours.'

'You are no Queen!' roars Cormac. I ignore his words, but not enough to let the pain it jolts through my heart go unfelt—a pain as familiar as a hug from Xavier, one I never wanted but could never escape.

General Steelborne stares at me, but his eyes show no emotion. I have committed far more than murder. I have committed treason, and he knows. He knows, Desmond knows, and the whole world knows.

Dorphne holds me as I walk, limping across the cobblestone ground. I look up to see the metal cube castle adorned with windows and armoured figures standing at each side. Two pillars reach to the sky, a staircase that leads to Caelumterra hidden inside them.

The castle is in shades of crimson, grey and black, with gold tracing the door that thunders as it falls, paving an opening into the castle. A river is still and eerily calm, with poison writhing in its depths, snaking around the fortress.

General Steelborne trails closely behind me—leaving

Lancelot to deal with a seething Sergeant Cormac. He puts an arm on my shoulder, and I turn to see his grim face.

'You have a lot of explaining to do, young lady.'

'Explain,' demands General Steelborne.

I washed until all the dirt and grime had been scrubbed away, leaving behind flushed, red skin. I changed from the tattered prison clothes into a pink corset dress with hems reaching my knees, and long boots with a blocky heel that thumps whenever I walk. However, I sit on my father's throne adorned in crystals jutting out through the hard obsidian, and my surroundings dim as an icy gale sweeps through the throne room.

Once a new ruler had been crowned, the throne would layer itself to suit the magical abilities of the monarch. Father's had been metal, and so had Xavier's—but I have not yet been crowned, and the metal singes my arms, but the burn only feels like the sun's warmth.

I wonder what my mother's powers were. Possibly a vampiress, or a sorceress like me?

'Victoria,' the voice is commanding, and anger seeps through me.

I have had enough of being made to feel guilty for no reason. 'You will address me as I am titled, and not as if I were your child,' I say through gritted teeth, but Steelborne doesn't waver.

'Much has occurred in the past few days,' Dorphne says quietly, her expression placid. 'Let her grieve like she should, and then she shall explain.'

I stare in surprise at her soft demeanour.

'There is no time for grievance. I want an explanation, and so does the rest of the world,' General Steelborne demands impatiently, fisting his hands together.

He is wearing a doublet that fit snugly around his muscular neck, a scar across his pale eyebrows, and silver hair that falls down to his shoulders.

Dorphne looks at me uneasily, and I know she wants to hear what really happened too.

'From the start,' Steelborne says when I open my mouth.

I shut it, then open it once more, and the words begin to flow.

'When Xaviour pushed me off that cliff three years ago—though I'm sure many witnessed it—none came to my aid upon the King's orders.' Steelborne winces. 'Ever since then, I have wanted to prove myself. To prove that I should have the throne and not Xavier. I was tired of being quiet and following Father's orders, letting others walk over me like I was nothing. I wanted to feel that power for once. The power of being in control of someone else.'

I bite my lip, considering my next words.

'I thought the feeling had evaporated, but it turns out it had stayed. Simmered in the depths of my heart, waiting patiently to be discovered.' I breathe in shakily.'So when the plan to Briarthorn Atoll presented itself, I was warped. Warped in the delusion I could steal the crown from under a war strategist's nose.'

Dorphne's eyes light up in shock, and General Steelborne cocks his eyebrows as if he had expected this all along. I fidget with my fingers.

'But Desmond had other plans. At first, when Father and King Thaddeus were murdered, I thought it was Xavier, despite him accusing Desmond and giving subtle hints that he was indeed the killer. Xavier and Desmond were working in cahoots, but of course, Desmond was smarter and ended their alliance.'

Killed Xavier, but I didn't say that. It was much easier referring to Xavier as someone who worked for another, rather than admitting that a power-thirsty figure as him should receive grievance.

I sigh deeply.

General Steelborne shakes his head in disappointment, and Dorphne purses her lips in anger.

'I trusted Desmond. I—'I cut off abruptly.

What happened between us stays between us. I swallow.

'In his room, I discovered a bottle of Wraith Berry concealed in his drawer and confronted him. He gave me some potion to knock me out and promised me time and time again that it was real. Everything between us was real. The trust. The promises. I didn't realise he would kill his own family to secure the crown.'

Dorphne gasps.

'And what did he promise you that made you so eager to trust him?' General Steelborne bites out.

His hands are clasped behind his back, a permanent frown settled onto his facade that marred his delicate features.

'He promised me my kingdom back.' *And he had fulfilled it.*

Dorphne opens her mouth to speak, but I silence her with a hand. 'But he wanted me to stay in Briarthorn Atoll.' I shake my head. 'I should have realised he meant as a dead body.'

Dorphne's grim expression falters at my words. I suddenly realise I know nothing about her or her past. Maybe she is empathetic, too trusting. But I doubt she hasn't gone through something.

'Don't say that, Victoria,' she tuts, her eyes are soft, but I can see the question that threatens to fall off her lips.

The rest of the royal family were dead. I could not say I aided in their murders, or even wished myself happiness at the thought of their deaths as I would be tried for execution. We all know who really killed them, yet the lone question lingers in the air, unsaid.

Who had killed Elysande?

'I pushed Elysande off the balcony and made a run for it.'

I wait for their reactions, rubbing my legs together. A cool breeze escapes from the outside world and into the fortress's threshold.

'And Desmond realised he could use you to secure not one but two kingdoms, so he played safe and exposed you among the folk, deciding to kill you in front of them all to show his power and your foolishness,' General Steelborne finishes.

I shift in my seat uneasily. *You are no queen.*

'That is treason,' he says quietly, and I can tell Sergeant Cormac appears in his thoughts.

It was a cowardly move to play, but I had no other choice. He would have killed me for sure.

I don't tell them about Queen Nyx. General Steelborne would kill me himself.

'So, you sought to take revenge on King Avalorian and Xavier, and it was all for power?' Dorphne seems to have recovered from her shock and finds her voice again, and I can only nod.

'What were you thinking?' General Steelborne bursts.

'You've got what you wanted now,' Dorphne places a hand to her temple, her soft features shrivelled in the orange light that illuminated from the chandeliers above.

There was no reasonable explanation, and they knew it too. I don't know what it really was either. It was something between hate and want. Want that spun into desire over everything else.

I wanted to prove myself, and I had. But now I had to prove my innocence for an act I had planned to commit.

'So what do you plan to do now?' Dorphne huffs. 'We obviously have no choice but to stay on your side, seeing we are to be put to death everywhere else.'

The way she says it makes my heart sink, and I stand up from the throne and walk off the dais, unable to look into her eyes. I step down the marble stairs, making my way to the red carpet and tall, obelisk-looking pillars, imagining them as walls of fire, coal and cobblestone drawing the way to the Stone Throne, guarded by the drooling, blood-sucking werewolves forced and strained to the Queen's every wish, every desire.

I had never seen the inside of Nyx's lair, but Mother had told me stories far more intriguing. Haunting.

I had lied to Dorphne. I had lied to all of them. I feel the startling blue eyes of hers following me as I pace the length of the room.

'We need to see what we are getting into first,' I say, looking up at General Steelborne expectantly, who sighs.

'Desmond will likely gather allies to wage war between our kingdoms. Of course, you are an escaped prisoner and a fallen queen, with a bit of convincing, he could get the Land of Fames and Caelumterra to participate as well,' General Steelborne says.

'So now we have to prepare for a war,' Dorphne concludes, glaring at me.

'And we have to contact Queen Nyx before Desmond has the chance,' I say.

'Are you crazy?' Dorphne bursts.

I stay quiet.

'Victoria, is there something you are not telling us?' General Steelborne's voice is soft but dangerous, like a predator readying to lurch on its prey.

'Desmond visited Queen Nyx, and I went along with him. She promised me she would help kill Desmond, and I made a silent vow to end her too,' I say slowly, cracking my knuckles.

Dorphne looks at me wildly. 'You're mental.'

'Not any more than her father was,' General Steelborne murmurs, and my heart rackets. They had no right to compare me to my father.

'If Desmond can kill a handful of my family and royal court, then he sure as hell can kill more. We need to contact the rest of the lands immediately. Twist the story he has told them, tell a part of my plan with Nyx—inform them of how I want to destroy her. I'm sure the Tribe of the Famished will need hefty convincing from Desmond, and Caelumterra may not participate at all.' I shoot a knowing look at Dorphne, who continues to stare me down with icy eyes.

Fear trickles down my head. What if they don't agree? What if I'm left to fend alone?

'And Queen Nyx, if she finds out?' General Steelborne asks.

'We have to keep it hushed, lure out Nyx when she kills Desmond, and I will have the Blood Crown,' I say, licking my lips. I breathe in sharply. I can taste victory.

'Please stop pacing, you're going to make me throw up,' General Steelborne suddenly whispers, green in the face.

I roll my eyes. 'Get the messages out. We have no time to waste. Desmond has most assuredly sent the letters out to the other islands already, and time is not on our side. We must be quick.'

I turn away from them, a piece of my heart cracking, another scar healing.

Power.

Steelborne gulps, and I grimace in disgust. I hope whatever he swallowed wasn't his own bile.

He nods his head and leaves for the door immediately.

'There's one more thing,' I say. Dorphne looks at me, and General Steelborne turns.

'As we escaped the dungeon, I saw Genevieve in a trance and Lorelei locked up in one of the cells.'

General Steelborne looks at me, astonishment playing across his face. 'You don't know?'

Dorphne looks back and forth between the two of us, unsure what to do.

'No?' I let out an embarrassed chuckle, fingers lacing together.

'King Desmond said they attempted to kill him on the day of the wedding.' I clench my fists.

Liar. Liar, liar, liar. 'Desmond assured me Genevieve had a concussion and Lorelei was with Prince Arnold,'

'And you believed him?' Dorphne cocks an eyebrow, and I feel heat rise up in my cheeks. She tries to catch my eye, but I avoid her gaze at all costs.

'We leave together. All three of us, tomorrow before sunrise.'

'You should call off the execution,' General Steelborne suggests.

I wait a few beats, not knowing how to reply. If I say yes, I'm risking my allies' trust towards me, and I can no longer keep my plan in motion. If I say no, in the thoughts of Dorphne and Steelborne, I will be a tyrant searching for power.

I choose my words carefully, knowing they would rather the world be in one piece than have a knife pressed to each of their throats.

'Then the rest of the world will be aware of Elysande's death and blame me for the rest, and no one will bother to seek Ferrumisle a second glance. Aetheria will be doomed for sure if our land—the land with power over bludgeons and bombs—has been demolished.'

It is a point, and General Steelborne knows it.

He breathes in, pursing his lips and heads for the door. I hear him sigh in annoyance, gruffly booming an order to one of the messengers to send out the messages. 'Where will we go?' Dorphne grumbles. Her arms are crossed deftly over her chest, the midnight robe adorned with glittering crystals for stars shimmering as it sweeps under her strength.

I smile grimly. 'We leave for Spelunca Mortuorum, the cave of the dead.'

I enter my room and discover Dorphne curved into a ball on my bed, and I hesitate before walking towards her. She turns as she hears the soft thump of my boots. The bed is shaped like a cave, crystals spewing out from all sides like jagged rocks daring anyone that lays foot on its grounds to enter. The soft, silky blanket in shades of pink envelops the bed as if it were the Red Sea.

It was the same as I had left it.

Atop, a chandelier glistens, painting the room a bright blue through the cyan drapes falling over the crystals. Black pillows ornamented with small red jewels at the corners sit on either side of Dorphne as she cuddles the last in her arms, cradling it to her chest.

'I'm sorry.' My voice comes out barely a whisper, and the silence that follows makes me crumble in my boots.

'You should be,' Dorphne finally says. 'I know I didn't tell you everything about me, but I did help you. I trusted what you said, back in the cave. That you were accused and framed for your actions.'

'You can just leave,' I say, secretly hoping she doesn't. With Dorphne around, I feel something. Maybe a bit safe.

'Victoria, this isn't about leaving. Even if I want to go, no one will be there for me in Fames. My parents died during the Hart's war.' She gives me a pointed look.

The war that raged because of Father, when he tried to turn Desmond against Thaddeus.

My heart sinks. I can't say anything. My mouth is shut, bound by guilt.

All I can do is let her sigh and continue. 'You may have been trying to prove yourself or get revenge, Victoria. But your family is the reason the world is in chaos. It always has been. Everything has gone upside down, and now Aetheria will have its final war.' She shakes her head, pitiful blue eyes looking into my own, pale and big.

'It's not the final war,' I say, but even as I utter the words, they seem false. If Nyx Darkryn partakes, everything will truly be destroyed, once and for all.

But she had to; otherwise I wouldn't be able to get the Blood Crown.

Awkward silence envelops us once more, and I know I have to shatter it before it cracks me.

'I don't want to trust people, but something in me always makes me do so. Maybe I think they'll be a better person, but I've learnt my lesson more than once.' I pause, and she slowly turns her body to me, tilting her head as she does so. 'I didn't know if I should trust you, and I still don't, but you helped me escape, you took the blows from the guards for me, you protected me like I was worth protecting.'

The words ramble out before I can stop myself, and something gnaws at my back.

A weird itchy feeling. Like I shouldn't be doing what I am doing. But I ignore it. 'I'm sorry for bringing you into this mess,' I say again. My voice is still croaky, but I hope Dorphne can tell I'm being genuine.

She exhales softly, arching a delicate, thin eyebrow. 'Very well.'

'So you'll stay?' I ask, hope blurring my words together.

'As what?'

I bite my lower lip. 'As my advisor?' I suggest, inclining my head to one side.

Dorphne bites the inside of her cheek. 'Alright.'

I pull myself onto the bed, and she intertwines our hands.

'So, what are we going to do when we meet Nyx tomorrow?' she asks.

Our hands linger together as we lie back against the pillows, staring at the ceiling.

'Fill her in on what has happened. I doubt she doesn't know.' I bite out the words grudgingly.

'Do you think she'll agree to fight?' Dorphne's soft voice carries, and it sounds like a melody to my ears after the ruckus in the dungeons.

'Of course she will. We will just have to plan how to defeat them all. How much of an army we can accumulate, when to attack, where to attack, all of that stuff,' I explain, waving my free hand about.

I turn to her 'What did your parents do?' I ask softly. Dorphne squeezes her lips tightly before answering, 'Worked for King Vorin. Mother used to be Arnold's nanny, and Father used to be a metallure.' My eyebrows shoot up.

'He's from Ferrumisle?'

She shrugs, nodding her head. 'Yes. Mother's from Fames though. She was an elf.'

I notice her pointed ears, and then I understand how she has so much strength, how she hauled me out of the tunnel and punched the guards who were muscular and heavy. 'You're an elf too,' I say in amusement. Her eyes twinkle mischievously.

'You're the first person who realised I was an elf and not a nixie.'

I smile. Nixies have pointed ears, and people often oversight their prowess in magic for strength, but few have the beauty that Dorphne bears. With her red hair flowing in long waves, she looks more a princess than I ever was.

CHAPTER XV

It is exactly midnight. The red carpet seems to stretch for eternity as we walk down the hallway. Framed paintings of Father sit as arrogantly against the wall as he did—even Elysande's—but Mother's is nowhere to be seen.

'Did we get news from Fames?' I ask.

General Steelborne clears his throat. 'None yet, My Queen.'

I nod and turn to him. 'Ready the carriages; we leave now.'

Dorphne's head lolls side to side before resuming its place at the edge of the carriage window, head tilted back.

The interior is embroidered with a ghastly, soft brown, and the flowery chandelier engulfs the carriage in its rosemary stench. The light that illuminates from it has been joint of more than a thousand shattered crystals, hardly noticeable as they are overlapped.

General Steelborne clasps his hands tightly in front of him. 'Do you not think we are trusting Dorphne blindly?'

By *we*, he means *you*.

'General, this is possibly the millionth time you have reiterated this question in the past ten minutes!' I bring a hand to my forehead, trying to calm myself down. General Steelborne sits opposite Dorphne and me as the carriage bumps against the rocky stones.

My heart rackets with fear, thumping against the walls of my chest as if attempting to break out.

After Nyx was banished, a land was created between Briarthorn Atoll and Ferrumisle. Jagged stones grew and darkness joined the lands. New creatures emerged, hunting our people until a land of dirt and grime formed, and Inferis became what it is today.

Not a whisper, nor even a wisp of smoke, has reached our people for centuries. None enter the Silva Cinerum unless it is absolutely needed, fearing the banshees that lurk in the graves of the dead and the howling werewolves that haunt the night.

General Steelborne stares at me keenly, and I know I have to give him an answer. He will call me a fool for trusting Dorphne so easily, so I choose the safest reply. 'I have more pressing matters to deal with than whether or not to trust Dorphne.'

What if Queen Nyx does not accept the offer? What if she chooses not to join our war? What if she acts as if I never visited her? What if she refuses to accept the promise she made me? So many questions, yet no answers.

'And please do stop fidgeting with your button. Queen Nyx cannot think for a second we are nerve-wracked by her very presence,' General Steelborne purses his lips, letting go of his undone button, and straightening himself.

'Do you think Queen Nyx remembers you?' General Steelborne questions again.

'How in Aetheria did you become General?' I round on him, astounded.

Steelborne sighs, and a small smile reaches his lips before he begins. 'I was your father's best friend.'

I hold in a grumble.

'We were young, and the Hart's Garden was always blooming with dandelions and sunflowers,' he pauses, his smile flickering, 'We were always together, and it was impossible to separate us. Avalorian always snuck me into the castle even if I was not allowed to.'

'Your father worked here, right?' I ask.

'For your grandfather, King Aemilius, yes,' General Steelborne replies, pushing a strand of hair behind.

'What created the rift?' I question, propping my elbow on the carriage window. I remember how Father used to snap at Steelborne and even refused to let him touch Xavier. But Steelborne practically raised me alongside Elysande, to listen, to nod, but to never say a word.

Thoughts of her body piercing through the stone now made me want to retch.

Help me!

But I didn't. Just like how I let Xavier die because of my pride. Because I envied him for the attention he received. The freedom he didn't deserve.

Steelborne's quiet voice carried in the carriage.

'After he became king and I took my father's place, he met your mother. They hadn't married yet, but after a few days in the palace, Calypso took a liking to me.' My lips part in shock. Calypso took a liking to General Steelborne.

My Mother *liked* General Steelborne. 'What?'

'It's not what you think.' Steelborne waves a dismissive hand. 'Avalorian soon found out and refused to marry her despite all his family's attempts. He never exposed her, even though he had every chance.

However...'

'Mother tried to gain Father's love back by bearing a child.' I continue for him. It's not until the words leave my mouth that I'm suddenly hit by a wave of anguish. Doesn't that mean—

'No, no, nothing like that,' scoffs General Steelborne, watching my face fall.

'But then why did she leave?' My voice comes out quiet and hoarse. I never bothered to think about my mother because it always left a sore place in my heart. I decided that not brooding over it altogether would make things better.

But now I see how much I do not know about Calypso. If I had thought about her, I would fuel my anger by thinking she had left me because she couldn't care less. Maybe it was that way. It sure seemed like it, and now General Steelborne had proven it true.

'No one knows, but some say Avalorian planned to have her executed.'

'But why?' I ask. I notice my fingers laced in my gown, threading with the silk. *Because you're a bastard.*

Steelborne chuckles. 'Like I said before, no one knows.'

I nod my head uncertainly, a faint smile tugging at the edge of my mouth. Maybe no one does know, but it seems General Steelborne has quite a clear idea of what happened.

A rumble against the rocky earth nearly jerks me out of my seat.

'We're nearly there!' calls out the coachman.

'Thanks, Felicio!' Steelborne grabs the side of the carriage, and I lay my head against the window, peering out.

Felicio comes from Fames, his blonde hair falling in curly masses around his long face. A sword is sheathed at his hip, a foulard wrapped around his face instead of his neck, causing his voice to be a bit muffled. He wears an ebony braccae and caligae, the pockets and stitches lined in gold.

Chocolate destriers gallop the carriage through the thorns and bones which were once grass and leaves. The world becomes gloomy, the moon disappearing behind masses of stone.

My mother is Calypso Berenice Magnus. My father is Avalorian Ironhart.

No, he is not. The general is hiding something from you.

I shake my head, frustrated. I need to stop thinking about her. She was in the past. He was in the past. They all are dead and gone and will never be back.

Breathe in, breathe out.

General Steelborne's calloused hand grabs mine, giving it an affirmative rub before it disappears. I close my eyes, willing my mind to clear.

Breathe in, breathe out.

No matter what happens, Queen Nyx has to be on our side. She has to continue to be our ally; otherwise no prophecy will be needed to predict our future.

I open my eyes, taking in the scene around me. I shake Dorphne as jagged rocks begin to appear, thunder rumbling in the sky as if it were a hungry wolf waiting to feast on us. Blinding lightning cracks the atmosphere as light blue fades into an endless void, not a star to be seen.

'Dorphne,' I gently shake her, and she moves a bit, mumbling.

'Dorphne,' I say again. 'Dor—' I shrink back as a terrified yowl erupts from her.

She whips around with a knife, pushing me against the carriage door. It swings open, and I grasp for the walls before I can be flung out. My hands burn, and it is with the intensity I remember that the doors are lined with metal.

'Steelborne!' I scream.

'What is going on back there?' yells Felicio.

The carriage jerks back and forth, and I hardly hear Felicio when he hollers over the roaring thunder, 'Fight all you want, but maybe don't put out the torches? Comes in handy for finding our way about, in case you forgot.'

I shriek, looking up to see that Felicio is indeed right. The wind slaps my face. The torches flicker with each bump, threatening to blow out any second.

I can hardly breathe, let alone hold on to the metal as it

singes into my skin. I feel my dress beginning to lift up, the coat around my shoulders failing to hold me down. General Steelborne drags Dorphne back as she suddenly goes limp, pushing her onto the seat before grabbing my hand and pulling me inside.

The door shuts, a deafening slam reverberating through the night sky. There is silence as I pant, General Steelborne fixing himself and dusting off what seems to be flakes of chipped paint.

Breathe in, breathe out.

I bring up my shaky fingers, failing to hold the trembles that course through me. They are purple from the metal. I hold them close to my chest, the prickles of heat still lingering amidst the cold air. We turn to Dorphne, who is slumped against the seat, ragged breaths cooling to faint gasps, her eyes looking into nothing before she jerks awake from her nightmare.

Before I can think, I round on her.

'What the hell was that for?' I stomp, and an exaggerated sigh escapes Felicio as the carriage quakes. Dorphne and General Steelborne exchange a look.

'What was what for?' Her voice is small at my accusing tone, blue eyes bigger than the sea itself.

'You held a knife against my throat. Were you trying to kill me?' I demand, taking a step toward her.

'W-what?' Dorphne looks to General Steelborne, flabbergasted.

'Victoria, I'm sure it was just a nightmare,' he says, placing a hand on my shoulder.

I stare at him. Did his scepticism just happen to vanish into thin air? He hesitantly shrugs, taking his hand off and flexing his fingers.

I sigh, shaking my head. 'I just wanted to wake you up because we're nearly there.' I point to the window, and Dorphne chews on her bottom lip.

'I-I should have mentioned it earlier.' She brushes her hands over her pants, and my stomach pools with guilt all over again.

'It-it's fine.' I take a step forward, hoping to move away from the door, but trip over General Steelborne's large foot. The carriage shakes, and I hear the destriers whinny in pain.

'Ay, everything alright?' Felicio calls out again. 'If you don't want to be stuck in the middle of nowhere, then try not to act like adolescents, please.' He sighs before muttering, 'We don't have extra Queens to replace you.'

Oh, I am so firing him.

I sit back down on the comfy cushions, but then the carriage screeches to a halt. I muffle a scream as I jerk forward, only catching myself in time before I hear Felicio's fading voice. 'We're here...' He jumps off the front, and I see him approach us with dark brown eyes the colour of hazelnut in the flickering firelight.

The door swings open, and I see what caused Felicio to quieten.

The mouth of the cave yawns wide, its jagged rock formations resembling monstrous teeth as if nature itself has sculpted a jaw hungry for unsuspecting souls. The darkness within seems to stretch endlessly, and the only light to be seen is the moon hanging above us all, the clouds shrouding and causing it to flicker off like a lamp at any moment.

'We can do this,' I say, but even to my own ears, I sound uncertain.

'I'll j-just be out here.' Felicio chuckles hesitantly before disappearing into the carriage.

General Steelborne rolls his eyes, making way to enter the cave. I follow him, trying to seem as courageous as possible. I lay one foot inside when a scream breaks the wind's hacking coughs, echoing through the woods. I turn abruptly, only in time to see our torches flicker and die and the moon disappear behind the canvas of clouds.

'Victoria!' General Steelborne pushes me outside, and I land against the grass on impact. The gash at my side stings, and all I can do is hope the stitches have not torn open.

'My Queen!'

I wince in pain as a terrified Felicio comes running toward me, attempting to stand. He holds out a hand, apologising profusely.

'Felicio, what on Aetheria are you apologising for?' I ignore his outstretched hand and pull myself up, groaning as I dust the dirt off my dress. I have an execution to commence, and I do not want to seem like a rag doll.

Felicio chuckles nervously. 'You see, my Queen, the trees may or may not have seemed like monsters, what with their branches having a striking resemblance to claws—'

'Felicio, get to the point.' I tap my foot on the ground impatiently, my heart still beating frantically.

He nods, scratching the back of his head before continuing. 'I may or may not have screamed.'

'Felicio!' I wave my hands in the air in frustration. 'You scared us! Could you not be more mindful of your surroundings?'

'I-I'm sorry,' his voice falters as I cut him off. 'You may be one of the strongest men in the army, but you most certainly are not capable of understanding when your emotions should be shown!'

I see the momentary flicker of hurt flash across his face before a hand grabs my shoulder.

'Victoria, that's enough,' General Steelborne says from behind. 'Do I give the orders or do you?'

Dorphne takes a quick step back as I turn on him, Felicio hesitantly staggering away, the shadow of his hair bounding behind him. General Steelborne stares me down, face rigid, but all I do is shake his hand off and make way to enter back into the cave, trudging through the long strands of grass.

It is dark, but the phosphorescent moss and lichen make the journey inside easier. For a while, rocks jut out and crystals hang from the cave's ceiling, water droplets dripping down until nothing but paved stones carve our way deeper. The scent of ash evaporated the pungent stench of gutter, and suddenly, the cool, midnight air transformed into a fiery heat nearly unbearable. I make way to remove my coat, turning to hand it to General Steelborne.

This place seemed to have aged centuries since I last visited.

He takes it unwillingly, glaring and draping it over his shoulder. I ignore him. There's enough light to pave our way, but not enough to see if my clothes are too badly stained.

'Walk faster,' I call to Dorphne. She's working her way through the maze of rocks a bit too slowly for my taste. Dorphne looks up, a hint of exasperation clouding her eyes before it vaporises.

'I'm trying,' she says, her voice strained.

Try harder, I think.

I walk further, the cave becoming a near furnace, met with a spacious room three times the size of our castle, pillars of coal rising from the flames licking the walls near the end of a brazen cobblestone door. A sharp bark echoes amidst the smothering fire, Dorphne letting out a gasp as I notice the three great beasts standing at the entrance of the Hall of Hell, snarling and drooling as if we were trespassers, waiting to lunge for our throats and feast the night away.

General Steelborne steps forward, walking past me to the gnarling stones embedded into the walls. Two devilish horns glow fluorescent in the fiery night, my heart snapping every bone in my body with its quickened pace, beads of sweat falling from my hair. I could feel my hair unravelling, the neat bun resuming its original attire: wavy unkempt locks.

I shake myself.

No. Now was not the time to shatter into smithereens. I will be standing in the sight of the most powerful and feared Queen in all of Aetheria once more—as a Queen myself—and I must seem as dignified as possible.

Breathe in, breathe out.

I fall in pace with Dorphne's long and quick strides as

General Steelborne bangs on the Hall's doors, kicking away the dogs, provoking them more.

Dorphne and I halt behind him, noticing the slight twitch in his arms. He grips one of the curved horns attached to the gong, pulls it back, and releases it with a resonating clang. The dogs' furious barking dies away as the bang reverberates through the wall of the caves, leaving a tense silence in its wake.

Then a sound of clicking heels floats through the air.

'Open,' commands a lilting voice.

General Steelborne takes a step behind me, Dorphne echoing his movement.

The hall doors creak open, a mechanism stirring about in the dark. I dare not look, for even the slightest hesitation could mark me as unworthy in her eyes. I instinctively step back, watching as the hall doors unfurl a creature commanding the greatest respect.

Her thin, jet, raven hair falls in wavy anguish, her pale face nearly the colour of death's call, a snubbed nose stuck in the air above lips that pursed in disappointment, with cheekbones that could possibly slice a finger in half. Shrewd, furious amethyst eyes gulp the world despite its size. Her figure is long and slim, thin, veiny fingers peeking out of an elegant white dress made out of the purest of white silk, draping gracefully and cascading down in delicate layers that whisper with each movement.

She finds my eyes, her head tilting as if to remember who I could be.

'Vic-tor-ia?' she articulates my name, as if speaking for the first time in years.

'Yes, my Queen.' I drop to a low bow, Dorphne and General Steelborne doing the same.

'And what brings you to my abode once more?' She stretches the o's, staring into my soul as I straighten myself.

'I may be mistaken to question your knowledge of the happenings in Aetheria,' I reply coolly.

Neither an answer nor a question.

'Ah, King of Briarthorn Atoll.' Nyx places a hand to her chest, letting out a cackle. 'Played you well, that one.' A wicked smile lines her creased face, ushering us inside.

I pull up a hand to halt the other two from following.

'You betrayed me,' I hiss. 'You never came to help.'

'Oh, I did say I would help at the right time, my dear,' Nyx drawls, placing a hand to her chest.

'The right time for my death?' I smile, lips tight. Her eyes narrow to slits.

I pass by her, nearly stumbling in shock because of her aura, gesturing the others to follow. It is cold like the snowy nights I used to play in as a child, but away from her, all I feel is the heat searing every part of my body.

'And who do we have here?' she murmurs, scraping Dorphne's chin as we enter into the mouth of a blazing volcano. Dorphne lets out a shaky breath and a fearful smile, looking up at Queen Nyx.

That's right. Show her you fear her. This way she shall be more willing to partake in the war.

I am hit with the stench of ash and a burning sensation as the boiling lava sears my skin. We are high up, but the volcano shows no mercy, spurting lava every few seconds.

We stand on a thick line of obsidian leading to the centre and three other pathways connecting on the other side of the chunk of obsidian.

'Dorphne and General Steelborne,' I say.

'Dor-ph-ene,' she breaks the name down, sizing her up before letting Dorphne pass through.

General Steelborne bows again before crossing, Nyx not bothering to give him a second glance as she follows us from behind.

'Your King plans war, does he not?' she asks, her voice holding an air of expectancy.

'Yes,' I answer simply, the fire spewing from the lava beneath us. The cobblestone is cracking under my feet. 'And he is not *my* King.' I bite out.

'You expect me to partake in this war?' Nyx asks again, ignoring me.

'I only ask for you to help me kill Desmond. I don't expect you to; I ask you to. Seeing as you have built your army, the crown will be yours with ease.' I pull my chin up high, back straight as I walk further into the boiling crevice.

There is silence as I lead the way to the centre, minutes stretching into what seems like hours.

A question gnaws at my head and before I can stop myself, I blurt it out. 'Has anyone contacted you in the past years?'

Desmond had said the rest of the Kingdoms had, but now I wasn't sure if I could believe anything he said.

Nyx sighs, the light click of her heels somehow louder than the average rumble of the volcano. 'Attempts have been made, but of course, none are worthy of my attention.'

None were of any use to her.

'So you are to say I have to kill the boy so that I may get my crown?' Nyx says when we are finally at the centre of molten lava.

The chunk of obsidian is crudely cut out, a rectangular slab of solid stone in the middle. She stands opposite us as we crowd over a table, with the map of Aetheria drawn on it.

'Yes,' I answered.

'But you would not be here just to inform me of this little... oversight.' She puts emphasis on the last word. 'Why are you really here, Victoria?'

Behind me, I feel General Steelborne stiffen. Dorphne has surprisingly not uttered a single word.

My breath hitches. 'Desmond has accused me of the deaths of my family and his own, and went as far as to imprison me in

Carcerem Regum Mortuorum. From what I inferred, the guards said he was to kill me the next day.'

'You escaped?' Nyx says, waving her hand at me.

Of course I escaped. How else would I be standing here?

'I did, and I brought Dorphne along with me.'

'Ah, and let me guess, your King turned half the folk against you in hopes of finding and slaughtering you,' Nyx blatantly says, shaking her head.

She sighs when I nod. 'I ask again, Victoria, what are you really here for?'

I let a beat pass, tilting my head to match her posture. 'What you plan to do, my Queen.'

Nyx cocks an eyebrow, a slow smirk touching her lips.

'Revenge. I plan to wage war against Briarthorn Atoll and kill all those who betrayed me, and take back what is rightfully mine,' I continue, smacking my hand on the table. Outside, thunder rumbles.

She knows what my true intentions are, but she won't kill me. Not yet. Nyx loves to play a little before murder.

'You have a plan?' Her voice is slithery, almost snake-like.

'Of course I do.' I straighten myself. 'I have already sent messages to Fames, and if you choose to partake, you can show the world who the true ruler of Aetheria really is.'

'Why would I do that? I have no need for revenge,' Nyx says slyly, bending forward.

'Desmond once said we are alike.' I laugh softly. 'This is what the fallen Queens do: make sure they redeem what is rightfully theirs.'

She stares at me, and a sudden burst of fear blooms in my heart. Her eyes are large with fury, a fire burning with such intensity I drop my gaze.

'What happened to the Queen of Ferrumisle?' She grows closer to me, pulling my chin up so that we are only a few mere inches apart.

'Dead,' I say. 'I am the remaining heir to the throne.'

Her eyes twitch, then suddenly snap with a glint of steel. It was as if a switch had been flipped, and a newfound intensity emblazoned from within.

'You lie,' she growls. I cannot see what is happening around me, but I wish I could.

I find her hungry eyes, 'I am Queen Victoria of Ferrumi—'

'You lie!' thunders Nyx, yanking away her fingers with force.

I stagger back, General Steelborne pushing me forward on impact. 'Pardon, Queen Nyx, but our lineage ends with me. Everyone else is dead. I do not und—'

'Your blood still lives!'

'Impossible! They are all dead!'

Nyx cackles, the laugh hollow and filled with mockery. The lava in the volcano begins to boil, bubbling towards us higher and higher.

'Victoria, we need to go!' Dorphne grabs my arm, General Steelborne pulling me back towards the doors.

'I know what you've done and what you aim to do, Victoria! You shall never be Queen of the world! I shall rise, and Aetheria shall fall, and everyone will fear my name! No one shall be Queen of the world except I, Nyx Darkryn!'

A cryptic cackle echoes through the cave as we rush out the doors, bumping into each other and breathing frantically. The beasts attempt to attack us, the biggest chasing behind us as we rush through the maze of stones and crystals. The soles of my shoes are wearing out, and the pressure of each footstep shoots a spasm of pain through my body.

'Felicio! Go, go, go!' I yell as we finally exit the cave. One of the ferocious brutes snarls and lunges forward, but General Steelborne quickly tears a bramble and forces it down the beast's throat.

Felicio hurriedly opens the door and resumes his position

on the destrier. I grab Dorphne's arm and pull her into the carriage with me, General Steelborne plundering in after us.

The carriage door shuts, and then we begin to jerk forward. A guttural howl reverberates through the woods, but a soft voice nurtures it into a low growl, commanding it to go no further. I watch as Queen Nyx lets her frail fingers linger around the brute's head before lowering to his neck, scratching him as he whimpers in pleasure.

The whimper turns into a yelp as a gush of blood wets his unkempt fur, fingers digging through the back of his neck and out the other end, slicing it clean in half. The crunch of bones is almost lost in the crack of branches as the carriage stumbles on, and as the beast's head lolls to one side and plops to the earthy ground, Nyx's devilish smirk never leaves her face.

My heart thunders in fear, racketing against my rib cage so brutally I can hardly make out General Steelborne's attempts at making Felicio run the carriage faster. But it is not my heart that seems to block out and drown everything else.

It is a voice; a voice that tells me Mother is alive.

The sun is rising, and we are nearing Ferrumisle.

'My Queen, you are in no position to enforce the execution,' General Steelborne says quietly. He tries to hold my hand, but I snatch it away.

Queen Nyx knew I wanted the crown. Well, let her. She'd kill Desmond for me, but we both knew she would have to remain cautious of her actions if she wanted to keep the coronet.

One slash of my sword and the Blood Crown would have been on the head of its last Queen.

'The price of treason is execution,' I answer coldly.

General Steelborne has the nerve to respond. 'Then you must be executed, too.'

'General Steelborne, might I inform you that if word of this escapes your lips, I shall hold another execution for mutiny,' I retort.

He scowls.

'I don't understand,' Dorphne mutters, plucking at the brown thread on the carriage walls. She's wrapped in a shell of her own thoughts. 'Do you want to kill Desmond for revenge or for power?'

I stare at her, widening my eyes. She doesn't hold my gaze for long.

'Maybe it's a bit of both,' I answer breathlessly, chortling.

The carriage rumbles to a halt, and the latch is unlocked. 'My Queen, please, the ceremony is to begin momentarily.' Lord Lysander stands outside in a deep crimson velvet doublet with a high-collared shirt underneath. He swings his long, flowing cape with a fur-trimmed mantle to the side, brandishing gloved arms.

Dorphne winces, looking at his feet.

I fear I have to agree, for polished leather boots do not seem to match all that well with the velvet-sheathed sword strapped to his side.

I plop down from the carriage, following Lord Lysander's lead. The sky is now a light yellow, stretching over the vast landscape behind the fortress. We walk into the dark hallway adorned with the crimson carpet, stretching miles with a dozen crystals at every centimetre.

Our family was too keen on boisterous bragging about failures.

We take a right, passing the keep, and from there does the first ray of sunshine pool in.

'All hail the Queen!' roars Admiral Lancelot from the open space below.

I walk into the arena, and I am met with a ruckus of chants. I expected anger at the deaths of the royal family, but no one seems to care. It's a circular box, and I tower over those beneath me. My dais juts out, a throne-like chair made of carved stone in the centre. I take a seat, and guards file in to stand beside me.

I spy the rest of the Lords and Ladies seated across from me in the arena. I can hardly view them well. They are mere tiny dots in my vision among the thousands that surround me.

Dorphne sits on a wooden stool beside me, while General Steelborne stands behind us, a sheathed sword at his hip. He is dressed in a black tunic and heavy trousers buttoned and lined in gold, connected with a balteus. He wears brown caligae as shoes. Surprisingly, his favourite red focale is not snaking around his neck.

'Where's your focale?' I ask, curiosity winning over me.

General Steelborne nervously tucks back a strand of his hair, which has been tied into a messy ponytail, likely in a rush when I hadn't been watching. 'It didn't seem right for the occasion.' His voice falters, and I wince, understanding.

Cormac had gifted him the red focale on The Hart's Maker Day. Ferrumisle celebrates it as a way to express our gratitude to one another every five years, to mark the bond created over time.

Seeing as how Elysande and Cormac had been exiled from Fames for plotting against the monarch, General Steelborne had been the kindest to him. Cormac decided to pass on his family heirloom to Steelborne, knowing he would keep it in the best care possible, just as he had cared for him.

Dorphne shakes me suddenly, and I realise the chants have grown louder.

'Kill him! Kill him! Kill him!'

I see General Steelborne's muscles tense, his sharp features stiffening.

As loyal as he is to me, I'm afraid I cannot pay it back.

Selfish creature.

The words Father had spat at me when I ate a cake and

refused to share it with Xavier came back at me, and I shake them out of my head.

Xavier.

He hadn't done anything, yet I had accused him and Desmond had killed him.

I nod my head, my heart heavy in my chest like it was a burden to be carried. It is.

Xavier deserved every dagger that gutted him.

I stand, the bushy, red cloak flowing around me with diamonds patterned across it in black. My once beautiful bun spews ebony strands from behind. I spread out my arms as my voice booms through the arena.

'Silence!' I demand.

The voices fade slowly, and then I notice the accusing eyes before a voice calls out.

'Where is the King?'

It reverberates through the arena and pounds in my head.

Where is the King?

Do they not know he is dead?

Do they not know they all are dead, and I am the only one alive?

My gaze follows the burly man with greying hair and a blue suit, and see his eyes hardening but never cowering. 'They are dead,' I say, enunciating every word.

Gasps erupt and murmurs arise, suspicious looks being thrown my way. Dorphne crosses her legs daintily, her back hunched in the gown she wore yesterday. Her head bows as if in mourning, but I don't rest my gaze too long on her.

I may be guilty, but for the sake of our Kingdom, I cannot expose my truth.

For my sake, I cannot expose my truth.

'A mere month ago, we visited Briarthorn Atoll,' my voice thunders across the arena, and the people lapse into silence once more. 'As far as the truth may seem, King Desmond, to whom I was betrothed, attempted to kill my family. He succeeded in doing so, wiping them all out before having me imprisoned in Carcerem Regum Mortuorum.'

'As you should be!' hollers out a woman. Bursts of laughter arise, and a small smile creeps its way to my lips. The horror I could do to Cormac to torture their souls and show them who's in charge.

I catch myself, blinking away the brutal thoughts, but the smile lingers. 'But I escaped, for the sake of our Kingdom. I urge you all to stay indoors, for this may be the last time you see daylight.'

My voice comes out smooth, but my words are rough, and the indication to them is clear as fear ripples through the crowd gathered.

It's like a domino effect. The fourth tier registers my words first, and my voice reverberates to the third, then to the second and finally the last. The twitching and wincing each humble peasant suffers does not go unnoticed by me.

General Steelborne cracks his neck, and I can see his teeth bared without sparing a glance behind.

'War is coming, Queen Nyx is rising, Aetheria is falling.' I clench my fists, hoping my gaze softens. 'I am doing everything in my power to gather the alliances I can. King Desmond wants me dead because I have a truth only the dead cannot reveal. I cannot promise your safety, but I can promise our victory.'

Uncertain murmurs arise, but even as I say the words, a bellow breaks the tamed crowd, and my gaze goes to the man who has been hauled to the centre, a rope hanging around his neck, hands tied behind his back. Without the cap, his black hair is a mess. A nightgown drapes over his loose figure, crumpled and a bit torn, showing signs that he was dragged out of bed.

'You listen to this woman? You believe she can be your Queen when she has the death of the rightful ruler on her hands?'

He spits on the ground, turning to me as unsure faces stare up, fear clouding their eyes. 'You are no Queen! You do not deserve this land. You do not deserve the throne!' He looks to the crowd, heaving. 'She fell into her brother's foolish traps to kill her. Who knows what lengths she'll go to if she trusts blindly? She is what her Father said, what Avalorian said—a pity born into pride!'

There is a silence so deafening I feel it will crack my soul. My breath comes out in quick pants, and it is all I can do to stop myself from killing Cormac myself.

The burly man who spoke up before lets his voice be heard once more. 'He is right! You do not deserve this throne!' He turns to face Cormac, spite forming in his eyes and a devilish grin capturing his blemished face as the crowd cheers him on. 'But your sister didn't either.'

To this, Cormac bares his teeth and tugs against the chains, cursing wildly. But I barely hear him. I barely register Dorphne's shove, or General Steelborne's failed attempts to calm me.

I breathe raggedly, heaving wildly.

You are no Queen. You do not deserve this land.

I clench my hands to my sides, standing stoically as the crowd decides their side.

He is right. You do not deserve the throne.

Anger burbles in my stomach. All my life, I had been doing one thing: being the dutiful princess I ought to be, knowing I would be Queen one day. But what I had overlooked was that when you try to change for the pleasure of others, you end up killing the person you really are.

You are your own prison and chance at freedom.

I hear my Mother's voice, but the crowd has taken their side, and it overpowers.

Their chants grow louder, faster, angrier.

'Kill him! Kill him! Kill him!'

She is what her Father said, what Avalorian said, a pity born into pride!

'Kill him!' I roar. The crowd clamours, hooting in approval. Instinctively, Dorphne shrinks back and Steelborne remains stagnant in a stature of shock.

There is the snap of bones and a hollow laugh from Cormac that morphs into a shallow scream before he goes limp, raised in the air. A fresh wave of ecstasy gushes through me.

Before I can catch myself, the words spill from my mouth. 'Guards, prepare for war! Only one can prevail as the rightful ruler of Aetheria!'

As the words register with the crowd, I turn and walk out of the brazen wooden doors, ushering the guards to leave. Dorphne and General Steelborne quietly trail behind.

'My Queen, do you not think you exposed a little too much?' Steelborne hesitantly asks.

'A bit,' I admit, but do not ponder on it any further. *Kill him!*

'That was unlike you, back there,' General Steelborne says again as we pass the Keep.

'I don't think I seem to care.' I reply pleasantly.

'Victo—' he starts again, but I cut him off.

'I will repeat myself once more, Steelborne. I am your Queen and you will address me as such. Now, wander along and attempt to brighten me with your presence when you have news from Fames or Caelumterra.'

I incline my head to one side, Xavier's portrait catching my eye.

'Oh, brother. I shall make you turn in your grave when I become Queen of all.' I sigh, a wild smirk pasting across my face. 'I so wish you were here to see this.'

CHAPTER XVI

'Remember who you are.'
'Who am I?' I ask.
'What you want to become.' Mother smiles.
'A Queen?' I look up at her expectantly.
I feel her silky locks before she lets out a chuckle. 'Better than any other.'

Mother is alive. Queen Nyx had said so—not really—but she said my blood still lived. Does that not mean she is alive? Everyone else is dead. Xavier, Father—if he really is my Father. I remember General Steelborne's high laugh and wandering eyes that gave away the lies his mouth formed as he told me that 'it was not what I thought.'

'Victoria?' Dorphne walks up to me from behind. I feel a shadow of a hand linger behind before it pulls back hesitantly.

'What?' I ask.

'News has arrived from Fames.'

I hunch over the map in the War Room, a bit stunned. After the execution, I immediately changed into a bouffant dress with a striking combination of crimson transitioning to a velvety black, with an extra train of ebony trailing behind. Sheer jet fabric drapes over my shoulders, a black satin sash cinching my dress at my waist, a small dagger ready at the hip. Sheathed, of course.

Silence envelops us, before I finally turn to face her.

'Already? I expected it to take a few days.'

Dorphne shrugs, her strawberry hair tied into a flimsy pony, a blush-rose dress delicately draping around her body in layers, the collar high until her jaw before it turns out like a blooming flower's petals on a spring day. Beads outline her waist and the circular overlapping layers fall elegantly around her.

I'm hit with a sudden flashback, remembering the day the waiter spilled the wine all over this dress, when the villagers had arrived to congratulate Xavier on his ascension. It was a beautiful and innocent gown for a beautiful and innocent soul, and it suits Dorphne just fine.

'Remind me to fire a ragged old dwarf,' I say, tracing my hand over the passage to Caelumterra.

'Why?' Dorphne says, indignation lacing her voice.

'I don't do incompetence.' I spit, matching her tone.

She says nothing more, instead grasping the wine bottles Felicio grabbed from the cellar, bringing them to the marble table. 'King Vorin stated he would be delighted to partake as your ally, but refused to mention whether Desmond has contacted him or not.'

'Then make him,' I answer simply.

'But why?' Dorphne shakes her head, casting me a sideways glance. She uncorks the bottle and places the glass tube to her lips, glugging the thick, red liquid down her throat.

'He may betray us in the middle of the war. If he has not received any form of letter from Desmond—which I am most certain he has—then he would have no reason to hide whether Desmond has contacted him or not.'

'But maybe Desmond bribed him and—' I cut Dorphne off, placing a hand to my temple.

'Vorin would be stupid to do such a thing. Fames and Briarthorn Atoll have never had a healthy relationship amongst one another, especially on the battlefield.'

Dorphne stares at me in shock when I address the King of Fames without his deemed title. I shrug it off.

After a moment, she shakes herself, looking me in the eye. 'And how do you plan to get this information out of King Vorin?'

'Force him to. I want answers by tomorrow, sundown. Whether you have to press a knife to his son's neck or hold him captive, I don't care. All I want is loyalty from one of Ferrumisle's strongest allies.' I bite out the last sentence.

Dorphne looks aghast at my suggestion. 'No one will respect you that way, Victoria.'

I manage a chuckle at her failed attempt to steer my ambition.

'What the people can't hear won't hurt them,' I rub my temple and revert my attention back to the map.

Briarthorn Atoll was only a day's trip to and from Ferrumisle. Neither of us had the resources or the land to spare space for battle, which only left Inferis and Fames. Inferis was too dangerous, considering Nyx's stronghold, and Fames was too fragile. One small flame could burn the entire land to smithereens.

Caelumterra was no good either. The Council had no interest in participating in any of the battles.

However, Prince William might take my letter into consideration.

'Do you think Queen Nyx knows of your plan to overthrow her?' Dorphne asks.

I don't look up from the map this time. 'You didn't hear what she said to me as we left?' I answer. She goes quiet. *I know what you've done and what you aim to do, Victoria! You shall never be Queen of the world!*

'So what are we going to do now?'

'Prepare for war against Briarthorn Atoll and Inferis.'

I focus my attention on the map again. The only place left was The Center. It had enough space and would be the perfect place to settle for war because it was brazen, with seldom any trees or bushes to lay wait in.

I notice a shadow hovering over the aged paper and look up to see Dorphne standing over me, her eyes clouded in confusion.

'What are you waiting for? Inform General Steelborne and the Palace Guards.' I usher her away, catching a glimpse of hurt scrawled over her dainty features.

'I'm not your servant,' she croaks out.

'Then what are you?' I purse my lips, raising an eyebrow in question.

'I thought we were friends.'

Friends.

I thought we were friends.

'We are nothing more than acquaintances,' I scoff.

Dorphne sighs, grabbing a bottle and heading out the door, her dress swaying. She mutters something almost sadly, but the words that escape her plump lips engrave in my mind sharply.

'We aren't friends—or acquaintances. Not until you fix your ways.'

I hold a basket woven with cane stalks, a handful of strawberries and two sandwiches neatly tucked inside.

'Here to apologise again?' she asks coldly.

Truthfully, no.

'No, I am not.'

I place the basket between us, removing the chequered red and white cloth and grabbing a sandwich. I don't bother offering Dorphne one. 'You willingly accepted to stay in Ferrumisle as my advisor.'

I bite into the soft bread, cheese bleeding into my mouth. I chew a bit more as Dorphne looks away from me before finally saying. 'I thought you treated your cohorts better.'

I swallow my bread. I have no answer, none that justifies my actions. It takes a few more beats before a reply forms at my mouth. 'War is coming. If we are anything but diligent, it is as good as losing the battle before it has even started.'

'You may have your—' Dorphne pauses, waving her right hand about before continuing, 'intentions, best at heart as they may be. Yet if you win the war, you wouldn't have won the throne.'

It doesn't take a genius to figure out what she really means. I place my half-eaten sandwich back into the basket, my appetite suddenly lost. The raw marks of my teeth are still embedded into the corner of the triangle. I pull the cloth over the basket, noticing Dorphne had not bothered to even ask for a bit of the delights I had brought.

Dorphne was right. The Lords and Ladies of Ferrumisle will be the first to target me, and quite practically any of the other lands. But there was no turning back now.

'When I have both the crowns—Ferrumisle's and the Blood Crown—they'll all respect me.' I say, clenching my hand into a fist.

'Victoria, I want to ask you a question.' Dorphne turns, grabbing my wrist as I make way to stand up. Out of the corner of my eye, I see a figure approaching. I try not to flinch at the ice touch of her skin, but I must give it away for she immediately pulls back her hand.

'You were bold enough to ask me so much. What's stopping you from pushing further?' I say evenly.

Dorphne shrugs. 'Are you sure that what you are doing is for revenge and not for the power to have the world all to yourself just because you can't let go of a foolish grudge?'

No, I want to answer. No, because people still think I am

undeserving. Because they think I will never be able to regain what I lost.

'Yes,' I lie. She will be safer not knowing the truth. She nods, but I can tell that she does not believe me.

'About earlier, what you said about us not being friends,' I say. Dorphne shakes her head.

'You really think we're friends?'

'I... don't know. All you've done is protect me, and be there for me. We spend time together, and as much as it kills me to say, I trust you.' I look away, fearing that I have revealed too much.

'What's wrong with trusting me?' Dorphne asks. She grows closer behind me, and with a sigh, I remember she has no knowledge of the happenings in court. She is not one of us.

'I was brought up to trust my family: my parents and my brother. I did, and one day, he betrayed me. Despite that, I still trusted people, even people whom I had no knowledge of. Desmond, I trusted him, and he betrayed me by calling for my execution. And you...'

The words linger between us, unsaid.

And you could betray me too.

'I would never do that,' Dorphne says, grabbing my hand. 'Whatever you go through, I'm here with you for it, as long as you promise to do the same. Stay with me. That's what friends are for.'

'But we haven't reached that level of intimacy yet,' I murmur.

Dorphne nods firmly. 'But we can.'

I turn to her, the flicker of a smile illuminating my features, but I don't have the time to thank her because just as I open my mouth, a messenger interrupts me.

'My Queen,'

'Yes?' I sigh.

'You have a message.' It is when he says this that I notice the hard edges and hesitant tone of his voice, and a bit of alarm. It is General Steelborne, I recognise with a dull thud.

'From whom?' I stand up abruptly.

He lets out an exhale before answering me. 'King Desmond.'

Deathly silence follows. The wind rustles my hair, a chill running down my spine.

'What would Desmond want with me?' My voice comes out barely a whisper. The answer is obvious. He wants to cower me. To make a fool of me. To kill me.

'He wishes to meet you in the Queen's Forest at exactly midnight tomorrow.'

'Why?' The words slip out of my mouth before I can stop myself.

'I think it would be best if you read the letter yourself,' General Steelborne ushers us to the castle gates, and I follow him begrudgingly. As much as I want to stop and turn back, I can't admit to him that I was looking forward to spending time with Dorphne. It was nice to have some company around, but he would be even more angered if he realised I trusted her.

But did I trust her because of our blooming friendship, or was it merely the thought that I could control someone beneath me?

'Where are you guys going?' Dorphne asks, catching up to us.

'The Commander's Office,' he replies stiffly.

'Why?' I reiterate.

'Are you not going to inform the Lords and Ladies of what is to come, so that they may assist you by harbouring the necessary weapons?' General Steelborne asks.

'You invited them already?' I exclaim, quickening my pace as I hear muffled shouts from the Office.

'It is the best choice. We do not have time,' he says, hand clamped behind his back.

My blood boils. He should have consulted me before allowing them to set foot in the palace. Our conversation at the execution was far from friendly.

General Steelborne makes his way to open the small wooden

door to the Commander's Office, but it is suddenly swung inward, and he stumbles before catching himself.

'We cannot do this any longer! We need to end it now, or never!' A woman with ebony hair and soft chocolate eyes faces us, her face morphing from anger to fear.

'Your Highness,' Lady Rhiannon gasps, quickly falling into a low curtsy.

I spot her husband, Lord Asher, hunched over a wooden table at the back along with Lord Lysander and Lady Emberlyn.

Lady Celestia sits lazily atop an obsidian throne-like chair, which I suppose is meant for the Chief Commander. Lord Auric stands beside Celestia, as nervous as ever. He drops his gaze as I push aside Lady Rhiannon and walk forward to the table, General Steelborne standing by the door and Dorphne following.

'Where is Admiral Lancelot?' I ask.

'The Chief Commander is out requesting the information you required from King Vorin,' Lord Lysander replies.

I nod curtly. 'Very well. What is it that you are all here for?' I ask, brandishing my hands. A look of confusion crosses over their faces. They could not know I need them. That is the last thing I need.

Lady Rhiannon hesitantly passes by me to stand with Lord Asher, and I try not to wince at the uneasiness her words bring to me.

We need to end it, now, or never!

No doubt they were talking about my reign.

'You have a message from your dearest King,' the mocking tone in Lady Celestia's voice is impossible to miss as she pushes forward the letter the six of them were ducked over, and I have to hold back my hand from striking that petty little face of hers.

The golden strands of hair fall meticulously curled around her shoulders, her deep blue eyes glinting with devilish mischief.

Her mouth is in a small pout, and Lord Auric taps her shoulder, a warning to stop.

Her pout drops momentarily before she says, 'And so that we may know what trouble you have brought to this land once more.'

'I might end my trouble through murder if you don't keep your pretty mouth shut,' I retort, glaring at her.

Celestia shrugs, handing me the letter, the crimson wolf seal broken.

I take it, but I do not read it. Instead, I hand it to General Steelborne and wait for Lady Celestia to get the hint. She rolls her eyes before standing and letting me sit upon the cushioned chair.

'Aetheria will be at war,' I say.

A ripple of furious murmurs erupts before Lady Emberlyn shakes her head. 'You finally have the throne and the first thing you do is end our world?'

'Not yet, Emberlyn. I'm sure it will take plenty of time for that,' I say sweetly. 'So how about you all listen to me instead of blabbering away? You know I can have you all killed, right?'

Lady Emberlyn purses her lips at the threat, her high cheekbones even more prominent under the single light above the table that illuminates us all, while her ebony hair blends in with the surrounding darkness. Though their clothes seem black, the Ladies seem to be wearing cherry gowns and the Lords are dressed in white surcoats with a gold belt, a sword sheathed to each of their hips.

'Yes, my Queen,' she answers stiffly.

Lord Asher softly raps the table, bringing my attention to him. 'When is the war supposed to take place?' he asks gruffly.

'As I'm sure you all read, King Desmond wishes to meet me tomorrow at midnight,' I reply, hands on the table.

'Alone,' Lord Auric suddenly says. All heads turn to him.

I realise he is still behind me, and I have to crane my neck to focus on him properly.

'Pardon?' I say.

'The King wishes to meet you tomorrow at midnight, *alone*,' Lord Auric corrects.

'So?' I shrug. 'It's no big deal; my men can hide in the bushes, as I'm sure his will undoubtedly too.'

'But you may be killed!' Lady Rhiannon gasps.

'Well, I'm sure it would be good riddance for you all, considering your job would be done,' I retort.

She is shocked into silence, but Lord Lysander does not back down. 'The point is not about your death, Your Graciousness; this is not how war is waged.

We have to be prepared. We don't discuss when it is supposed to take place; it can occur at any time.

The first strike could be the moment you leave the land!'

'It would be foolish to leave us unprotected!' Lady Celestia cries from the back.

How I wish it wasn't.

'That is why I expect you all to be sufficiently armed.' I slam my fist down on the table, and the room goes silent.

'I asked you all to listen. I do not care about what opinions you have. The war is not only between us and King Desmond, but Queen Nyx as well.'

'All the more stupid to leave for Queen's Forest!' Lady Celestia scoffs again.

'Celestia, I would request you to keep quiet before I silence you myself,' I grit out.

Lord Auric seems taken aback, retreating into the shadows once more.

'Your Queen is right. She has to meet King Desmond. For all we know, he may want a truce,' Dorphne speaks up from behind. As foolish as the excuse may be, I pass her a ghost of a smile.

'A truce to have the Queen's head to leave our land alone!' Lady Emberlyn matches Dorphne's icy tone.

'Can we focus on the solutions instead, Ladies?' Lord Lysander impatiently says. 'We not only have the King of Briarthorn Atoll against us, but Inferis as well. If Queen Nyx is ready to fight, she could strike at any time.'

'How on Aetheria did you have the courage to ask her to aid you so blatantly?' Lord Asher asks.

My, these irritating souls. Why, on Aetheria, must they know what I plan to do and how I intend to carry it out?

'That is none of your business. All I want right now is peace, and for that, we need to eliminate Queen Nyx, no matter how tough it may seem. Lord Lysander, I would like your insight on how we could achieve this,' I say roughly.

Lord Lysander too is a war strategist. He helped Father with his plan to steal the Blood Crown a few years back. Unfortunately, Father's pride took him too far, and the first time he decided not to follow Lord Lysander's plan, it got him into a pool of trouble. The next time, he did not consult Lord Lysander at all and ended up in a pool of blood.

I knew better than to do that.

'It is possible Queen Nyx has already informed King Desmond of her participation, but whether as his ally or not we do not know, and that is what he may want to discuss with you in the forest,' Lord Lysander replies.

Strange as it might be, it never occurred to me that Nyx would tell Desmond. She does like the element of surprise, but it could be a possibility.

Lysander takes out his sword, pointing to Inferis on the table. 'Inferis is two hours away from Ferrumisle and three hours from Briarthorn Atoll. The Queen's Forest is only a mere one and a half hour away from Inferis.'

'What is the point you are attempting to make?' Lady Celestia sighs.

'I believe what Lysander is trying to say is that the Queen's Forest is closest to Inferis, so if the Queen visits the King of Briarthorn Atoll, there is a vast likelihood of there being a full-fledged attack on Ferrumisle,' Lord Asher explains.

'Are you suggesting we go forward with the mindset that they both are allies?' I ask, rubbing my head. It was beginning to throb.

'It would be the most plausible explanation,' Lord Lysander confirms. 'If Queen Nyx and King Desmond join forces, they will end you, and Queen Nyx will have her crown after killing Desmond.'

'But we don't want that to happen,' I say, raising an eyebrow.

'Yes,' Lady Emberlyn says, surprising me. I almost forgot—she too is experienced in battle. Before marrying Lord Lysander, she worked in Fames.

I address Lady Emberlyn, 'You have fought against King Desmond. Do you agree with Lord Lysander?'

'Yes,' she repeats. 'If you do wish to meet the King of Briarthorn Atoll, I would suggest you send a messenger informing him you would like to meet elsewhere.'

'How about she does not meet anyone? I thought we had come to that conclusion,' Lady Celestia says.

'I for one agree with the Queen. Celestia, if she does not meet the King, it would make our land come across as weak,' Lady Emberlyn stiffly replies.

'Which would cause them to underestimate us, and we would have the upper hand,' Lady Celestia counters.

'Rule number one of war: never underestimate the enemy.' Lady Emberlyn's voice raises a pitch or two, smacking her hands on the table. She was right. Underestimating Desmond would be a foolish thing to do.

'And you think you know so much?' Lady Celestia matches her tone.

'We tried the same tactic with King Desmond, and it failed

brutally. It was by sheer luck that we escaped with at least as much of our army as we did, especially since that was at the beginning of the Throne War,' Lady Emberlyn hisses.

'There you have it! Why should we trust her if she failed the King before?' Lady Celestia says triumphantly.

Lady Emberlyn's face gushes a bright red.

'Enough!' I trail around the table before coming to stand between the two women. My eyes are tired of moving back and forth between them.

'Celestia, no one has asked for your judgement. Lady Emberlyn is absolutely correct. I must meet King Desmond.'

'And as a matter of fact, King Desmond is not one to be left waiting. Whatever he wants to say could be invaluable to our planning, and angering him by delaying a response could make his actions even worse,' Lord Asher says.

'I agree,' I answer. 'Where do you suggest I meet King Desmond?' I turn to Lady Emberlyn.

She clears her throat before answering. 'The Centre.'

A clamour of disagreement bursts from all the Lords and Ladies, even from Lord Auric.

Just as I had thought, I knew it would be the perfect place.

'The land is brazen! How is she supposed to protect herself?' Lord Auric bursts.

'If there are no places to hide, there are no secrets. Both sides shall be transparent, although there is no doubt an army shall be waiting at the borders of Briarthorn Atoll,' Lady Emberlyn remarks.

Lord Lysander watches his wife thoughtfully. 'She is right. The King will have no choice but to arrive alone.'

'That is, if he agrees,' Lady Celestia grumbles.

'I'm sure he will. If he does not arrive, he will lose the element of surprise, as we will be ready for any attack to come,' Lady Emberlyn clasps her hands in front of her tightly, looking to Lord Lysander for support. He nods. If Desmond does appear, there is a chance he may attempt to divert my attention before launching an attack. But I know that even if he does show up, he would not allow his army to raise a finger against me—unless it was his own.

'My Queen, are you positively sure you want to meet the King?' Lord Lysander asks.

'Yes,' I say. 'I need my strongest men at the border of Fames. We shall go through their land to avoid any disaster in our own.'

Lord Asher nods, readying to leave. 'I need as many weapons from the armoury as possible, and as many trained metallures.'

Lady Rhiannon bows her head, a gesture to say she heard.

'Emberlyn and Lysander, you two must devise strategies with the army after my... meeting with Desmond. I will need Lord Lysander to come along with me.'

'Yes, my Queen,' he says.

'Lady Celestia and Lord Auric...' I pause, thinking about what they could do. 'Train the strongest and most unpredictable stollars.'

'Do you want them to die?' Lady Celestia bursts. 'The most unpredictable will explode on the battlefield in seconds!'

Lord Auric shifts in place. 'Your Majesty, I think—

'I didn't ask for what you think or don't. At least their lives will come in use and they will die with honour,' I retort, pointing to the door. 'You may leave now.'

Lady Celestia rolls her eyes and Lord Auric hurriedly nods, following behind the rest as they file out the door quietly.

The door thuds shut, and General Steelborne makes way to stand opposite me next to the table. Dorphne takes the chance to comfortably sit upon the chair.

'The letter,' I hold out my hand as General Steelborne digs in his pocket.

'It has to be here somewhere...' he smiles uncertainly as he searches in his other pocket. His silver hair is left open and bobs around as he hunts in his surcoat.

'You lost the letter?' I stare at him, astounded.

'Already?' Dorphne's light accent carries through the room, stifling a giggle.

'Did you take it?' asks General Steelborne.

'Why would I?' Dorphne scoffs in indignation.

'Ah, here it is,' a white paper roll is clumped in his fist when it emerges from the pocket of his pants.

'You shouldn't have left the letter in the room with them,' I say, grabbing it as he hands it over.

'One of the guards took the letter from the messenger when he arrived in the morning and could find neither of the Royal family members. The Lords and Ladies were early for the execution, and so the guard entrusted them with the letter.' General Steelborne explains.

'How do we know it's not a faux?' Dorphne asks.

'She has a point,' I mutter, unfolding it.

The paper crinkles. 'They seem to be planning my death already.'

'Your father assigned spies to follow them after Lord Lysander's plan failed.' He coughs at the last word. 'He had a hunch that they were trying to kill him.'

I feel like someone has taken a dagger and dug it through my chest. 'Father never told me.' My voice comes out quieter than I expected.

General Steelborne's eyes soften.

'Don't get distracted by the past,' Dorphne says from behind. 'Read the letter, come on.'

I nod, swallowing the lump in my throat. My heart beats erratically as I smooth out the yellow paper, neat flicks of the words devouring the letter whole. I already knew the gist of the contents, but then why was I so worried?

'The letter isn't going to bite you, you know?' Dorphne says.

I sigh in frustration, flapping the letter out on the table.

'Ruler of Ferrumisle, I hope this letter finds you in the best of health.'

Dorphne lets out a snort.

'I trust you have safely arrived at your abode, and as much as I wish to let you rest from all the commotion over the past few weeks, I am deeply concerned about a certain matter that has arisen amidst us.'

I resist a scoff. I most definitely did not arrive safely and have had barely a few hours of sleep. But a question lay ahead: what matter could be so important he wants to meet me alone?

I continue, pitching my voice a bit louder. 'I ask you to meet me in the Queen's Forest at exactly midnight tomorrow. The matter is of grave importance; thus I cannot expose it by quill or messenger for fear of being intercepted. I ask you to come without forces of any kind.'

'It's a trap; no one is blind enough to not see through those honey-dipped words,' Dorphne scoffs, coming to stand behind me.

I continue, reading out the next line. 'I understand if you choose not to associate yourself with me any longer.'

General Steelborne mumbles.

'What?' I ask.

He shakes his head in confusion. 'Associate? Why use the word associate?'

The pieces suddenly fall into place.

'Is he asking for your alliance?' Dorphne gasps. 'Is he really asking for a truce?'

I can't believe my eyes. Desmond wants us to be his ally?

'I trust you will make the right decision. None can know about this. Yours truly, King of Briarthorn Atoll.'

We stand in momentary silence.

'It might really be true. Look,' I say uncertainly, pointing to the signature. 'He has not addressed me with my name or as a Queen. Nor has he addressed himself by his name, to take precautions.'

'There is no address either.' Dorphne looks to General Steelborne.

'The letter arrived by messenger?'

He shakes his head. 'The messenger informed me that the letter had come through a Hræsvelgr.'

A hræsvelgr. A giant that can take the form of an eagle.

'But what if this letter was sent months ago and was intended for the King of Ferrumisle?' Dorphne asks.

'Why else would it be delivered now? Besides, then King Thaddeus would have expressed who he would like to meet. He would not have communicated by writing you or ruler.' I answer.

Wracking silence fills the room, thundering in my ears.

Is this really what Desmond wants to talk about? Alliances? Does he think I am a fool for accepting such a thing when he betrayed me?

I hear a faint whistle.

'Are you sure you still want to go, my Queen?' General Steelborne asks. My heart rackets. After a beat, I respond.

'Yes. Ready the carriages. We will go according to plan. My army must be settled at Fame's borders.'

'I will inform Drótt, my Qu-'

A thundering quake shakes the palace, the earth vibrating with fury. Dorphne shrieks, and I hear hollers and shouts from outside.

Everything jolts, the map falling to the floor and my head feeling dizzy. The door bursts open, and Felicio comes running in.

'Queen Victoria, there has been an attack,'

It takes a second for the words to register.

'Attack? What do you mean?' I ask. Lord Lysander had been right. But it couldn't be Desmond, could it?

Another rumbling shake reverberates through me, the crash

of a bomb so deafening it sweeps me off my feet. Felicio grabs my arm before I can fall.

'Who attacked?' I shout over the noise.

'My Queen!' Lord Lysander comes rushing in. The dim light above us all crashes into smithereens.

'We have to get her to safety!' Lord Asher appears from behind, and Felicio responds by ushering me out.

'Wait, no! Who has attacked?' I try pulling away from Felicio, but my attempts are useless.

'Guards!' Lord Asher roars.

But then the rumbling abruptly stops, the palace still shaking. The quakes ease to a low hum in the earth, and the clamours outside cease. Dorphne sighs in relief until a voice echoes around the room.

'This is the King of Fames,' I wince at the noise, discreetly slipping out of Felicio's grip. 'I have come to make an offer.'

An offer? I hold my breath, waiting for him to make his statement. General Steelborne shakes his head, and even though I know what King Vorin is about to say, the ice in his voice sends a shiver down my bones. 'I want your Queen. I want your Queen in return for your puny land!'

'So puny you want to conquer it,' Felicio snorts, rolling his eyes. A ghost of a smile lifts at the edge of Dorphne's lips before slipping away. I take in a deep breath. How weak must our defence have been that the King was able to penetrate our forces?

'For now, this castle will be mine. There is no use in calling for your guards. They have all been locked up. My men have already begun scouting the northern parts of Ferrumisle. I want to meet your Queen by midnight; otherwise, all your land will be is rubble and blood, just like your royal family!' A cackle bursts before morphing into coughs, and I have to cover my ears until the microphone is taken away from him.

'What does everyone have with meeting at midnight?' Felicio says again, and I groan.

'What do you think happened to Lancelot?' General Steelborne suddenly asks. Admiral Lancelot. I completely forgot about him.

'By the looks of it, he may be in Fames Prison, or he may be dead,' Lord Lysander casually answers.

Lord Asher stiffens beside him.

'Is the Queen all right?' Lady Rhiannon runs up to us from the end of the hall, and I spot Lady Emberlyn and Lady Celestia at her heels.

'Yes, she is,' General Steelborne affirms.

'And she will not be going anywhere any longer,' Lady Celestia says, perking her lips.

'I will leave tomorrow, no matter what happens,' I say, folding my arms.

'My Queen, you cannot possibly think of going anywhere when our land has been invaded by an allied nation with foreign guards swarming our palace. We need a place to lay low, and you need to talk to King Vorin!' Felicio says tiredly.

'A messenger can be sent to King Desmond, asking him to visit us, since the other possibility is void,' I retort.

'And you really think he will risk his life to come here?' Lady Celestia sniffs.

'Yes, because I'm equally sure Lord Lysander will hold off King Vorin long enough to give him the thought of retreating, unless he changes his mind, of course,' I reply sweetly, and Lord Lysander stiffens.

'Oh God. Who do you plan to send as a messenger?' Felicio questions.

'I do not trust anyone, so the only person I can send—' I turn to General Steelborne, whose face fleets in panic.

'Me?' he asks stupidly.

'Yes, you,' I say. 'Inform King Desmond of our current situation. I will try to talk this mess out with King Vorin.'

'But—'

'No buts. King Vorin is either calculated or mad, and if we do not obey him, we are not only risking our lives, but everyone in this land,' I say firmly, pursing my lips tightly.

'Oh look, she finally thought about us,' Lady Celestia murmurs. I ignore her, my heartbeat spiking.

'What does this have to do with King Desmond?' Lord Asher sighs.

'As far as we know, King Desmond wants to form an alliance with our land.'

Lady Emberlyn seems shaken. I hope I don't look as surprised as I am. I expected them to have figured it out already, what with staring at the paper for so long.

'But why?' she asks.

'As I'm sure we all know, the reason was not stated. That is why I have to meet him tomorrow.' I pause before continuing, 'General Steelborne, do not be so flustered; I will be fine.'

I reassuringly pat the General's shoulder before resuming. 'And if things get too messy here, I'm sure King Vorin won't mind his head on a pike.'

CHAPTER XVII

'Oh, look who we have here,' mocks King Vorin.

I make my way outside the castle, Lord Lysander and Dorphne at my heel. Felicio stands by my side holding an unsheathed sword. King Vorin breaks into a cackle.

'There will be no need for that, young man. We come in peace.'

His silver hair is thin and gelled back, wearing a marine blue coat lined with white cotton at the neck, his grey eyes forced to be a prominent feature amidst his sharp cheekbones and thick, snowy eyebrows. A white shirt is tucked into sleek pants the same colour, hidden under the coat. Unlike most kings, he has not grown lazy and continues to fight in any battle that may occur. Thus, the flat stomach.

'I'm sure trying to destroy our castle was for peace,' I remark, and King Vorin shakes his head.

'You mean I *failed* to destroy your castle,' he corrects me, gesturing to the still-standing fortress. The setting sun casts a low shadow over us all. A pillar has been bombed, but nothing more.

'Poor display of warfare from your side, although I'm hardly sure it can be called warfare anymore.' I smile as King Vorin's brows furrow into fury. He was well known for failing to hit his target, and it had become a joke between royalty and lords and ladies alike.

'Speaking of warfare, what brings you to my land?' I casually ask, halting behind the fallen wooden door. It had been cut down, the ropes frayed. King Vorin stood some few metres away, a carriage pulling behind him. Fames was home to a land of many creatures, some of which I never knew even existed, and each species had a lord or lady to be their leader, but not both.

'I hear you want to form an alliance with us,' King Vorin says.

'And that you have already accepted,' I continue for him. His lips purse before resuming.

'Yet, it has come to my knowledge you attempted to kill King Desmond.'

I stiffen.

'What, may I ask, would I expect of you if you chose to slaughter your own ally?' he finishes.

'That was Avalorian's plan.' I refer to Father by his name. Hopefully, it will make me seem more detached from the ways of my family. 'He wanted Xavier to kill Desmond, and I only attempted to kill Desmond for his murderous acts towards my family.'

'Leave you to do all the dirty work, eh?' King Vorin chortles.

'But what I don't understand is why you came all this way just to ask a simple question whilst attacking innocent victims?' I ask, clasping my hands in front of me.

'It came to my notice you intended to threaten my reasons about keeping Desmond's contact with our land a secret from you.' King Vorin cocks an eyebrow.

'Well, certain precautions have to be taken, don't they?' I reply sweetly, not missing a beat.

'Where is Admiral Lancelot?' Felicio suddenly asks from behind. His voice is muffled under the helmet, but despite that, I hear his teeth grinding together.

'Oh, your messenger? Don't worry, he will arrive soon. I just wanted you all to bear a bit of punishment for attempting to have my head.' He smiles sickly, and I widen my pathetic grin, acting a bit shocked before ushering him inside.

'Of course. My apologies for keeping you waiting so long outside. Come, enjoy our hospitality. Let us discuss matters over a goblet of wine, shall we?' I say, snapping my fingers.

Felicio sheathes his sword with too much force before guiding the King into the castle. At least he doesn't contradict the fact about being our ally.

I'm about to turn when the carriage door squeaks open and I see a woman with sleek, oily hair the colour of a raven's feather step off the carriage. She hoists an umbrella adorned with raven feathers, yet is dressed in all white. It is a contrast from her shocking blood lips and wide crimson eyes, deep black circles enunciating them even more. Her blocky heels create a hollow sound as they click over wood, halting before me.

'Ah, Victoria, we meet again.' Lady Drusilla drawls. 'Or should I say, *Queen* Victoria?'

She bows curtly before standing. 'Come, it is nearly dark. What causes you to stay out for so long?' She pouts before smiling. 'Am I really that worthy of your attention?'

Drusilla links our arms together as Lord Bardulf Conri, the Lord of Werewolves, emerges.

His bushy beard is enough to tell the time is near. In a mere two weeks, he will be a stray wolf just like all the rest. They will be forced to roam in the Centre where no one can be harmed. But I fear in two weeks there may no longer be an Aetheria.

I mask my emotions with a soft smile matching Drusilla's, leading her inside the castle, Lord Bardulf following close. The banquet hall is just a few rooms away, and candlelit lamps light our way through. General Steelborne has managed to exit the castle through our underground passages, carrying my message by letter, as I'm sure Desmond would hardly pay heed to him at all and would not trust Steelborne if he brought my greetings through word.

Desmond would agree.

Anything to have a chance at my neck.

'How does it feel to finally be Queen?' Drusilla suddenly asks. I'm a bit taken aback. Of all the things I expected the Lady of Vampires and Vampiresses to say, this was not one of them. But then again, a Lady always wants more.

'Conflicting,' I answer truthfully. There is momentary silence, the thumping of Drusilla and Bardulf's clumped boots with the soft pat of my heels against the red carpet.

'What of the other Lords and Ladies?' I question, steering her to the right. I can hear the clamours and laughter from the Banquet Hall.

'Only the most influential were to arrive, considering your services are more powerful than many,' Drusilla drawls, placing a hand to her chest. I cannot deny what she said. We do have the most militarised land out of all.

'Where is Prince Arnold?' I ask again. It strikes me as strange that he has not arrived; I was sure he would have questions about Xavier's death, considering how close they were.

Drusilla shrugs, but Bardulf's scratchy response surprises me. 'He will arrive momentarily.'

I nod, not sparing a glance back. My smile falters as we enter the banquet hall, where the Lords and Ladies of Ferrumisle and Fames are bustling and laughing. Wine sloshes around in their goblets and rims their mouths a light red, voices pitched high as they interact with King Vorin.

We walk towards the small crowd, but because of the music blaring from the band and the overlapping voices, I am left unheard.

'King Vorin,' Drusilla coughs, and the King's attention reverts to me.

'I believe we have amends to make,' I say loudly.

'Ah, of course. Lady Emberlyn, we shall meet later,' he nods to Emberlyn before following Lady Drusilla, Lord Badrulf, and me to a small table near the corner of the room, large enough for five but small enough to share a secret or two.

King Vorin sits opposite me, and it is with unease I realise he may be a foot taller than I expected. I almost feel cowered in his presence.

'So it is agreed, we have an alliance?' I ask, starting the conversation without a moment's hesitation.

'Yes.' King Vorin confirms, pulling a chair to take a seat. 'Our troops confirm that Queen Nyx has made no move to leave Inferis, although the banshees and nixies have been spreading quite a plague of harmonious wails.' King Vorin shudders.

'It is a warning,' I say, looking around at all of them. Drusilla and Bardulf take a seat. 'The time is coming near. My troops are being prepared for the war ahead, and our land is to begin fortifying tomorrow morning.'

I drum the wooden table with delicate fingers, tilting my head as I reveal the shocking information to them. 'And we may have another alliance on our hands as well.'

'Another?' King Vorin looks at me suspiciously, grey eyes clouding in judgement, and I shake my head before explaining Desmond's letter and request to them all.

'And you are sure this is not a trap to lure you out into the open and fire?' King Vorin asks.

'No, I'm not. Which is why a messenger has been sent to King Desmond informing him of our thoughts.'

'You sent your most trusted advisor?' Lord Bardulf glares me down with fiery orange eyes, sizing me up and perhaps questioning my stupidity.

'Yes, for he knows how to protect himself. I have no worries. Killing him would mean acting on emotions and would only make Desmond seem craven rather than powerful. If he has the Blood Crown, why can he not look me in the eyes and drag his sword over my throat?' I raise a delicate eyebrow, challenging him.

Lord Bardulf only scowls, grumbling as King Vorin asks, 'Say tomorrow is not a trap, how will you convince King Desmond to destroy the crown?'

Destroy the crown.

In all my plotting, these three words had never appeared once.

I laugh, hoping they do not see through me. But seriously, who in their right mind would want to destroy the Blood Crown? If that is what they came here to do, then I'll play along until I have to snap their necks in half.

'Desmond is smart. When the time comes, he will give up the crown and destroy it for himself. As arrogant as he may be, he would not risk the rest of the world for his power.' Even as I say the words, self-loathing washes over me like a cold bath on a winter's day, sending shivers down my spine. The hypocrisy in me is one any individual would surely admire.

'And how do we know you will not turn on us if you somehow retrieve the crown?' Lady Drusilla clamps her hands in front of her, long pink nails stretching out an inch, clenching together as they turn red.

'If King Vorin has accepted my alliance, I'm sure you trust him enough to follow my lead,' I say instead, smiling as wide as I can, my cheeks aching in pain.

A rumble reverberates through the palace floors, quaking my insides. The hilt of a sword or two strikes the stony ground, a hollow sound echoing. A clatter of footsteps can be heard scuffling towards us. A few gasps escape the wandering ladies, and Lady Drusilla stiffens. I have to resist the urge to smack my head, for before I turn around, I know that the one and only person who can elicit such a response is Prince Arnold.

'Queen Victoria,' a voice stiffly calls me from behind, but it is far away, booming through the hall. The soft whispers of the ladies evaporate into thin air, swimming around to fall onto the suspecting ears of another. I turn, widening my smile.

'Why, Prince Arnold.' I place emphasis on Prince.

It takes only a few long strides before we are mere feet apart, piercing green eyes digging into mine. His deep marine velvet robe glistens with gems no bigger than a millimetre along each diamond point, concealing the white dress shirt tucked into ebony pants. Arnold holds a crystal-studded sceptre in his right hand, the other crammed in his pocket.

'We need to talk.' He does not give a second glance to Drusilla or Bardulf, only nodding once at his father. Arnold's golden chestnut hair is sleeked back with what seems to be aloe vera.

His guards behind him look tired, and they struggle to calm their shaking hands.

'Of course. Come along,' I usher him to follow and hear a grunt before the clump of Arnold's knee-high boots cautiously falls into step behind me. Passing the Lords and Ladies, Lord Lysander casts me a grim tight-lipped smile, whilst the others ignore me.

Lady Celestia scoffs softly, holding her head up high. I expected a reassuring grin from Lord Asher or Lady Emberlyn, but none came, and my heart sinks a bit.

Only a bit, though. Not enough to inflict any pain.

I find Felicio leaning against the wall, and he sulkily looks away as I pass by him.

'Get into shape,' I hiss. 'Make sure everything stays in order and nothing goes wrong.'

He rolls his eyes, muttering something under his breath. I glare at him before quickening my pace, suddenly aware of Arnold's shadow tickling my back.

We exit the hall, and I immediately turn left for the Palace Gardens. What better place to reunite with Prince Arnold than to remind him of the time he helped Xavier push me off a cliff? A sinking feeling erupts in my stomach, as if a stone is pressing against my gut. I am very well aware that Arnold could try killing me, but I shake off the sensation.

'Where are we going?'

My stomach constricts tighter, but panic tinges his voice. He's still the scared little boy he once was.

'The Palace Gardens,' I reply, pitching my voice a notch higher with a little bit of enthusiasm. I can't see him, but I've known him long enough to guess his bushy eyebrows have been pulled into a fearful frown.

After what seems like an eternity, we reach the Palace Garden doors. They are tall, towering even over Arnold, carved from birchwood and polished until they seem like marble. Two golden brass doorknobs stick out in the dim candlelight of the corridor, and eerie shadows form on the carpet below us. I see Arnold's silhouette rub one foot behind the other.

'What are you here for?' I ask him quietly. My voice carries in the hall, light but slithery. I take a few steps forward, making way to pull open the door while concentrating on Arnold's outline. His shadow mirrors my movement, and when I tug open the birch handles, it comes back as smoothly as metal gliding over skin.

Arnold brushes past me into the garden, the grazed grass crushing under his boots. I notice his guards lingering in the back, ready to follow, but I put up a hand before they can do so. I step into the cold breeze, allowing it to blow through the layers of my dress. All my frantic nerves die away, and I feel my erratic heart slow. Without looking back, I let the doors shut, a thud reverberating through the earth.

The evening has faded into midnight, the waning crescent looming over us ominously. I hear Arnold breathe in shakily before he speaks.

'I wanted to have a little chat. About the night Xavier passed,' Not killed, not murdered. Just passed.

And just like that, the wind calms into a cool blow, then gradually, it transforms into a small puff of breath. The whistling subsides, and the trees still. It was as if a feather had finally made contact with the flowery earth after a horrendous hurricane. All around us, brambles and sticks lay untouched from the boys' last game.

It has been years since I last came here.

Xavier had been murdered. Desmond had killed him.

But that is all I had ever thought of it as. A murder. I didn't vow revenge. I ran. I ran and ran and ran so I wouldn't befall the same path they all did. It had gotten me what I wanted. To be Queen. But it never brought the respect I desired.

Did I even stop to think about Xavier? I always brushed it aside. I never really tried to mourn, I was just... I was just what? Afraid? Afraid that when I thought about him all the guilt would come crashing down on my heart and splinter and crack it, hijack itself into a confounding puzzle so much so that I wouldn't be able to put myself back together?

'It's just that I hadn't really met Xavier since, you know, the inci-'

I feel a dagger dig through my chest and gyrate, slicing my soul with each twist and turn. How long has it been since I last thought of him? The sudden realisation catches me off guard, and it must be evident on my face because Arnold stares at me wide-eyed.

'Sorry, did I say something wr-'

'No! No, no,' I hesitantly chuckle, embarrassment washing over me. A Queen should not be acting like this. I look around, spotting the cliff. The ragged, crumbling old cliff that had led to the acknowledgement of my family's betrayal and the burst of my rebellion.

I glance over to Arnold, who violently shakes his head. 'Maybe we should just stay he-'

I grab him by the arm and drag him forward anyway.

'Victoria—' Arnold muffles a yelp as I lock arms with him, pulling him down before he can embed himself into a tree. His muscular physique flexes under my palm, and I pull away immediately. We brush past a few bushes, winding our way around the poppies and lilacs that litter the garden in feverish colours.

Arnold's fingers wrap around my wrist as we finally reach for the cliff. A single, bony bark of a tree is perched slanted, a lone leaf withering away. Silence envelopes us, Arnold's heavy breathing barely noticeable as my own throat constricts.

Never did I ever think I would be standing over my own grave.

'So,' I swallow, 'what did you want to ask me again?'

Arnold opens his mouth, then closes it. Then suddenly, he begins fumbling with his coat.

'What on Aetheria—' I take a step back as he removes and flourishes his cloth over the ground. It lands with a hard thwack, before he makes way to sit.

'Come.' He taps the open space next to him, and I reluctantly settle down, gingerly pulling my dress up an inch for a more comfortable position.

The warmth of his body seeps into the cloth and tingles my body with familiar energy. I remember lying beside Desmond, but as quickly as the thought appears, I push it to the depths of my mind.

'Xavier,' Arnold says. 'I wanted to talk about Xavier. What exactly—happened?'

I sigh, then launch into the epic expedition which had taken place merely a week ago. Throughout this time, Arnold's expression remains passive, only crumbling when I mention Xavier's gut-wrenching death.

'Nathaniel killed him?' Arnold clenches his hands into tight fists, clawing at the soil in the ground. It gives way in his fingers as he attempts to hold it.

'And Xavier really did kill King Avalorian and Thaddeus?' Arnold asks again when I don't reply.

'Desmond killed them. Desmond killed them all,' I grit my teeth, begging my heart to blow off steam. Fury. What a tiring emotion. It really is an art to keep it fuelled.

I continue to explain our plan, how Desmond has contacted me and how King Vorin agreed to the alliance after a minor setback.

'That's Father for you. Will do everything and nothing to assert authority,' Arnold sighs, cracking his knuckles. The sharp noises rupture the air like lightning, and I wince at every split.

'How will you inform him of your change in setting?' Arnold asks, looking to me.

'I sent General Steelborne,' I answer. He nods, flexing his arms, his jaw firmly set.

'What's wrong?' I ask, tilting my head. 'I understand why Nathaniel would kill Xavier and King Avalorian, but why kill Elysande?' Arnold chews his bottom lip, searching my face for a reaction.

I don't give him one. I've had enough talk, making way to stand up. 'Some things are best left unsaid.'

Confusion clouds his complexion before he shakes himself. He looks away, blinking in what seems to be shock. When Arnold speaks, his teeth grind against each other.

'You've changed.' I choke out a laugh. 'You barely know me. Was I so petty that I grabbed your attention?'

Hurt flickers across his eyes. 'I didn't mean to insult you.' He pulls himself up, glaring at me.

'Like I said. You barely know me. Why would I be insulted by a common remark?'

Pity settles in my stomach, flooding to my lungs. Oh, how much I *have* changed. That young girl who would once listen to everyone because she was told to, only to soon be the Queen of nothing. What was all this even for? To prove myself worthy to a crowd who will never believe me?

But I vowed to make them surrender in belief—and I will.

If Desmond really wishes for an alliance, three kingdoms against one would for sure mean victory.

Queen Nyx is fuelled by vengeance. She will be blinded by it when she sees the world come against her once more. I fidget with the collar of my dress, impatiently waiting for His Highness Arnold Lou Vorin to dust his coat and throw it over his shoulders.

'Did they bury his body?' he suddenly asks. I turn and begin walking, playing with my fingers, attempting to covet the humiliation that tinges my face. I nearly trip over my dress in my hurry, but Arnold catches me, wrists encircling my arm.

'You don't know, do you?' His voice is low, threatening.

'They said they buried him,' I say, not daring to look in his eyes, hoping my voice comes out cool.

He lets go of me, scoffing. 'Some sister you are.'

'Some brother he was,' I retort, but guilt fishes in my stomach all the same.

'And you're sure you didn't kill Xavier?' Arnold perks an eyebrow, and I nearly gag.

'I would never kill Xavier!' I try to keep the panic out of my voice. Why was I so worried, so guilty?

'He tried to kill you. And I can't believe I'm saying this, but—' Arnold shakes his head, digging his hands into his pockets. 'The girl I remember would have always been kind to even the worst. The woman I see in front of me would do anything to secure her crown.'

And just like that, the fire roars alive in my chest once more, decapitating all the nerves that trembled me.

A small, mirthless smirk plays on my lips. 'Oh, really? I'm

ecstatic about your humbling observation. But I really was
hoping for a more... queenly title.'

'You mean the Queen of nothing? You will not have anything
any longer, Victoria! Look around you! Look at the mess you
have created! All because of one little problem?' Arnold roars,
wrenching the words out of his mouth. His hands are out,
balled into tight fists.

'Little problem?' I burst. 'Xavier stole my throne! Xavier
took my power! Xavier took everything I stood for and reduced
me to ashes!' I scream.

I am aware of the heat coursing through my veins, the
trepidation spreading across Arnold's face.

'Would you sit there and let someone break you until you
were nobody?' I bellow, waving my hands about furiously.
'Because I did. And look where that got me. Look who I am now
because of everyone around me!'

I unsheathe the dagger hidden under the crevices of my
dress, whipping it around and rushing at Arnold with it.

But he is fast.

He pulls his sword from the air and our knives clang
together, echoing through the quiet night.

'Victoria,' he says calmly, but his eyes are filled with alarm.
Good. He has every right to witness the monster I have found
within me.

'Victoria, don't do this. Victoria, don't do that,' I mock,
easily dodging a blow he aimlessly strikes. Another deafening
clank bursts into the air. 'And I—I,' I can't bring myself to
say the words.

'And you listened,' Arnold offers, and I bring down my
dagger hard onto his shoulder, only to be rebounded by the
impact of his sword.

A crash reverberates.

I push back, finding my ground once more, soles digging

into the soil, crunching the flowers that once embellished the garden. We prowl each other, breaths ragged.

'And I listened,' I repeat. I lunge forward again. A crack of his sword elicits a sharp scream from me as I feel the thick liquid ooze out of my cheek. The skin where the metal has contacted burns in agony, but instead of cursing, I laugh. I laugh a horrendous, monstrous laugh. 'Well, Arnold, where did that get me?'

My breathless words have Arnold staring at me like I'm crazy. Nobody ever said I wasn't. 'To become a madwoman,' he snorts in reply.

'Yes, a madwoman. So, whose fault is this?' I pout, striding forward. With every step I take, Arnold retreats.

'There's a reason princesses are meant to be petite,' he growls, and my wrath spikes up a notch, my heart dancing in rhythm with our feet, frantic and angry.

'I am not a princess!' I roar. The dagger comes clashing down, and Arnold falls backward on impact. I can hear the scuffles and terrified whispers behind the doors we are so far away from. The door that determines Arnold's fate.

If it unbolts, he shall live. If it remains shut, he shall die.

Oh, the pleasure I will feel when I reduce him to rotten flesh and bones.

I dodge his every blow, swiping and slashing as he backs further and further, clinging to the dirt to save himself from my blade. Finally, the last blow renders him unarmed. His sword flies, but I feel the satisfaction only when the realisation slaps Arnold in the face of where the sword has landed.

'Brings back old memories, doesn't it?' I sigh pleasantly before correcting myself. 'Sorry, I forgot you never experienced this.'

I bend down, pulling him by the collar. He lets out a soft whimper. I scoff, pushing him back. Arnold yelps, only saving himself in time as the rubble crumbles under his weight. Even the slightest tremble could cause the cliff to give way.

'You know, I should be more considerate.' I giggle, moving away from him. The rock cracks irreparably.

'Victoria, please—' Arnold pleads. He tries to follow, but another crack splinters his way.

'It's okay, Arnold. It'll be a quick death,' I assure him, smiling sweetly.

'Victoria, please!' I raise my hands in the air, the dagger falling from my grip.

'No!' His voice thunders through the night, the doors bellowing open as frantic shrieks echo. I halt, snapping out of the scene.

Luckily, the cliff doesn't.

'Father!' Arnold yells. He gropes forward, but that just might've been the biggest mistake of his life. Second only to planning a private chat with me.

The cliff gives way, and a rumble reverberates through the night. 'No, Arnold!' King Vornin roars as the guards behind him run forward to save his son.

'You witch!' The King rounds on me, but for some odd reason, I feel no fear. I stare him dead in the eyes as he stalks towards me, before a hard crack splinters the air and everything goes black.

CHAPTER XVIII

'She's a monster!' someone roars.

'Arnold, plea-' another voice says.

'Please what, Father? She tried to kill me!' interrupts the other.

'We have an alliance, son.'

'Break it! You weren't there when she bashed me with a single dagger! You should have seen the hatred in her eyes! I wasn't staring at the girl I knew four years ago. I was fighting a goddamn monster!'

I feel strangely numb. I try turning, but a spasm of pain snatches a strangled gasp from my throat. The voices die as the mattress squeaks under my pressure. There is momentary silence, a vacuum of sound that only amplifies the chaos in my mind.

'Arnold, if you really claim she is as scary, then why do you intend to have this conversation here?' hisses King Vorin.

'Because I'm not scared of her. I'm scared of the burning rage inside,' Arnold answers.

I'm half dead, but even I groan at the stupidity of his explanation.

'Arnold, are you stupid? The burning rage inside her is what makes her a monster!' King Vorin exclaims.

'So can we leave? This woman is nothing but a misunderstood soul that is already wrecking our world! If we agree to participate in this war, Aetheria will be no more!' Arnold argues.

I can barely breathe, let alone understand what is happening. I catch a few more mumbled exchanges of words before everything returns to pitch black.

'Victoria? Victoria?' Frantic arms shake me awake, and I muster all my strength to open my eyes. I feel like I'm reliving the night Desmond drugged me to sleep.

'What?' My voice comes out sharp. I focus my blurry gaze on the young woman in front of me.

Her face is pulled into one of disappointment, fury melting her emerald eyes.

'Where were you?' I ask Dorphne, the words coming out mumbled.

'Shadowing you so you wouldn't do something stupid, which you did.' Dorphne's lips settle into a grim line. 'Although I'm surprised you never asked about me.'

I open my mouth to answer, then shut it abruptly.

Xavier stole my throne! Xavier took my power!

I groan, shaking my head. I feel like I'm being thrust backward, and my hand instinctively touches the burning sensation on my head. I feel something wet and pull my hand away to see hot, crimson blood. I look up at Dorphne questioningly, but all she does is stare.

Then it all comes back, as sharp as the dagger must have been for Xavier, plunging into my gut.

My stomach sinks, and the scenes feel so vivid, so real as I see Arnold crumbling down with the cliff, a sense of unease clawing at me. *Where did that get me? To become a madwoman.*

My blood surges at the memory, but I bury it under the rest of my pain.

There's a reason princesses are meant to be petite. I am not a princess! Even now, I can still hear the roughness of my voice.

The hard edges of my words. The seething anger coursing through the string of retorts I spat.

But nothing could miss the fact that I had lost control. I had lost control of the little ball of fire inside me years ago, but now the little spark was a raging forest.

I knew it would get to me somehow. Sometime. But it felt so surreal. So unlike myself, yet the very being I was meant to be. I feel my lips part as the hollow words whisper raspily in my head.

'Is this what change feels like?'

Dorphne blinks, tilting her head to make sense of what I was saying.

So much pain fury, and frustration built up until my heart exploded, shredding muscle and skin inside my chest until it was new and whole, red but void.

But I cannot even make sense of it myself. If this is change, if this is who I am meant to become, it satisfies me.

I haven't been oblivious to the changes in me. The demanding nature, the commanding attitude, the seething fury I resort to the moment someone attempts to cover me in grime—yet it feels like freedom. The taste of fresh air after being let out from a prison I was locked in for decades.

It's okay, Arnold. It'll be a quick death.

What had gotten into me? What had made me so desperate that I wanted to kill him? I search for a reason, scour the depths of my heart, breathing raggedly as Dorphne helps me lay back down.

I am hyperventilating, and she frantically calls out for a name I cannot decipher. Maybe Lady Emberlyn. Or General Steelborne.

I see a nurse walk in, her face drowning in panic as she places a hand on my pulse. I strain to do the same, to see what had caused her such alarm.

'At least a hundred and seventy-five beats per minute!' shrieks the nurse.

Fear gushes through my body.

I try to make sense of what has happened. Try hard not to focus on the fact that I could die.

Why? Because of fear.

I killed Arnold. I had broken our alliance. But hadn't I heard him just now? Just a few moments before I was shaken awake by Dorphne?

I toss around, cracking my fingers nervously. The sound whips through the air, I'm sure, but it is barely audible inside the chaos of my head.

I hear a small scream. The blanket is ripped off my body and the cold envelops me warmly, like I am no stranger to its attitude. A hand is placed above my left breast, and a frightened nurse calls out, her voice strangled.

'One hundred and ninety-one!'

The sudden realisation gashes me across the face. Arnold stands over me with a dagger, and I tense at the impact. I touch my cheek, the hot sensation immediately subsiding after coming into contact with my frozen hands.

When I pull my hand away, blood seeps through the cracks in my skin, trailing down in thin, crimson streams.

Everyone goes stagnant, yet time ticks by. My heart thunders on. Faster than what I'm used to.

'That,' he says gravely, 'is for trying to kill me.'

How had he survived?

His eyes are filled with venom, loathing, and every other vile emotion I could possibly think of. For some reason, I feel nothing. I don't feel the need to punch him or grab his neck. A part of me had been expecting to be beaten up by Arnold, but this wasn't what I had in mind. He really is too much of a kind soul.

But his words aren't, a small voice hisses.

And then the thought I had been needling through the carpet for appears as clear as day before my eyes.

I had not tried to kill him because I was mad at him. I tried to kill him out of impulse. Because I wanted to do it again. Because the thought of having control over some situation appealed to me.

And although the very thought of this inhumane monster inside me chills me to the bone, I cannot deny that the sheer satisfaction I felt throughout was brutally piquant.

'What happened?' I finally ask, voice hoarse. For a split second, I watch as Arnold's hard eyes soften, but just as quickly as the barrier dissipated, it was put up once more.

The nurse beside me sighs, dropping my wrist. 'My Queen, it is best if you stay in bed and shun your duties until you are well again,' she suggests.

Her ebony hair is tied up neatly in a bun, a gem gleaming on each of her hands. Her fingers are long and bony, the phoenix sprawling across her bare neck. The clothes she wears have no design. It is all plain black, nearly blending in with the dim torchlight of the dungeon.

'Dungeon,' I repeat softly. My heartbeat picks up again. I look wildly around for bars, the victims of Desmond. Genevieve and Lorelei. Xavier. Anyone.

'Victoria!' a voice snaps me out of my thoughts. I turn to Dorphne, who cups my face in both of her hands, forcing me to stare into her eyes.

'We're fine, you're fine,' she digs her fingers into my cheekbones. 'We aren't there anymore,'

I take a deep breath, closing my eyes before nodding my head, swallowing.

Beside me, Arnold scoffs. 'Victoria needs reassurance? I'm the one who nearly died tumbling off a cliff she pushed me from!'

'Stop whining,' demands Dorphne, placing her hands on her hips. There's the accent again. Her words are rushed, pronouncing the letter 'o' as a 'u.'

'Don't tell me what to do, girl,' Arnold spits, and Dorphne

lands an equally painful strike across his face, a smarting sound echoing. I stare at her with wide eyes, Arnold staggering back in shock.

'What was that for?' he finally gasps, clutching his red cheek.

'For acting like I'm lower than you are. How the hell did you not die?'

Arnold recovers quickly, his face stony. 'Father saved me in time. Slid across the slide of the cliff and grabbed my hand while our soldiers helped us up.'

You witch!

I shake my head frantically, remembering the anger scrawled across King Vorin's face.

Dorphne lets out a chuckle. 'Would've been nice of you to join your mother in hell.'

'I am your Prin—' Arnold stalks forward, his face flushing red, matching the colour of his bruised cheek.

'Son,' a voice cuts through the chaos.

I pull myself up slowly, grunting when I see King Vorin appearing beside the boulder door. The slab of stone crumbles as it slides to the side.

I manage to sit upright, and a brick of dizziness slams into me. *You witch!* The nurse grabs a cold cloth and applies it to my cheek. The water drips down the side of my face, some drops clear, some drops pink.

'I see you are healed, Queen Victoria,' King Vorin raises his eyebrow, passing a pleasant smile as he comes to sit beside me on a cobblestone stool.

'Not as much as Arnold is,' I manage to bite out.

King Vorin ignores me.

'I think it is time to reassess your alliance with Ferrumisle,' Arnold says sharply, turning to his father.

'I think not,' I croak out, something like desperation crawling into my voice.

He must have noticed my despair, for after a beat, King Vorin replies, 'I think—yes.' He stifles a cough.

'We will disappear,' King Vorin says simply.

'And you think the Council would protect you?' I cough over my words. The nurse presses the wet cloth tighter to my cheek. Crusts of blood fall to the bedding.

King Vorin was planning to escape to Caelumterra before the war began. 'Why, yes,' he answers, eyeing me with a devilish gleam. 'They would protect us and make us more powerful. Queen Nyx would not dare to hurt us.'

'Think about it, King Vorin. You really want to sit back and watch the rest of the lands die at the hands of Queen Nyx? You think you can escape her wrath, hold the deaths of millions on your hands, including your own people?' I taunt, my voice wheezy.

He shrugs.

I try again, raising my voice a bit. 'Queen Nyx will know.'

'Not unless you are dead,' Arnold retorts. I chuckle, my laugh morphing into a cacophony of coughs.

The nurse flinches.

Dorphne places a hand over mine.

'You can't run,' I rasp. 'We have you surrounded. One wrong move and your Kingdom can fall.' I cough again, doubling over. I barely avoid the metal rods.

I wheeze, pulling myself up. 'She will not stop until she has the neck of every King and Queen in Aetheria. You think the Kings and Queens before, who came down to help five thousand years ago, stopped the war?'

I look up to see the dawn of realisation stretch over the father and son's faces. A grim smile tugs at my lips. They could not disobey me now.

Their Kingdom would be tarnished by the time they left. They would have no time to prepare for anything.

'The admiral.' Arnold kicks the bed hard, and I jerk with impact. The nurse glares at him, but he rolls his eyes at her.

'It's okay, Father. Leave Fames. We can escape,' Arnold says, turning to his father. King Vorin looks around slowly, as if trying to process the information.

'We cannot just abandon our Kingdom, son. We have a duty.'

'So? Father, she tried to kill me!' Arnold flails his hands about, and I see the guilt glisten King Vorin's eyes. He's trapped. A rush of adrenaline gushes through me, and I feel the same impulse I had when I nearly killed Arnold.

It was triumph; it was power. This is everything I could have ever asked for. But I didn't ask for just this—I asked for more.

'Very well then,' Arnold says. 'So the alliance is broken?'

I cannot even fathom what Arnold has just said.

Dorphne stares at him, green eyes wide in disbelief, then she curses loudly. 'How in Aetheria is he a prince! I always told Mummy he was dumb!'

The very thought of his stupidity makes me yearn for Desmond. His calculated responses, his ingenious mind.

'No, it's not,' I whisper again.

'Yes, it is?' Arnold looks uncertainly towards his father, and King Vorin shakes his head.

'She is right,'

Arnold's face falls.

It's like watching him tumble over the cliff all over again. The shock in his eyes, the betrayal, the fear, the realisation that he was about to die at my hands.

How much more did I need to feed this insatiable desire of mine?

King Vorin sighs.

'Are you really going to trust this psychopath over me?' There is deafening silence. It bounds off the dungeon walls and echoes in my ears like the echo of a gong. Even Dorphne goes quiet.

'Forget it.' Arnold shoves his chestnut hair out of his face. I watch as he mutters something under his breath, taking his coat from the carved ledge.

'Son, I—'

'I said forget it, Father.' He swings the coat over his head, making way to leave the dungeon. He looks back, glaring at me, then returns his gaze to King Vorin.

'You're making a big mistake, Father.'

King Vorin looks away, a cough burbling up in his chest. He sighs, turning around to move the boulder.

As he does so, I hear the patter of footsteps.

Urgent footsteps. They are lofty and chunky, and as they grow closer, I know immediately who it is. I push off the bed, and the nurse gasps, urging me to get back in. I feel fine. I am fine. This pathetic nightgown fails to make me look anything other than a ragged teenage girl who has no clue what is to be done in her life.

Before I can warn him, General Steelborne collapses into Arnold, who lets out a yell of pain.

'Steelborne, what happened?' I say, my words mixing with Dorphne's gasp: 'Are you okay?'

General Steelborne wheezes, getting to his knees. The nurse hurries over to him, hollering out orders to the rest. He is bruised and his face is swollen. Blood clumps his clothes, that are torn from the seams.

'I'm fine.' He gives me a pointed look. He breathes in, then out, before saying, 'King Desmond needs to meet you.'

'What?' I breathe.

'He said it is urgent. You need to go now. To the Centre.' He doubles over in pain.

'Steelborne, why?'

'Victoria, I said go—now!'

I shake myself, turning to Dorphne. 'Get my clothes. And Felicio.'

'What about Lord Lysander?' Dorphne asks.

'Prepare the army,' I order, almost missing her question.

'Why? You're just meeting Desmond,' Dorphne argues.

I round on her, fury igniting my blood as if it were gasoline, spreading to every part of my body. 'Do what I say and get the work done. Now!'

This was the perfect opportunity to steal the Blood Crown. Even if Nyx didn't kill Desmond, I would, and what's better than having twice the revenge?

Victoria Ironhart,
Day 2,

~

Woe has harboured more than sadness;
it has evolved into hatred,
into madness,
for sadness leads to a thirst to prove oneself,
thirst is an adequation of desire—an ambition so cruel,
and for me, desire dawns vengeance,
A retribution that provokes a revolution.

~

I think I'm crazy.

I don't think it's that hard to believe, honestly.

The thoughts that have been bursting forth in my mind are strangely enticing—delicious.

It's like I can taste the blood melting in my mouth; the victory on my tongue. I was so close. I was so, so, so close. I would finally have everything I ever wanted: the world.

But I was going to do something else.

Burn Aetheria. Burn Aetheria to the ground and watch as the flames devour the lands whole, lapping furiously and burning all those who dare wrong me. Those who dared to betray me even when they knew what I went through.

I was going to burn Aetheria to the core, and when I did, I would be able to hold the ashes and say I had the world at my feet. They are already trapped—all of them. I know it.

Once I have found them, I would make them witness their home burn, and then I would smoulder them next until only I remained, until the Council was forced to succumb to the horrible realisation of their foolishness at writing my destiny the way it should never have been.

CHAPTER XIX

The carriage wheels crunch the forest leaves as we ride through Fames. It has nearly been an hour since we left Ferrumisle. Dorphne had brought a blood-red leather suit for me to wear, puffed at the cuffs in black and laced with gold. Nothing but a singular crown rests on my head, bejewelled in carbonado and silver. My hair had been tied in an elegant bun so that the silver wouldn't sear through my head.

'Was it true?' Dorphne suddenly asks.

Felicio rides the carriage, and General Steelborne sits opposite us.

'What?' I wring my head a bit, arching a brow.

'That you sent Admiral Lancelot to be captured on purpose?' Dorphne rephrases, her face scrunched in confusion.

I laugh. 'No! I had to threaten him with something. It's a matter of quick thinking, really.'

'Why did you have to threaten him?' General Steelborne asks, looking from me to Dorphne. She blanches, so I respond. 'Arnold was testing my patience.' Steelborne stares at me for a moment before understanding dawns across his features.

'Victoria, you cannot go around trying to kill your alliances,' he says softly.

'And I cannot let them keep degrading me for who I really am,' I retort, leaning on the window.

'No one is degrading you, Victoria,' Dorphne starts, but I cut her off.

'They have, and they always will. And the only way to make them see that I am worthy of my throne is by bearing the Blood Crown.'

It is midnight by the time we cross the border of Fames.

'You must approach with caution,' warns General Steelborne. I make my way to leave the carriage before two arms grab me from behind, dragging me into a hug.

'Don't let him kill you,' Dorphne whispers fiercely into my ear. I tap her hand lightly, and she lets go.

'I'll be fine. Make sure the army is prepared if an attack is to be orchestrated.'

General Steelborne nods curtly, then I take off into the darkness.

'You came,' a low, husky voice erupts from a shadow behind me. The moon is lit, but only three quarters.

'Yes, I did.' I turn, catching sight of Desmond. His pale face is illuminated in the moonlight, his mustard eyes a vibrant gold boring into me.

I can hardly make out his hair from the rest of his body, but the slight curve at the top shows it has grown. I notice a scar dragging above his eyebrow, the black blood crusted.

'Why did you want to meet?' I ask, the question that has been gnawing at my mind ever since the letter arrived.

'Wrong question, *Venefica*.' The name sets my muscles on fire.

'Tell me,' I hiss, stalking closer to him.

'If I answer yours, will you answer mine?' he asks, turning

away from me. This man. Did he not realise we were mere days away from doomsday?

'Tell me.' I bite out the words. Desmond stares at me uncertainly, a flicker of fear crossing his eyes.

He begins to walk away, ushering me to follow. The land is brazen. No trees, no bushes, no villages. Nothing. But the moment he steps out of the darkness, I notice why the curve of his hair has been so prominent.

Nestled in the mass of his ebony locks is the only golden crown in Aetheria, glistening arrogantly. The jewels atop are nothing short of magnificent, no matter how many times they are seen by the naked eye.

'You brought the crown?' I gasp, pulling a hand to my mouth.

'To protect it in case an ambush occurs at Briarthorn Atoll,' he says matter-of-factly, picking up the Blood Crown to brush a hand through his hair.

'Blood?' Desmond says, squinting his eyes. A breeze brushes through my hair, but the crusted blood sticks some of the ebony strands firmly to my forehead.

'What?' I shake my head in annoyance.

'How did that happen?' He leans in to touch the slit, but I move away immediately. The ground suddenly seems interesting, the vivid cracks mimicking those of a high magnitude earthquake, and I can't help but feel like wanting to fall through them.

Silence envelops us. A sudden urge to beat him and snatch the crown off his head nags at me, but even as I think it, I know I am much too weak to fight off his strength.

'Tell me,' I reiterate instead.

Desmond kicks a stone, fisting his hands at his side before he turns to me, agitation evident in his eyes, his tone adopting an unnatural urgency unlikely from the Desmond I knew.

'Nyx has contacted me, offering herself as an ally.'

Just like I had predicted, I barely hear the rest of Desmond's words, which come rushing out of his mouth like a house being devoured in flames.

'I am no fool, for I know she will kill me the moment she gets the chance. I asked you, Victoria, to meet me in the Queen's Forest at exactly midnight because I no longer want your soul. I beg for a truce, for this war cannot be won with each of us against the other.'

'When did she contact you?' I ask sharply.

'A few moons ago,' Desmond tilts his head. 'Why?'

'Nyx and I had a pact,' I hiss, anger boiling in my veins, bubbling my blood. I wasn't surprised that Nyx had put the both of us against each other. I was still worked up over the fact that he had used and betrayed me, offering Nyx the opportunity he himself had warned me not to commit to. I point an accusing finger at him. 'You did too, to help cover up your murders and secure the crown for your own. She would support you in your disdainful pleas when you say you didn't kill them.'

Desmond nods slowly. 'Let me guess. She betrayed you and attempted to bring me to her side?'

I nod. 'She tried to turn the plot. She wants us to end up killing each other in wrath, exactly like you said.'

Desmond strides toward me, his steps deliberate, grasping both my hands with an intensity that sends a chill down my spine. 'Victoria, please.'

A distant rumble of thunder reverberates through the air.

'You really think I'll trust you?' I spit, trying to pull away.

'Victoria. Nyx has been trying to get the crown through you,' Desmond says softly. His words make my blood run cold.

'Your General retold your tale of ambition.' Ambition. A kind word for desire.

'Give me one reason—one reason I should join forces with you,' I say fiercely, tugging away from him.

'Queen Nyx has been playing both of us. You know she has. From the moment she agreed to become your ally, she has been using you to get the crown. The moment we turned on each other was the time she decided to strike. Are you really going to continue to feed your unhealthy obsession of proving yourself just to let the world around you *burn*?' His hand grips my chin, forcing me to meet his gaze, those piercing sunlit eyes searching for something—anything—in mine.

'No,' I whisper, the word like ash on my tongue.

It seems with every breath I take, I lie. *Yes. Yes, yes, yes, yes.*

I will not stop until I have redeemed my soul and body for all the torture they have succumbed to over the last twenty-four years. Does he really think a little speech will obscure my path to achieving eternal glory? From proving everyone else wrong?

He must see the reluctance in my eyes, for he shakes his head and sighs. 'Once everything around you has burnt, the only entity you will beg to be discerned by is death.'

A clap startles the shivers out of me.

It is slow, deliberate and echoes through the emptiness.

It startles me, my heart lurching in my chest. The sound is sharp, slicing through the tension, setting my nerves on edge.

Desmond immediately drops my hands, his teeth baring as he curses softly under his breath. My legs stiffen.

'Queen Nyx,' Desmond turns to her, slowly—as if he were to placate a ravenous wolf—smiling tightly.

He bows, one hand behind his back. No.

The Blood Crown. I will myself to follow his actions, and Nyx watches with a famished glint in her eyes.

'Took long enough for you to figure it all out, Victoria. It really is a shame,' she tsked. 'I expected more of you.'

Really, Victoria, I expected more of you!

Father's blatant words echo in my head, but then I remember, he is dead.

I could laugh at his death, really.

I straighten my back, a smirk playing at my lips. 'I hadn't expected such cowardice from you, either, Queen Nyx. Sitting in a cave for more than five thousand years, really, you would think an evil sorceress has better things to do than sulk around.'

Nyx's devilish smirk slips, replaced with a scowl that speaks volumes. 'My army awaits at the border of Inferis,' she addresses Desmond. I feel my hands burn. How dare she ignore me.

'Hand over the crown, and all will be safe. Fail to do so, and you shall see your universe burn before your eyes,' Nyx chuckles softly before adding, 'unless you perish first.'

'Why do you want the crown so badly?' I beat Desmond to the question.

Nyx turns to me, but her gaze is wandering, as if I am nothing but a mere peasant.

'You, of all people, should know, Victoria. When an individual is not given what they deserve, they will fight with every ounce of their power to earn it. And that is what I am doing. I deserve this crown. I deserve the power. I deserve the world. I deserve the universe itself!'

She wipes away the strands of white hair that mar her chalky complexion. Nyx is adorned in black, the dress hugging her figure loosely, her large ears poking from under the nest of her hair.

'You said we were alike, Victoria,' Nyx hisses, licking her lips. 'See who you shall become when you fall once more.'

'You alone hold the title of the fallen Queen,' I snarl, hands fisting. Nyx growls at the tag.

'You don't need the crown, Nyx,' Desmond says. She rolls her eyes, strolling forward lazily.

We step away from her with every stride she takes, our legs moving in unison as Desmond tries to reason with Nyx. It won't work. I know it won't. There is no use in reasoning with a mind bent on revenge and redemption. A dove flies overhead in the void of darkness.

'The Blood Crown chose Briarthorn Atoll for a reason. We are not powerful. We are merely meant to be its protectors.'

Nyx cocks her head to one side.

Desmond continues. 'I came out here to destroy the crown. It has been the source of war ever since your disappearance.'

Looks like someone realised his mistakes a bit too late for the world's taste, didn't he?

That's why Desmond wanted to meet me. He knew Nyx would stop at nothing, so he decided to destroy the crown. Such nobility.

I could never fathom doing such a thing.

Turn over the Blood Crown—what foolishness. Why give up such an artefact when you could have it all?

'Please, Queen Nyx, you have to see. Fighting over such matters will lead you nowhere.'

My heart rackets furiously.

But it did lead somewhere.

'We can form a truce, and with all our powers, Aetheria shall thrive better than any world in this universe.'

Her eyes soften.

Something was about to happen. Something bad.

There is momentary silence before Nyx drawls, 'If you have completed your words of wisdom, am I free to attack you?' A lazy smirk crawls over her face. She giggles.

It hits me with sudden ferocity how much Nyx's striking features resemble Dorphne's.

I grab the hem of Desmond's shirt, breaking into a run before Nyx shrieks into the night air.

'All hail Queen Nyx! Run, little princess! You can't hide from the truth anymore!'

Desmond chases behind me as the nixie remains stagnant, rooted to the ground. She does not move, yet with every passing minute, my legs begin to ache, and it seems like we have not run even a metre away from her deathly stare.

Run, little princess! You can't hide from the truth anymore!

Her threat simmers in my mind. It sizzles and engraves

itself into my brain, and it only becomes worse when I realise the message was for me.

Not for Desmond. Not for the Aetherians.

For me.

I am hyperventilating by the time Desmond shoves me behind a boulder.

I can hear every breath Nyx's army takes behind her. Each shallow intake of air is like a single dragon stomping across the Centre, shaking not only my body but my soul as well.

'We don't have much time.' Desmond breathes violently, rubbing his face aggressively.

I stare at the crown on his head.

'Victoria!' He shakes me, and I jump, turning to meet his eyes. I feel disconnected. Strange.

'I called both armies,' Desmond says, and I remember the dove that flew overhead us.

'How long will they take to arrive?' I say, my vision blurring, bringing my arms to wrap around me.

My teeth were chattering. Thunderous hooves echo from all sides as Desmond pulls me up.

'Victoria!' I hear Dorphne shriek. I tremble, falling to the ground. I feel so cold.

Dorphne drops beside me.

'Fight, Victoria. Fight for your land,' she whispers.

Fight for yourself, Victoria. Fight, fight, fight.

I heave off the ground, slipping. Dorphne catches my arm once more, a forlorn smile spreading across her face. I can hardly hold on to her, my sweaty hands refusing to linger even a second on her ghostly pale skin.

'Come on, Victoria.' She pulls me up, grunting as she throws one of my arms around her neck and the other around Desmond's.

He holds my arm tightly, possibly reassuringly.

But all I want to do is snap off their heads.

I'm fine. I can do this alone.

Desmond nods to Dorphne, and we walk out from behind the boulder, Quen Nyx standing miles away.

'Her voice felt so close,' I murmur, head nodding, and Desmond stiffens his grip on my arm.

The rest of our armies crowd behind us, and I feel General Steelborne's shadow beside me. I groan, writhing out from Desmond and Dorphne's grips.

I grasp my head suddenly, a whistle blowing deafeningly in my ear.

'Ah, finally! I was expecting this to take much longer!' Nyx cackles, raising her arms in the air, and Dorphne stiffens.

'We must begin the coronation! I see you have made your decision,' she drawls.

My heart drops, and I slowly close my eyes. No.

'There will be no coronation, and most certainly no decision has been made in your favour,' Desmond growls. The points of his teeth draw blood from his lips.

'Oh,' Queen Nyx pouts. 'But I wasn't talking about myself. For me to become Queen of Aetheria, my crown must be retained by my heir.'

A dozen arrows shoot my heart, cracking it completely, and I drop to my knees, quivering.

I wasn't talking about myself.

No.

Please, no.

A hot tear streaks down my face, and I hold in a terrified scream, wracking my body back and forth. I feel hands come over me, but crystals spiral loose.

Screams and hollers echo around me, but I am in my own world. I can't watch. I don't want to see. I clutch my chest, pressing, pinching, punching it, finally screaming into the open air.

I want to drag my sword through her a million times until she dies the most torturous death alive.

Why me?

I stare down Queen Nyx, sobs cracking my face. I can tell my lips are blue, but so are the tips of my fingers.

I clutch my hands tighter, drawing blood from my palms.

'Come, dear. Show your friend what a true princess looks like.'

Breathe in, breathe out.

I can't. I bite my tongue, spitting out blood as I draw in air faster and harder. Nyx opens her arms wide, a beckoning smile searing through her flesh.

I can feel my jaw drop. My surroundings blur. I cannot hear anything. I cannot understand anything, and I most certainly cannot comprehend why a tear trickles down Dorphne's face as she walks forward, only turning once to meet my eyes.

It takes years. Or at least it feels like it. It takes so long. So, so long for me to fathom all the events. For Dorphne to reach Queen Nyx, for her to place a brambled crown crusted in gold over her head. For me to suddenly understand that another person I trusted has failed me.

She was no elf. She was a nixie.

Dorphne was Queen Nyx's daughter, and Queen Nyx was Dorphne's mother.

I had so foolishly, oh, so stupidly let her into my fortress and into the taverns of my heart.

Dorphne hugs Queen Nyx tightly, as if relishing the fact her mother was an evil sorceress trying to take down the world. She had saved me. She had been there for me through and through. She had stood up for me. We were friends. I trusted her.

That wasn't my fault, Venefica.

Desmond's words thunder in my mind.

I want to break down into pieces. Rearrange myself and put it all back together. Maybe it would ache less. My head throbs as I attempt to stand, and Desmond catches me in his arms. I shove him away, dizzily unsheathing my sword.

I see at least three of him standing in front of me.

Once this registers, I feel my brain die.

Like it has been switched off.

Because I don't feel like myself anymore.

I feel inhumane.

I shake my head vigorously, the bun untangling into a mass of slithery hair.

'You idiot!' I lash out. Everything is an echo. I can hardly make out anything except for the way Desmond stares at me.

In shock. In fear.

'You had to bring the bloody crown out into the open?'

'Victoria, I—'

I can feel Nyx's eyes boring into me in amusement.

'Don't speak to me like I'm a child, Desmond! I have had enough! Give me the crown!' I snarl, lunging for him.

He pushes back, and I fall into the dirt. I try again. Again and again.

Just smile and wave.

My crown topples off my head. Someone hollers out an order. I hear an explosion. Someone calls my name. I feel arms grabbing me as they pull me away from Desmond, whose demeanour remains unfazed.

You are not worthy of the crown!

I hear clamouring and screaming. I see Desmond run out into the open. I see him brandish his sword fiercely. I see his army cheer him on. I struggle against the arms. A blurred face comes into view.

'Go!' I cry at Dorphne, my voice cracking. 'Leave me be!'

Hot tears run down my cheeks as I flail against her.

General Steelborne pins me against the floor as I attempt to fight him off. Another scream reverberates. Another cackle.

Another menacing order. Another thunderous response. Another crash and another bang.

My hand snakes its way to his back, and I unsheathe his sword. Steelborne's eyes open wide as I strike him across the gut, and he staggers back in shock. I growl, lurching up from the ground. Dorphne backs away immediately, and I smirk.

'Let's play a game,' I taunt. 'You run, and I chase.'

I lick my lips. Maybe this is what Queen Nyx had meant by I could no longer run from the truth.

Because I am her.

This is who you are now, Victoria.

She was right.

Dorphne screams as I run after her. More explosions. The ground giving way beneath me. I can feel the spirits of the dead consuming me. The wind whips my hair, and adrenaline rushes through my blood as I finally slip and pull Dorphne down under me.

I let the sword plunge wherever my arm wills it. Dorphne tries to thrust me off as she dodges the blows and the blade smashes from each side on the ground. It is hot. My knuckles are bloody. It takes me moments to register that we are on the edge of the land, a chasm opening in front of us, and that we could tumble down together any moment. That's alright. If I go, she goes too.

I can taste her blood in my mouth, oh.

'I truste-'

'Stop!'

A voice thunders through the air.

It is like lightning. It came and went.

I feel like I'm hallucinating as I turn to see who the person may be.

It sounded like Desmond. *Then why is everyone looking around for the caller so wildly? Why am I not sure if it is him?*

I finally spot it. Not the person, but the crowd gasping and tumbling backward. We are far away from the voice, or at least I feel like we are, because now as my vision focuses, the mob parts. I spit on the ground, standing up in annoyance.

Dorphne pushes away from me, gasping and wheezing.

I stumble a bit, hand on my knees as I jerk forward, grunting.

'Will you come out already?' I snarl.

'Of course,' the voice says again, brightly. But when the crowd parts and I see him standing there, my knees buckle and I collapse to the ground.

I begin trembling all over again.

I could kill myself.

Desmond catches my sight first, bound together by rope.

Then Queen Nyx. Dorphne lets out a strangled gasp and I nearly gag at the bloodied sight of her. Nearly.

She deserves it.

And so does Desmond.

Then I see him, and all the fight evaporates from my body.

His face is marred, splattered with blood, and his hair is just the way it used to be, unkempt without a crown. There is a hole that has been sewn together at his gut, his complexion ghostly.

I let a choked sob roll down my cheek.

'Why couldn't you stay dead?' I whisper, my legs shaking.

Xavier smirks.

'Well, sister, that isn't a very nice way to reunite with your dear old brother, is it?'

CHAPTER XX

Desmond Nathaniel Thorncrest

I gag against the ropes that bind me.

The taste of my own blood bleeding in my mouth is unbearable. Damn that brat. I thought Victoria said Metallures could be killed with crystal. I look over to Nyx hopefully, who has been unconscious for half the duration of our little war play. Her head hangs limp, but she is hardly breathing.

Xavier had emerged when I split from Victoria and ran in the opposite direction, where Nyx had been standing. I loathe people who refuse to parley in battles. I'd rather die with honour than be safe. Half my soldiers had been slaughtered by the army of banshees, nixies, and vampires, and just when I thought I had Nyx cornered, a blood-curdling scream echoed, and the sharp crack of bones before Nyx was lying in a pool of blood, Xavier behind her.

He was no pleasant sight to behold.

I twitch, biting down, but the gag only sinks further into my mouth until I cannot even chew.

I didn't surrender. It was only when the tip of my sword began to curve and snake its way around my neck that I realised my stupidity.

Xavier's outstretched hand curled, tightening the hold on my neck. I could still feel the specks of blood running down in hard flakes across my neck and onto my clothes.

It was burning hot here.

Xavier had promptly smirked and wrenched the crown off my head. He didn't wear it, though, and it hung around his wrist like a bracelet too big for even the largest man. He wore nothing but a suit, and I recognised it to be the same one I had killed him in. I vividly remember asking him how he was here and if I was hallucinating his reappearance.

'Why, I am from a lineage of sorcerers, fool.'

'But how did you protect yourself?'

'So that you can prevent it from recurring?'

A clatter snaps my focus back to the scene at hand. I want to curse and roar into the open darkness. Victoria has gone crazy. She is a monster. I could see it in her eyes from the moment she appeared in the Centre.

I knew Nyx would be there—she'd already gotten a whiff of the plan when I sent that general and threatened to expose his secret to Victoria. I made it seem like Nyx would be able to kill Victoria and me, and she would finally have the Blood Crown.

I anticipated her murdering Victoria, but not this. Never this.

Xavier throws the Blood Crown into the middle of the two of them.

I hear a small gasp escape Victoria's blue lips.

It goes quiet.

Too quiet for my liking.

Victoria, don't be an idiot.

But even as I will these words, Victoria stares at Xavier like a lost puppy and lunges for the crown.

She is ragged, her clothes torn and tattered, and her face is drugged in dirt. She looks about the same as when she escaped the Dungeon of the Dead Kings, yet somehow everything about her has changed.

Victoria is wild. I can see it in her eyes as I struggle against the binds, watching her grasp the crown and place it on her head. A victorious cackle leaves her throat, echoing through the night sky. It is even darker than before, and the moonlight illuminating the two siblings makes them seem as menacing as any other villain.

The crown glows, resisting her touch, but she forces it down, glazing it in crystals so that it can nestle in her wild hair smoothly. It obeys. She closes her eyes, breathing in the air.

But then I see a figure behind her.

'Victoria!' A voice screams. I turn to see Nyx's daughter

collapse to the ground and cover her eyes as Xavier lunges behind Victoria.

The guard tying me down grunts as I suddenly shove against him, the rope around my neck loosening. I tug off the binds, blowing a punch to the vampire's face and a knee to the gut, the sweat on my hands making it harder for me to mindlessly shove the gag off my face as the guard crumples to the floor, heaving.

Everything happens fast—too fast.

Xavier pivots Victoria around, and when she finally opens her eyes, he yanks the crown off her head, and it is with a burning intensity I see the shape of the edge of the land take form—ragged, as if it had been torn apart.

There is a look of finality in Xavier's eyes as he pushes her, and she goes hurdling off the side, screaming.

'Victoria!' I roar, my throat ripping. I run, adrenaline pumping through me as I heave and pant, knocking Xavier aside as I try to grasp hold of her, but then the cliff crumbles and gives way, the last look in her eyes chilling me to the bone.

There is no guilt, there is no remorse, there is only a sadness I am incapable of explaining, and I know I will never have the chance to ask her what it was for because as the rocks begin to break down, sinking into nothingness, she follows. She follows, and down goes everything she ever worked for. Herself, her crown, her Kingdom.

It shatters my heart, crumpling each tiny piece and forcing me to swallow my betrayal a hundred times over before bringing me to my knees. Someone pulls at my hand, urging me to move.

I'd lived thirty-one years, but I saw my life die before my eyes.

Victoria falls.

And then she just keeps falling.

TO BE CONTINUED

AUTHOR'S NOTE:

For the best experience, I recommend reading
Victoria's diary entries from **Day 2** to **Day 10**.
I promise, you won't see what's coming.

ACKNOWLEDGMENTS

Alhamdulillah.

None of this would have been possible without the help of Allah.

My first book, published?!

I want to thank every single one of you who picked up this book to read it, and those who helped make this dream come true.

My parents, thank you for your endless support and for always listening to me rant about how my characters should be, allowing me to brainstorm and suddenly get the most amazing ideas from nowhere, and helping me with every little thing to achieve my dreams.

To Shaziah Shamim, my book cover designer, thank you for bringing my unruly sketches to life and delivering such a fantastic book cover.

To Nisha Sanjeev, thank you for helping me out through the whole process of editing and publishing, and for the encouraging comments I received from you and my editor, Diya Sanjeev. Once that email came around, I shed tears of joy because I really believed that my book would not end up anywhere, and yet here we are.

My friends, my cousins, my family from everywhere; thank you for supporting me, pumping me up and congratulating me for every little milestone I made to get this book written.

To some very specific people who always liked a new reel, always commented, and always made sure they were updated on every single thing, gave me feedback and just in general even asked me about my book or attempted to guess the plot and give me an idea or two, (you know who you are), it meant a lot. You don't know how happy I was to see that people are actually interested, even if it was just a few of you.

To my best friends Hamdan, Aliza, Minal, Zara, Emaan, Hayaa, Raniya, Sarrinah and Bilal, thank you for being there for me from the very first day. Every milestone I achieved was celebrated by these people through encouraging texts, ice creams, flowers and a comment that read: 'I can't wait to read this!'

To Helen—who I met online—thank you for your endless support towards The Blood Crown and insightful glances into anti-hero protagonists and unhinged antagonists. You made me feel like my writing was worth something and that it could lead to great interpretations of the morally grey world.

To Mishel—who I also happened to meet online—thank you for every encouraging comment you posted on my reels, and for every text that told me my writing was great.

And finally, to my teacher. In Year 7 all the way to Year 10, I want to thank Miss Mahjabeen for pushing me to speak and do the thing I loved the most. She always gave feedback on the smallest poems and best stories, and hyped me up to take the smallest opportunities I could find. She plays a major role in helping me discover my passion for writing, and I cannot describe my joy at being able to fulfil my dreams in front of the one person who was there to see it all.

Once again, thank you to everyone who was there to see The Blood Crown transform from a dream to what it is today.

ABOUT THE AUTHOR

Muzainah Shahrukh Yasin, better known as M.S.Y, is a 15-year-old Pakistani author of The Blood Crown, currently based in the UAE. She began her writing journey at 13, publishing short stories and poems on an online platform. At 14, she completed her debut novel, The Blood Crown, which is now published. Muzainah has won multiple awards in school for story, scriptwriting and broadcasting, and has co-directed two school plays. She has also been featured in Gulf Today, one of the UAE's top three broadcast newspapers. When she's not writing, Muzainah enjoys painting, exploring new ideas, and getting lost in the worlds of her imagination.

Follow her journey on Instagram at @authormsy.